A Secret in Salem

Sheri Anderson

Based on characters from *Days of our Lives*,
originally created by Allan Chase, Ted Corday, and Irna Phillips

Days of our Lives
Publications

Published by Days of our Lives Publications, an imprint of Sourcebooks, Inc.
P.O. Box 4410, Naperville, Illinois 60567-4410
(630) 961-3900
Fax: (630) 961-2168
www.sourcebooks.com

Library of Congress Cataloging-in-Publication Data:
Anderson, Sheri.
  A secret in Salem / Sheri Anderson.
     p. cm.
  1. Rich people—Fiction. 2. Women fashion designers—Fiction. 3. Married people—Fiction. 4. Family secrets—Fiction. I. Title.
  PS3601.N5465S43 2010
  813'.6--dc22
                              2010035795

Printed and bound in the United States of America.
VP 10 9 8 7 6 5 4 3 2 1

For Esther and Cliff, who taught me the value of love, family, and romance…I miss you.

1   *SHAWN AND BELLE*

ALTHOUGH HE'D BEEN HALFWAY AROUND THE WORLD, SHAWN Douglas Brady had never seen a fleet of ships like this one. While the blue-and-green-striped sails of his 45-foot Nicholson were usually impressive, he felt like a moth in the midst of monarch butterflies. But then, he was in Monte Carlo, the playground of the rich and famous.

Surrounded by Italy and France, it had the smallest, most exciting beachfront in the world at only 3.5 miles. Occupying only 1 square mile of land, the principality was considered the gem of the Riviera, if not the world.

Monte Carlo? Were they really there? It had been over a year since he and his wife had left Salem—on the yacht the *Fancy Face IV*, bought for them by Belle's magnanimous father, John Black—for their adventure. Shawn, the handsome but oft-troubled son of two of Salem's finest, had married the blonde spitfire Belle and then had an adorable daughter, Claire. But Belle had often fallen through the cracks in their social circle, which was dominated by her manipulative and malevolent half sister, Sami. So she was thrilled to take to the high seas. They needed an escape, and John knew that seeing the world from this vantage point would give his daughter and son-in-law a new perspective.

"Belle, get up here!" Shawn shouted excitedly. "You and Claire have to see this!"

A curly-haired moppet popped out from the galley.

"Mommy's in the head, Da'!" Claire squealed.

"Then you get up here, now!"

Shawn grabbed his daughter and hoisted the little girl onto the beautifully defined shoulders that topped his sinewy, tanned body.

Claire giggled and pointed at the mass of sailboats, cruisers, and yachts that filled the harbor. "Wow." Claire giggled. "Even bigger than in Crete! Those sure aren't 'stinkpots.'"

Belle made her way up from below. Though a bit wobbly, when she looked around her, she was totally overwhelmed.

"Unbelievable." She gasped.

"Both the scene and our daughter. For a three-year-old, she's a well-traveled little girl."

"Not little, Da. And I'm four—almost!"

Belle, looking a lovely shade of chartreuse, stroked her daughter's hair.

"How you feeling?" Shawn asked carefully.

She smiled wanly. "As good as I look?"

Uh-oh, Shawn thought.

"But—damned excited to be here."

Shawn knew why. One of those yachts would later be holding a lavish sweet-sixteen party for Dalita Kasagian, the daughter of über-rich Serge Kasagian, and Belle's fashion idol was going to be there.

"Olivia Marini Gaines," he stated emphatically. "OMG."
With that, Belle puked all over the deck of the yacht.

2 MARLENA

THE MASSIVE PALE PINK DOOR TO LA JOLIE CLINIQUE SWUNG open, and a beautiful blonde of indeterminate age made her entrance.

The petite redhead behind the reception desk immediately suspected an American but had been taught to never assume. The clientele came from every corner of the world, for every conceivable nip and tuck—and some not so conceivable. It was called *medical tourism*, and Geneva was one of its capitals.

"Bonjour, Mademoiselle," the receptionist said.

"Bonjour," the blonde replied. Then, in English, she said, "Marlena Evans. I have an appointment with Dr. Masters."

"Please fill out this form, and we'll be with you shortly. Mineral water with lemon? Or perhaps a glass of champagne?"

"Water will be fine, thank you." Marlena smiled. *They certainly know how to treat their patients.*

As she glanced around the waiting room, Marlena noticed that the clientele were deserving of champagne in crystal flutes, or at least they thought they were. As they reclined in overstuffed down chairs with footstools, the red soles of their Christian Louboutins reeked of money.

Marlena settled in and looked at the clipboard. She knew these forms well, having offered hundreds, probably thousands by now, to her patients back in Salem. But Salem didn't seem across the world at this moment; it seemed as if it were in another galaxy.

Marlena was in Geneva, home to some of the most well-respected clinics in the world. And not just "spas" like the one she was nestled in.

She shook her head as she saw the information they wanted. Height. Weight. Color of eyes and hair, and ethnicity. Skin type. Allergies. Medical history. She laughed softly to herself. Do you think they'd believe the number of stab wounds, pregnancies and miscarriages, accidents…the demon possession? Yep, even demon possession. Anything could happen back in Salem, and while some of that life washed over her like a nightmare, it had all been real when it happened. *Very real*, she mused. But, at this point, none of it mattered.

∞

Marlena's name was called, and she was ushered in for a consultation with Europe's most discreet plastic surgeon.

Dr. Masters looked as though he had stepped out of an L.L.Bean catalog. Roughly handsome with tousled salt-and-pepper hair and a bit of scruff. His hands were the only things that gave him away. They were beautifully manicured and welcoming as he shook her delicate but strong hand. He flashed a warm smile and surveyed her quickly.

"Not sure what it is you're here for. You have amazing skin and look to be in terrific shape."

For a woman your age, that's what he means.

"And I don't mean for a woman your age."

To her surprise, Marlena blushed. *Can he read minds too?*

"Seriously. So many women—and men too these days—come in here needing a nip or tuck. Sometimes it seems crazy," he added, touching her face gently. "You've probably heard about Serge Kasagian's extravaganza tomorrow. Hence the full waiting room. But I wouldn't want to change this face. Perfect nose, lovely full lips, great symmetry…"

She knew she should interrupt as he took in her well-toned body, but the compliments felt good. Wonderful, in fact. *Is it a surprise that the most competent, attractive, even beautiful women—even psychiatrists like me—need to hear them?* she wondered.

"Great—uh, symmetry," he said again as he examined her body. Marlena suddenly realized his American accent was perfect.

"You from the States?" she asked, already knowing the answer.

"Montana."

"Ah, I'm originally from Colorado—most recently, Salem."

"Massachusetts." He nodded. "Home of the witch trials."

"A different Salem," she countered, then quickly changed the subject. Her Salem was much too confusing to explain in a sentence or two. Suddenly she felt as if she were flirting, which she had no intention of doing, no matter how hot this doctor was. "So, I'm actually here about scar repair and tattoo removal."

She noticed he cocked his eyebrow.

"Not mine. My husband's. He has a tattoo of a phoenix on his back."

"Which you hate." Dr. Masters smiled.

"I always said I didn't care..." she said, tears forming in her expressive hazel eyes. "And I don't...But now I think it may be killing him."

3   *JOHN*

TO THE OUTSIDE WORLD, JOHN AND MARLENA'S RELATIONSHIP was back on track. Living as man and wife in Switzerland.

The first time they met, he was wrapped in bandages from head to toe, having undergone extensive plastic surgery. He was suffering from amnesia and had no memory of who he was.

From there, his life story made Jason Bourne's look like a kindergarten fairy tale. But from his time as a blue-collar cop to his initiation into an elite international spy organization to his role as chief of a multimillion-dollar company, there was only one constant: his love for Marlena.

Their love affair was wildly passionate, tear-jerkingly romantic, and often so turbulent it tore them apart. They had other relationships—even other marriages—but their magnetic field always wrenched them back together.

John was always Marlena's hero. Until he was paralyzed from the neck down.

Fortunately, the paralysis wasn't because of a brain stem stroke, which would have meant he'd never regain movement in his limbs. That tragedy, known as locked-in syndrome, kept its victims from moving anything more than their eyelids. Instead, while John's paralysis was totally debilitating, he had retained a small bit of movement below the neck. They hoped for more someday, but for now it remained just a hope.

John's paralysis stemmed from his being injected by a lunatic of a still-unidentifiable fluid. Science and technology have given the world some of the greatest cures and inventions of all time but have also placed havoc in the hands of demons.

Marlena had left that morning, after telling John she was going to Geneva for a meeting. He had nodded. Since moving to the Alps, she'd occasionally done some consulting. Once a psychiatrist, always a psychiatrist. It's said that head doctors are more screwed up than their patients, and at times the outside world might think his Doc's life was a little wacky. But he knew better.

"You should go," he said in the throaty voice that was just above a whisper. "Doc'll be back soon."

"And you, rest," answered the tanned and lean brunette whose hands had just slid over his entire body.

"Thanks, Tara, for everything," John said.

"Will I see you tomorrow?" she asked with the Dutch accent he found oddly appealing.

"If Marlena's in Geneva, absolutely." He smiled. "I like where this is headed. You're a real pro."

Tara moved to the birdseye maple armoire in the corner of the bedroom and slid open a drawer, taking out five crisp one-hundred-dollar bills. Then, noticing Marlena's cream Mercedes driving up the winding path to the estate, she slipped out of the bedroom.

What she hadn't noticed was the car following Marlena's. And although John gazed through the floor-to-ceiling windows of his massive bedroom, neither did he.

∞

"Of all the estates in Lausanne, this is the most impressive I've ever seen," Dr. Masters said as he entered the foyer behind Marlena.

"John always wanted me to have the best," Marlena responded quietly.

"He obviously thinks you deserve it."

The house was indeed amazing. Named Maison du Noir—the House of Black—it was a contemporary glass, wood, and steel structure that miraculously complemented the lush hillside over-looking historic Lake Geneva. Outsiders felt the name was depressing, but it was John's last name, not to mention his condition for the last few years.

"My life's never been about money."

"Why doesn't that surprise me?" he quipped.

"When you can buy anything you want, nothing has value," Marlena added as she placed her cream alligator bag on the side table.

"Yet you spent beaucoup bucks on an OMG," he noted.

Was he gay? Why would he know the cost of an OMG Grace handbag?

"No, I'm not gay. My wife loves handbags," he replied to her quizzical expression.

He actually can read minds. Wait.

"Wife?" she said, realizing there was a hint of disappointment in her voice. "I mean, you're not wearing a ring, not that all married men do, and not that it matters."

What was she doing? He was there to see her husband.

"John's room is this way," she added, clearing her throat.

They made their way up the winding, free-floating staircase that encircled the living room. Behind her, he couldn't help but focus on her shapely legs. He also knew she was flustered, and he liked that.

"And the handbag? Actually, it was a gift, Dr. Masters," she tossed out casually. "And a knockoff. I'd never let anyone spend $25,000 on a purse."

∞

It took less than thirty minutes for Dr. Masters to finish his examination of John. John's medical records were updated on a daily basis by the nurses who had quarters in the three-bedroom guesthouse on the edge of the property and took round-the-clock shifts.

"Wanna tell me what this is really about?" John asked, staring at Marlena, who had moved to the window.

"Dr. Masters's specialty is plastic surgery," Marlena evenly stated.

John knew exactly what that meant.

"Did she tell you I've had the tattoo removed three times, Masters, and now it's darker than ever?"

"Obviously not a standard ink."

"Bright guy."

"It's reacting to a chemical in your system that hasn't been identified," Masters stated plainly, not about to let John intimidate him. "We need to find out what that is."

"Simple as pie, right?"

"My wife's a chemical biologist, and she's doing some remarkable studies. I'll take a scraping of the tattoo for analysis; then I'd like her to see you."

Wife. There's that word again, Marlena thought.

"Maybe we could have a foursome."

"John!" Marlena said admonishingly.

"My sense of humor's a little shaky these days, Doc," he apologized.

Dr. Masters removed a small case from his pocket. Using a sterile knife, he quickly took a skin scraping from the area around the tattoo, nicking John in the process.

"Hope it's not too painful," Masters said.

"Not after all I've been through," John answered. Then he added, "Send your wife around, unless you want Doc to bring me to her."

Masters knew Marlena could do that. Not only was the bedroom set up with every conceivable lift system, it had voice-activated commands for lights, heat, sound, and entertainment modules. He knew they had to have a state-of-the-art van for John to travel when the whim hit him.

"Your call," John replied.

Marlena was pleased. At least John was receptive.

"Could I bring you some dinner?" Marlena asked John.

"Not hungry. Didn't sleep much this afternoon, and after all this, I think I need a rest," John answered.

"You've got one lovely wife, Mr. Black," Dr. Masters said.

"Call me John. I don't like formalities."

John also didn't like the way Dr. Masters looked at Marlena. He also knew this was a man Marlena could relate to, if he were ever out of the picture.

"Then you may call me Blake," the doctor answered. He then followed Marlena out of the room.

"You came a long way, and I truly appreciate it," she said softly, meeting his gaze. "He's a good man, really."

Really, Dr. Masters thought to himself. "As far as his paralysis…" he began cautiously.

"Able to move his hands and arms slightly, but that's all," she interrupted.

During his examination, repositioning John to study the tattoo, Masters had realized John was moving on his own; his muscle tone was more than sufficient to hold his weight.

"A good man," he reiterated. *Then why was John Black lying to his wife?*

4   *CHARLEY*

MONEY ISN'T TO SPEND ON THE FRENCH RIVIERA; IT'S TO BURN.

Vegas conjures up images of wild gambling, sexual liaisons that would make even Paris Hilton blush, parties, drugs, and rock and roll. All that pales in comparison to the extravagant debauchery of the French Riviera.

While the old money of Europe stays discreetly behind centuries-old gates, the new money is out for everyone to see. Fat Russian mobsters spray topless, tanned beauties with thousand-dollar bottles of Dom at La Voile Rouge. Jet-setting celebrities, hip-hop artists, and the noveau riche fill the clubs and casinos until the wee hours of the morning. Boutiques catering to their moneyed clients' every whim will close at the drop of a ten-thousand-euro advance to pamper their most loyal customers.

OMG was one of those shops.

How odd it was that Olivia Marini Gaines, once heralded as the designer of choice for the Clinton-era *Town & Country* set, was hotter than Louis Vuitton had ever been. Passion for the beautifully crafted Vuitton bags covered with gold LVs had been replaced by ones covered with OMGs.

Olivia didn't mind. In fact, she ate it up.

Unlike her husband, billionaire hedge-fund owner Richard Gaines, Olivia loved the spotlight. As a child, she had wanted to be a dancer and performed with Il Corpo di Ballo del Teatro alla Scala, the resident classical ballet company in Milan. Lithe and lean, with exquisite form, she had been the upcoming star of the ballet school until puberty cursed her with 34DDs. What a curse! Later they became her blessing, and not just for the drooling stares she got when walking the streets of Milan.

Olivia's father was a tailor, her mother his muse, and in fashion-conscious Milan, he had worked with every major designer, including Armani, Gucci, and Valentino. With nips and tucks of the finest fabrics on the planet, he worked magic on his daughter's blossoming frame.

Olivia had a great eye and took note of every step of the process. When her father died unexpectedly of a heart attack, she had been devastated. She had also vowed to follow in his footsteps.

By twenty, Olivia Marini had her first smash collection. It was the '70s and rock-glam fashions that dominated the runways. Olivia's line had a twist. The minis and cropped jackets were of the finest fabrics and leathers, with the OMG logo in platinum thread. There were also colored diamonds and other precious jewels tucked *inside* the hems. No one but the owner knew which gems they were or what they cost. To own an OMG was like being one of the super-rich who bought stolen art masterpieces and hid them in their basements. Not everyone could afford one.

Richard Gaines could.

Called Richie by his closest friends, he was front and center at every major house during Fashion Week. He bought the entire collection for his seventeen-year-old buxom Swedish mistress and agreed to back Olivia's burgeoning design firm. That is, if she married him.

Olivia was an independent, gorgeous creature. Flowing black hair, olive skin, and thick lashes she batted whenever the calculation caught her. She also loved money and the idea of being Mrs. Richard Gaines. Who cared if Richard had a reputation as a womanizer and had been married three times by the age of forty? His body was toned and tanned under his Brioni suits, and his friendly blue eyes mesmerizing. He was also known for showering his women with the wealth he'd obtained all on his own.

The wedding was two weeks later on his 198-foot megayacht, a yacht tiny in comparison to the one they owned now.

While Richie concentrated on his London-based international banking business, Olivia dived into her design firm. She immediately changed her logo from her scripted initials OM to OMG. Yes, she had relished the fact that in the metaphysical '70s, her initials were the oldest and most sacred sound found in yoga, but changing them to OMG shone the spotlight on her as Richard Gaines's newest (and she knew, very last) tantalizing wife. Little did she expect that it would eventually become one of the most popular acronyms in history.

Oh My Gosh, Oh My Goodness, Oh My God!

She loved it, and she adored her new, flashy husband.

As for Richie's reputation as a womanizer? Olivia claimed he was totally faithful, but deep down, knew better. There were things she would never do sexually that he craved, and whether on hops to Rio or during what he said were late-night business meetings anywhere in the world, she suspected—no, knew—that some dark beauty or two were making him happy.

Olivia was happy too. She relished the money, the prestige... and the three beautiful children who were her ultimate trump cards. Jackson and Chance Gaines, born two years apart, were well educated, well mannered, and well respected. And they were total hunks. Like many of the sons of the megawealthy, they were often seen on the pages of the tabloids, partying with Lindsay, the Olsen twins, or whoever was hottest at moment. When on business in Los Angeles, they stayed at Chateau Marmont and hung out at Soho House or Voyeur, watching the topless dancers slither on poles and paying thousand-dollar bottle tabs to stake claim to one of the prestigious tables. In New York, it was the Ritz-Carlton in Battery Park. Hip, with gorgeous views of the Statue of Liberty and close to Wall Street, where they did the bulk of their business.

Although Olivia loved her sons with all her heart, the gem of her life was her daughter, Charley.

∞

Charlotte "Charley" Gaines, who by fifteen had often been compared to Angelina Jolie, was actually Olivia's opposite. She had the same flowing dark chestnut hair, but her skin was like flawless porcelain, with eyes a clear blue with hazel and brown flecks. Her temperament was more like her father's. She didn't grab the spotlight; the spotlight grabbed her. She also had no desire to be in the banking business like her brothers. She was content to be behind the scenes, behind the lens of a camera.

At eighteen and a graduate of Choate Rosemary Hall in the States, one of the most exclusive prep schools in the world, Charley was spending a few precious months with the family. She actually loved their sprawling vacation home nestled in the hills of Monte Carlo, and Olivia was letting her work on the marketing campaign for the next summer collection while she helped out in the boutique. It wasn't just nepotism; Charley had her mother's incredible eye.

As for Charley working at the shop? Richard and Olivia both believed that all three children needed to develop a strong work ethic. So ridiculously rich or not, all three kids worked alongside the normal folk every summer. Charley with her mother and the boys with dear old Dad.

"Diddy and his entourage are running late," Olivia told her daughter as she hung up her platinum iPhone.

"They're usually on time," Charley said, surprised.

"They'd planned to helicopter over from Nice, but with so many people here for the party, a Bentley brigade felt safer."

"And more flashy," Charley added.

"He can't help it if he likes people to know he's successful," Olivia said, smiling and crossing herself. "What says success more than a one-of-a-kind OMG handbag?"

Charley knew her mother was right. Even other top designers craved them.

Diddy and his posse were out of OMG in less than thirty minutes, after spending over $87,000. They made quite a stir as they exited the Lalique crystal doors. Paparazzi were at a safe distance—but everywhere.

It had always been common to see them in Monte Carlo, even though they had restrictions. The principality had security cameras of its own scattered throughout the entire area. Aside from hoping to keep its residents and tourists safe, Prince Rainier wanted to give at least a modicum of protection to the celebrities who'd added such panache to the mile-square city.

Diddy, his off-again, on-again girlfriend, Kim, bodyguards, and several of Diddy's kids headed to the dock for the skiff to the hippest new superyacht, *WHY 58*, the latest in luxury. The yacht was shaped like a horseshoe, and light flooded in on every deck. It wasn't as huge as the nearly 400-foot *RM Elegant*, which he'd rented numerous times, but it was just him and his family there for Dalita Kasagian's sixteenth-birthday bash. He wasn't performing this time; he was just a guest. Besides, everyone had ridiculously scaled yachts. This was an eye-catcher.

The guest list was a who's who of young Hollywood and the international jet set. Everyone from the *Twilight* stars and the Kardashians to Princes William and Harry with off-and-on girl-friends Kate Middleton and Chelsy Davy would be there.

Performing? Nick Jonas, Demi Lovato, Miley Cyrus, and *American Idol* "loser" Adam Lambert. Rihanna would make an appearance, only after assurances that Chris Brown was nowhere in the south of France. Jay-Z and Beyoncé had made sure Kanye had him in Los Angeles, recording.

All were paid to be there, of course, flown in on private jets by Dalita's nouveau riche daddy. The price for entertainment alone was over five million dollars.

It was going to be one enormous, gaudy, pretentious bash.

When Diddy swept out the door, one tourist did manage to snap a picture. Shawn and Belle were in the courtyard outside the opulent, petite boutique located to the right of the Hôtel de Paris, and he had his iPhone. Not a platinum-gilded one like Olivia's, but technologically just the same.

Belle didn't care about Diddy. She couldn't believe she was within yards of her current designer icon, Olivia Marini Gaines.

When she was one of Basic Black's top designers, Belle had a soupçon of recognition. Her designs were clean, crisp, and safe.

Olivia's designs were clean and crisp too but never what you'd call "safe." Like any of the great actors who always concealed a secret within a character, OMG had them too. Many of them.

From the secreted jewels in the hems to the numbers and addresses of all the hottest clubs sewn on the labels, OMG designs were always a surprise.

"I think she's in there," Shawn said, giving Belle a nudge. "Go in and say hi."

"Are you insane?" Belle replied.

"Sometimes I think he is, Mommy," chirped their almost four-year-old.

"Let's go," Belle begged, then ducked behind Shawn as Olivia exited the shop with Charley behind her. "Please."

Shawn knew his wife well, and when she was feeling insecure, he knew not to push. They'd had enough ups and downs in their relationship, especially when it came to the triangle they had endured with his wealthy nemesis back in Salem, Philip Kiriakis.

It was also nearly time for the evening summer concert, and patrons were streaming into the palace courtyard.

"Come on, CB," he said as he swooped up his increasingly weary little girl. "Let's find you a hot dog."

"Steamed mussels, Da," she pleaded. "With *pommes frites!*"

"Four next month, huh?"

"Yup!"

The roar of Olivia's Aston Martin DBS caught Shawn's attention, and he turned to see that Olivia and her daughter were leaving. For the first time, he got a good look at Olivia's pride and joy, sitting in the passenger seat of the custom shiny yellow sports car. He'd heard of the young heiress before but had never actually seen her.

She took his breath away.

As Olivia pulled away from the shop, Charley caught his eye and flashed her perfect smile. In that split second, Shawn felt as if he knew her.

∞

It didn't take long for Claire to gobble down the dinner they'd brought back to the boat. She was dozing off on her plate when Belle joined her and Shawn at the teak table in the main cabin.

"She made you that nervous, Belle?" Shawn questioned his bride as she returned from the head.

"To quote our daughter—yup!" Belle answered. "Do you mind putting her down for the night?"

Shawn kissed Belle on the tip of her nose and carted the little one to the back of the yacht. It was only a matter of feet. This wasn't a megayacht, after all. The three separate cabins gave them enough space to move around in, but even Shawn would have to admit that at times the quarters got tight for two adults and a rambunctious almost-four-year-old.

Shawn and Belle were especially careful with Claire, who'd endured a tumultuous first few years and once nearly drowned at the hands of her mother's ex-husband, Philip. Although Claire was only two at the time of the accident, she seemed to have adjusted. But they still always feared being on the water would bring back terrible memories in the mind of their precious little girl.

Within minutes, Shawn was back.

"Out like a light," he said, whispering so as not to awaken Claire. "Even with all that's going on up there," he added, nodding to the deck. "Join me?" he asked with a smile.

Belle was exhausted but decided not to argue. She knew that every now and then she needed to give in.

Monte Carlo Harbor was rocking. August in Monte Carlo was the most spectacular time of the year. Tourists from around the globe rubbed shoulders with the few thousand permanent residents and swelled the population to over a hundred thousand. Most of them stayed in rental homes, villas, and the magnificent hotels that dotted the coastline. Others lived on the hundreds of boats, from thirty-footers to the block-long yachts with live-on crews numbering in the dozens, most of which bobbed quietly and empty during the low season.

"Welcome to paradise, Tink," Shawn said as he helped Belle

to the deck. There was a chilled bottle of Veuve Clicquot, Belle's favorite champagne, and fresh strawberries.

"Got this idea from your mom and dad."

Belle's eyes clouded.

"It's gonna be okay," Shawn said in a comforting tone.

"Mom says he's better, but I'm not sure," Belle answered, and then added, "You know my mother. Always keeping a stiff upper lip for us kids, whatever she's going through."

"We've got a week until we see them," he said as he popped open the champagne. "For now, let's just think about us."

Shawn kissed her, his tongue darting inside her mouth. She smiled warmly and then kissed him with more passion.

"I love you, Shawn," she said with conviction.

"Same back."

They sipped the Veuve Clicquot.

"What should we do until then? There are so many places to see. Any thoughts?"

"You already know," Belle answered.

"The aquarium, the museum, of course—oh, and Club 55 is supposed to be amazing. It's a two-hour trip by sea, but Princess Stéphanie's there whenever she's home. Or La Colombe d'Or. Great food and real Matisses, Renoirs—all those guys—bolted to the walls, and it's less than an hour to get there by boat."

Belle laughed. "As if you care."

"You do."

"It's really not our scene, but thanks." She brushed the brown floppy hair from his forehead, then added knowingly, "Tell me where I really want to go."

"Princess Grace's grave."

She nodded. "How she influenced fashion is still phenomenal. Like Katharine Hepburn or Coco Chanel."

"To die so young...such a tragedy," she added.

Shawn clinked his Riedel champagne flute to hers, the only two nonplastic glasses on the boat. "But a great love story."

Belle looked into his eyes. As impetuous as Shawn had been when they were teenagers, he could be incredibly romantic.

He slid his hand under the back of her polo shirt and pulled her close. Then he unfastened her bra with a flick of his fingers.

Belle knew where this was going and bristled slightly, which he felt. They'd only had sex once in the last few weeks.

Just then, brilliant fireworks exploded in the Monte Carlo sky.

Through the shower of silver and gold, a bright yellow streak caught Shawn's attention.

It was Olivia's Aston Martin convertible winding its way up the hillside.

Looking closely, he could see Charley's hair flowing freely in the wind.

5  *MARLENA*

It was nearly midnight when Marlena looked at the clock. She'd been tossing and turning in her bed for over an hour, but her head was spinning, and she couldn't sleep.

The Pratesi linens and down comforter covering her DUX bed were luxurious and comforting. John had insisted on the best for her, of course. For Marlena, however, his arms around her was all she wanted.

Restless, Marlena crawled out of bed and went to sit at the Biedermeier desk that looked out to the lake. It was a beautiful moonlit night.

"Why does this make me feel even more alone?" she pondered, then shook off the thought as she noticed there was a new text on her BlackBerry. It was from Belle, texting that she and Shawn were safely in the south of France.

Marlena kissed the phone, then flipped through the photos Belle had recently sent her from her round-the-world journey. It had been much too long since she'd seen her youngest daughter in person, and she hadn't held Claire since the precious thing was a toddler.

Of all her children, Belle had a special place in Marlena's heart. She could never voice that to anyone and would deny it if asked, but because she was Marlena's only biological child with John, it was true.

Her twins, Sami and Eric, had seemed to always have strong, independent lives since they popped out of her womb. Sami, so mercurial and uncontrollable, with her constant neediness and desire for control, rarely leaned on her mother. Ultimately she was as headstrong as Roman, the man who had once swept Marlena off her feet and who she'd always love in some part of her heart. Eric, more sophisticated and intelligent, flourished away from the lifestyle of Salem and his divorced parents. Marlena had also raised two stepchildren, Carrie and Brady, as though they were her own.

Belle was named Isabella as a tribute to the luminescent young woman who had borne Brady and who John had married when Marlena had been presumed dead. Isabella, who had succumbed to the torture of pancreatic cancer, had a beautiful soul, and so did her namesake.

As Marlena studied the photos sent by Belle, she thought she heard voices coming from downstairs. Wide-awake now and curious, Marlena took her black silk robe that was draped over her chair. She slipped it over her trim body and, as she did, caught sight of herself in the full-length framed mirror. The luxurious fabric fell softly over her still-toned breasts.

"Not bad for an old broad," she said wistfully. To think she'd borne three children who now had children too.

Smoothing the fabric with her hand, she welcomed the touch

of flesh against her body, even if it was her own. Her hand lingered for a moment, until she was distracted once again by the muffled sound of arguing.

Wrapping the robe securely around herself, she headed downstairs.

∞

The house was dark except for the security lights that lit the path as Marlena made her way to the kitchen. She could hear only one voice and recognized it as that of John's night nurse, Desiree.

In the dimly lit kitchen, Marlena could see the statuesque brunette on their landline. She was wearing a short robe, and her hair was tousled as though she'd just gotten out of bed.

Desiree lived in the guesthouse, and Marlena was deeply curious as to what she was doing there in her kitchen. She realized Desiree was blasting someone in her native French.

"What do you mean you have no idea? It's my money, and I need it now," she sputtered in French. "Papa, three of my friends are desperate too, and none of us can get our cash. I don't care about your rich friends! It was you who suggested that investment!"

Desiree was near tears and slammed down the phone. "*Merde!*" she shouted. Then she nearly jumped out of her skin when she saw Marlena in the open doorway.

"*Docteur* Evans." She gasped.

"I didn't mean to intrude, Desiree," Marlena said calmly. "Are you all right?"

Desiree stammered, "My cell phone went dead, and I had to call my papa. It was an emergency. I'm sorry."

"Don't be, it's fine," Marlena answered. "I didn't mean to eavesdrop, and my French isn't quite that good, so don't worry."

Marlena was being kind. She recognized enough to know it was a major blowup with Desiree's father, one of Paris's top surgeons, and that it involved money.

"I have three friends who are going to hate me," she sputtered.

"Would you like to talk about it?" Marlena asked.

Desiree hesitated. Yes, she would like to talk about the news she'd just heard. But each of John's employees signed a strict confidentiality agreement Marlena didn't know about, and she was afraid where the conversation would go. With her entire savings down the tubes, not to mention her father's, she couldn't afford to lose this job.

"No," Desiree answered flatly, then quickly changed the subject before she started to cry. "Would you like me to check on Monsieur Black?"

Marlena thought for a moment, then shook her head. "He's sleeping. Would you like some tea? Or a drink?"

"Thank you, but I need to be alone," Desiree answered quietly. "*Bonne nuit, Docteur* Evans."

"Night."

Desiree exited through the servants' entrance.

Now Marlena was alone, and she didn't like it. As beautiful as her environment was, she needed someone to talk to.

She checked the clock on the Viking range and computed the time difference.

"Six fifteen in Salem."

Even though it was after midnight in Lausanne, it was late

afternoon in the city where Carrie and Austin were still visiting.

Flipping through her phone contacts, she stopped before reaching Carrie's number.

"Alice Horton," it read.

Few would realize that Marlena had Alice's number in her phone and that the two continued to talk fairly frequently even after she and John had left the country. Alice always had sound advice for the psychiatrist everyone else turned to.

Alice Horton. The matriarch of Salem was gone now too, and Marlena felt a twinge of guilt for not having attended the funeral. She also knew that Alice, so deeply devoted to her family, would never have wanted Marlena to leave John's side. Carrie and Austin had gone in Marlena's stead.

After a moment in thought, Marlena opted not to call her daughter. What would she say? That she was lonely? So very, very lonely.

∞

John's room was silent except for the hum of the monitors that kept track of his condition.

Marlena moved into the room as if on cat's feet.

John, the man she loved more than life, was still. He looked as he did so many times throughout their marriage. Even in sleep he had the aura of a hero.

The bed, specially built for him, wider than a double and longer than a queen to fit his six-foot-two-inch frame, was inviting.

John was lying on his side. Marlena assumed he'd used his remote system to reposition himself.

Gently, so as to not wake him, Marlena slid into the bed behind him.

She wanted to reach out and touch the phoenix tattoo she'd brought Dr. Masters to see. Instead, she merely stared at the strong, muscular shoulder she'd leaned on for so many years.

For a few moments it felt right.

For her.

For John, it was torture.

He could feel the heat from Marlena's lithe body, and his breathing began to quicken.

Fearing she was agitating him and he'd awaken, she quickly slipped out of the bed and glided to the door.

"Why?" she whispered and then disappeared before starting to cry.

John rolled over on his back and stared at the ceiling.

He didn't dare let her know his condition.

Not yet.

6  *CHARLEY*

THE SUN WAS JUST BEGINNING TO RISE WHEN CHARLEY WENT out on her terrace overlooking the entire city and boat basin to take in the day.

The view always inspired her. While the city was just coming awake, it sparkled as light gradually flitted across the deep blue water of the Mediterranean.

Sailors everywhere are traditionally early risers, opting to take in the stillness of the morning and smell the saltiness in the sea air as they bob gently in the liquid glass that surrounds them. Then there were the sailors in Monte Carlo—party central—who often came home when the sun was coming up.

Although Charley could party alongside the best of them when times called for it, that really wasn't her scene. She wouldn't even be going to Dalita Kasagian's soiree, except her daddy was giving OMG solid white gold key chains as party gifts, and it would be tacky for her not to be there. Serge Kasagian knew how to ensure everyone invited would show up.

That was necessary, though; people didn't just not like little

Dalita; they basically detested her. Squat and chunky, with unruly black hair and a thick nose, she had no personality because she'd never been required to have one. Her parents showered her with everything she ever wanted, including gorgeous gigolo boyfriends in their early twenties.

Charley had a privileged life too, but the summer jobs her father made her and her brothers work had helped ground her. Clean living always had appealed to Charley, and she loved the outdoors. She was a star on both the varsity tennis and girls' soccer teams at Choate and hiked daily, even during freezing Connecticut winters.

Charley slipped back into her room and changed into the simple workout gear that accented her classic thoroughbred body. She had long legs, a high, rounded butt, a sculpted torso, and perfectly formed round breasts, unlike her mother's notorious gazongas.

Pulling her mane into a breezy ponytail, Charley exited to the hall, then trotted through the expansive belle epoque villa on the way out for her morning jog.

The door to Richie's home office was slightly ajar as Charley passed by. It wasn't unusual for her father to be up early, and she could hear him on the phone.

"Direct all inquiries to Jackson; he's covering this," Richie said as he hung up the phone. The tone in his voice was overly clipped, which wasn't like him.

Charley peeked in, startling him.

Richie was wearing his standard Ralph Lauren Purple Label sweats.

"You okay, Daddy?" Charley asked.

"Couldn't be better." He smiled.

It was obvious that was a lie.

"Want to jog with me?" she said, knowing not to probe. As warm as Richie could be, he was a private man. "It's a brilliant, brilliant day."

"There'll be plenty of them," he responded. "Come here."

Charley trotted to her dad, and he hugged her tightly, then held on just a second too long.

"I'm going to have a busy day, lovey," he said. "See you at Dalita's party?"

"Wouldn't miss it." Charley groaned.

"Good girl," he responded. "But you always are."

He kissed her sweetly on the forehead, and she knew it was time to go.

"Ta," she said, blowing him a kiss as she exited.

Looking back into the office, she saw her father lean back in his massive leather chair. She'd seen him distracted before, especially since the worldwide recession, but this seemed different.

Then, maybe she was imagining things. She just loved him so much.

Charley passed through the kitchen, where one of the three housekeepers was assembling the tray of freshly squeezed juice, soft-boiled egg, and toast that she brought every morning to Mr. Gaines.

Kelsey, a fresh-faced Portuguese twenty-year-old, offered a glass of bright orange liquid to Charley, who downed it.

Everyone in the villa had their morning rituals, and this was one of them.

"*Obrigado*, Kelsey," Charley offered.

She'd learned long ago that addressing a foreigner with at least a few words in her own language went a long way.

"*Não há de quê.*" Kelsey nodded appreciatively as Charley disappeared through the back door.

✺

Olivia was working out with her Czech trainer by the pool when Charley jogged past. Olivia did her best to stay in immaculate shape too. It wasn't easy, as her landing gear was down on the way to fifty, but what the exercise didn't fix, plenty of discreet surgeons could keep taut.

Surgeons like Dr. Blake Masters.

Charley blew a kiss to her mother and burst into the hills overlooking the basin.

More of the harbor was awake now.

Cutting through the water in the distance was the blue-and-green-striped mainsail of the *Fancy Face IV*.

7 SHAWN AND BELLE

BELLE STOOD ON THE BOW, CLAIRE AT HER SIDE, AS THE *FANCY Face IV* cut through the choppy water.

"Whee." Claire giggled as they rode the waves as though they were on horseback, matching their rhythms to the water's rise and fall.

"Whee!" Belle responded. "Hang on tight."

Belle had never realized how much she could love one little girl.

The wind whipped their hair as Shawn called from the wheel. "You two okay?"

Belle was feeling a bit better this morning, but still queasy from last night's champagne and sex that had lasted into the wee hours. No, she hadn't really felt like making love. It seemed to be the last thing on her mind lately. Especially after what had happened when they were in Egypt.

Belle had been having bad cramps that morning in Egypt, so Shawn insisted she spend the day pampering herself. He had suggested she relax in the spa at the Four Seasons Hotel while he took Claire on a barge ride through Dr. Ragab's Pharaonic Village.

In the hotel's opulent lobby, she had run into Philip. Yes, that Philip, Philip Kiriakis, her ex and the thorn in Shawn's side, was in Cairo on a quick business trip for Titan Industries.

It had been wonderful seeing an old friend from home, whatever the outcome of their last encounter. They had spent the afternoon near the bright blue stained-glass window in the Tea Lounge, eating sumptuous Turkish treats and talking. She had never told Shawn; she knew he'd have gone berserk, so she kept the brief encounter to herself. Belle also knew Philip wouldn't mention it to anyone in Salem, especially with all the ups and downs he and his new wife, Melanie, had been through.

But the memories of that afternoon lingered. When she looked in Shawn's eyes, the omission of that meeting made her feel guilty. Not the best emotion to feel when her husband wanted to make love.

Belle had also been extremely tired lately, especially keeping tabs on a precocious three-year-old. Plus she'd been working on her designs whenever the sea was calm enough for her sketches to convey what she had in her head.

They were sketches she hoped she'd be able to show Olivia Gaines. She still couldn't believe she hadn't had the nerve to go into the boutique to introduce herself yesterday. Then again, Belle wanted to approach her idol professionally, not in her white shorts and Top-Siders with her daughter and husband in tow.

"Mommy, look!" Claire squealed, breaking Belle's concentration. "More helicopters!"

Indeed, the celebs were on their way. For Dalita Kasagian's party on the 421-foot yacht.

The *Fancy Face IV* cut into a huge wake, spraying Belle and Claire with water. The two were drenched.

Belle was pleased this wasn't the day she'd meet Olivia.

∞

The sun was full and warm and dried off Belle and Claire quickly. The temperature would reach nearly eighty degrees today, so it indeed was brilliant weather.

They'd been en route for over an hour, when they pulled into the harbor at Cannes.

While Shawn dropped anchor, Belle got herself and Claire dressed for the day.

"You guys ready?' Shawn called into the main cabin.

"Yup," Claire responded.

Shawn had lowered their dinghy into the water. It was a miniature version of the boat—named the *Fancy Face IV and a Half*—and they took that in to the bustling seaside resort.

It cost Shawn a pretty penny to dock the tiny dinghy during high season, but the hundred-dollar tip was worth it.

"Hungry?" Shawn asked as he rubbed Claire's tummy. "How 'bout the Carlton?"

Belle wasn't hungry, but the thought of sitting at the beach restaurant of the famous hotel and sipping a Ramos Fizz sounded lovely. They would be rubbing shoulders with *nouveau riche* tourists who came to the hotel known internationally as the hub of the Cannes Film Festival. Those who were there not only to dine, but to see and be seen.

Not long after they served, the moment Belle clinked her

glass with her husband's Bloody Mary, they suddenly heard, "Shawn? Belle?"

Running up to them from La Croisette were Shawn's half sister, Chelsea, and Abby Deveraux.

"Hey, little one," Chelsea said as she hugged her niece tightly.

"Auntie C," Claire answered, hugging back. "Who're you?" she asked Abby.

"You don't remember me?" Abby answered, feigning hurt. "I'm your Auntie's friend Abby from Salem."

"So-rry." The little girl shrugged.

"What are you guys doing here?" Shawn asked.

"Nice to see you too." Chelsea laughed, flashing her big brown eyes.

"We could ask you the same," Abby chimed in.

"Just one—fabulous—stop on our world tour," Belle answered.

"And—" Shawn said, looking for an explanation.

"Abby's here covering this huge party for Spectator.com," Chelsea answered. "It's on Serge Kasagian's yacht. He's some mega-wealthy industrialist or something. It's supposed to be a very big deal."

"We know," Belle said. "We've seen his aircraft carrier. By the way, is Max with you?"

"No," Chelsea said, motioning her hand back and forth. "We're kind of comme ci, comme ça at the moment."

Although Chelsea and Abby were best friends again, Abby's crush on Max was always a sore subject between them.

Belle let it drop. Max and Chelsea were an off-and-on kind of couple.

"Spectator.com, huh?" Shawn interrupted, changing the subject. "I didn't realize that was you."

It shouldn't have been too much of a surprise. Abby, the beautiful young blonde, had journalism in her blood.

"Mom and Dad." Abby glanced at Claire. "Remember Jack and Jennifer—"

Claire shrugged again.

"Anyway, when they wanted to do an online site for the paper, I asked—no, begged—to do it," Abby said. "We've done okay," she added modestly.

"Okay?" Chelsea said incredulously. "You guys are almost as big as TMZ."

She high-fived her best friend.

"What can I say? People like me." Abby smiled wryly.

"We're going to the party," Chelsea said, indicating her Nikon. "I want a shot with Robert Pattinson."

"We'll be in the press area outside the party," Abby corrected.

"But if anyone can get in, you will," Chelsea added.

"Da's taking me to ride go-karts at Buggy Whip," Claire chimed in.

Buggy Whip was the most popular attraction for kids in the south of France, and to her, that was better than any lousy old birthday party on a boat.

"Then we head back and hope to make it to St. Nicholas Cathedral," Belle said with hope in her voice.

"Princess Grace and Prince Rainier's graves." Chelsea nodded. "I remember you were a fan."

"Yuck," Claire replied.

The maître d' approached.

"Americans, yes?" he said without the disdain he most certainly felt. "Will you be joining your friends?"

"Oh, no, we won't, Michel," Abby answered, making sure she read his engraved name badge. "We have to get ready for the Kasagian party. But thank you so much. Hope we weren't a bother."

Abby slipped him a fifty-dollar bill.

"*Mais non*, Mademoiselle." He smiled. "Join us anytime."

He glided off, and Chelsea gave a knowing look to Belle and Shawn. "What can I say?"

"We have to jam anyway," Abby reminded her friend.

"Have you seen your folks yet?" Chelsea asked Belle carefully, knowing she and Abby had to scoot.

"We're going up there in a couple of days," Belle responded.

"Give them my love," Chelsea said carefully, not wanting to pry. "And we're here until Monday," she added, indicating her cell phone. "Let's figure out something."

Shawn stood. "Absolutely. It's crazy we don't keep in better touch, Sis."

"Crazy," Chelsea answered.

Dropping her Coach bag and camera on the table, she gave her big brother a warm hug.

"Chels!" Abby called as she snared a taxi.

Chelsea dashed off and into the cab as the waiter presented Shawn with the bill.

"Whew." He whistled. "But worth every penny."

Kissing his wife, Shawn added, "Now let's get our party started."

Claire and her da high-fived, not seeing Belle surreptitiously putting her hand to her forehead.

The three got up to go, and Claire noticed Chelsea's Nikon still on the table.

"Da!" Claire squealed. "Auntie Chelsea needs her camera."

But it was too late. Chelsea and Abby's taxi had disappeared down La Croisette.

8   *MARLENA AND JOHN*

EVERY DAY HAD ALWAYS BEEN A FRESH START FOR MARLENA. SHE was one of those people who had always been endlessly optimistic. Marlena's mother, a stoic Scandinavian, had raised her daughter to live with the belief that the world can throw you a million challenges, but life goes on. Through even the most difficult times, there is a light at the end of the tunnel.

Marlena wanted to believe that desperately, but the challenges were getting harder and harder.

In the crisp morning air of Lausanne, Marlena strolled through the vineyards on their property. When she was home—and now Lausanne was their home—she did it daily to clear her head. Picking a handful of grapes, she smelled their sweet aroma.

The scent was heavenly.

Her cell phone chirped, indicating a text: "Need 2 c u."

It was from Dr. Masters. She found herself smiling.

"*Docteur* Evans, I'm so sorry," she heard behind her.

Marlena jumped, covering the screen, feeling a twinge of guilt. It was Desiree approaching, and there was deep concern in her voice.

Marlena's knee-jerk reaction was, "Is it John?"

As a doctor, Marlena knew that tone.

"No, oh, *mais non;* he's stable this morning," Desiree assured her. "I've had a family emergency—that call last night—and I have to visit my father."

"In Paris." Marlena nodded knowingly.

"There's a flight at two. I'll be back the day after tomorrow. Please don't fire me," she rambled.

"Of course we won't," Marlena said, surprised that Desiree would even suggest that. "I can cover whatever he needs until Kristina gets back."

Desiree knew John wouldn't like that.

"Is that a problem?" Marlena asked, based on her reaction.

Before Desiree could answer, the sound of a car approaching caught their attention. It was the day nurse, Kristina, and she was several hours early.

"And problem solved." Marlena smiled reassuringly.

"*Merci,*" Desiree said as she looked heavenward and crossed herself. "And thank you too," she added to Marlena.

"How are you getting to the airport?" Marlena asked a bit too quickly. "I have to go into Geneva, so I could take you."

"Are you sure?" Desiree asked. The cost of a cab would be expensive, and the train schedule was tight.

"Absolutely. But we'd better hurry."

Marlena surreptitiously glanced at Dr. Masters's text before slipping the phone into her pocket.

Heading to the house, Marlena felt her face flush.

What am I doing?

∞

John sat up on the end of his bed, watching the exchange between Marlena and his nurse in the vineyard.

In one of his many incarnations, he had worked out of Salem's branch of the ISA—the International Security Alliance. While working for the secret spy agency, he had honed his observational skills. John knew how to read people.

Especially his wife.

He knew Marlena's every move, including the shifting of her weight, the tilting of her head, and the touch of her finger to her lips. She was anxious, and there were so many things for her to be anxious about.

They had not had sex for well over a year. His paralysis was at the hands of a crazed psychiatrist who had been treating him for a condition foisted upon him by his nemesis, Stefano DiMera. Stefano, who had been revealed to be his half brother, was a man so evil that everyone in Salem knew him to be capable of the deepest, most convoluted deceptions. For now, John had to accept that he was indeed Stefano's blood relative, and if so, his own brother was ultimately responsible for this debilitating condition, a condition so vile that it had left him virtually unable to perform even the most mundane tasks and also the most important—making love to the woman he cherished more than life.

But in the last few months, John had made impressive strides in his recovery. Improvements Marlena knew nothing about.

The confidentiality agreements he'd made with every person he hired made that possible. Ultimately, he was paying the bills, and money talks.

Watching Marlena from this vantage point made him feel safe. Slowly, he got up from his sitting position and stood.

After taking a phone from the pocket of his pajama bottoms, he dialed a familiar number. He moved cautiously to the edge of the window as the phone rang, keeping an eye on Marlena and staying out of her line of sight.

Shirtless, his sinewy body and well-defined abs were confirmation that he was in better-than-average condition.

"It's John, and I need to see you," he said to the voice on the other end of the phone. "When?" he said incredulously. "As soon as humanly possible."

John noticed Marlena and Desiree heading back into the house and abruptly ended the call.

With a slow but steady gait, he made it back to the bed just as Marlena reached the top of the stairs.

Thinking John was resting, she knocked lightly.

"John?" she said.

He cleared his throat as though he hadn't spoken for a while. "Ah, come on in."

He settled back into the elegant chocolate-colored sheets, and Marlena entered.

"Desiree needs to go into Geneva, so I'm going to take her," Marlena said calmly. "Kristina's already here and said she'd cover."

"Kristina's good; that's fine."

"Anything I can get you before I go?" she asked.

"You'll be home late?"

"I may do some shopping," she said, "and have a quick bite before coming back."

"In other words, yes?" he said, cocking his eyebrow.

"Maybe," she said, then quickly corrected herself. "Yes."

"Have a good one."

"I will," she answered.

A good what? Trip? Supper? Tryst with Blake Masters?

She shook off the thoughts that were making her stomach flutter, and kissed John on the forehead, then headed out the door.

John noticed her flick her hair as she glided out of his room.

Where are you going, Doc? he thought. Then he took out his phone once again and dialed.

"Tara, hi," he said. "You available? Marlena won't be home for hours."

9  *JACKSON*

THE HEADQUARTERS OF FINANCIAL GAINES GROUP, LLC, WERE ON the forty-first floor of One Canada Square in the London Borough of Tower Hamlets. Also known as Canary Wharf Tower, the skyscraper was not only the tallest building in the United Kingdom, but home to major media and banking institutions from around the world.

At the age of twenty-eight, Jackson Gaines, the oldest of Richard Gaines's children, was second in command of the business. Favoring his mother's side of the family, he had dark brown hair that matched his eyes. He was also lean and fit and, like his father, over six feet tall.

Movie-star handsome, he was impressive and imposing as he stood looking out his office window at the drizzly morning. He focused on the dome, the postmodern structure that would be housing the 2012 Summer Olympics and where ITV just completed shooting the wildly popular *Britain's Got Talent.*

"Think they'll have this crappy weather for the 2012?" Jackson asked the pretty petite blonde who sat at his computer, busily and efficiently copying files.

"Pardon, sir?" she responded.

"The weather," he repeated. "Sunny, but still bloody drizzle and fog. Guess it's why we all love the south of France."

He was making small talk, and she knew it.

"Have you been there?" Jackson asked.

"No, sir," she answered, not looking up. She thought he was flirting, and she couldn't help but be intrigued. But as hot as he was, this was business.

"Done here."

Jackson turned his attention as two men, around thirty or so, entered from the conference room.

"And I," the girl responded, moving back from Jackson's desk.

The three agents of the Financial Services Authority had been there since seven this morning.

She shrugged, shaking her head. She'd found nothing out of line.

The two men simultaneously did the same.

Jackson laughed. "I guess that means we're good?"

The taller of the men adjusted his glasses. "The figures all checked," he said evenly.

"I'm sure you understand," added his companion apologetically.

"When it comes to people's investments, you can't be too careful." Jackson smiled. "Especially when it looks too good to be true."

"Since the Madoff scandal—" the bespectacled agent started.

"No problem, guys," Jackson interrupted. "But if you're finished here, I've got a plane to catch."

"We're done," the blonde responded.

Jackson hit an intercom switch on his desk.

"Jules, can you see them out?" he asked.

A statuesque redhead who could have been a supermodel in another life appeared in the doorway and indicated for them to follow her.

"The main elevators are dodgy this morning." She smiled. "Let me take you to the private elevator."

Jackson winked at the blonde as the three intruders were ushered out, a gesture that wasn't lost on his assistant.

When he was alone, Jackson's demeanor changed from one of confidence to concern as he slipped his iPad into his new Asprey portfolio. Something felt wrong in the pit of his stomach, but he didn't know why.

His phone rang. The ringtone was "We Are Family" by Sister Sledge, and he knew right away it was Charley. She'd put that in his phone, and he had vowed to change it but hadn't bothered. Truth was, he liked it, and his wallpaper image of her making a funny face usually cheered him up.

"Hey, Sis," he answered.

"Puh-lease tell me you're coming tonight," she pleaded.

"What's tonight?" he teased.

"I cannot be there without you and Chance." She pouted.

"We're on the one fifty-five, arriving in Nice at five. Plenty of time," he confirmed.

"Are the girls coming too, or will I have you both to myself?" she asked.

"Your brothers are flying solo, Sis," he said, unaware Jules appeared behind him in the open doorway. "With this crowd, we'd be bonkers not to come stag."

Jackson didn't see Jules's reaction. She was one unhappy camper.

"We're meeting Dad for drinks at Mont Agel. Then we'll come up to the villa and go together," he insisted.

"I'll be waiting."

"Love you," he closed.

"Madly," Charley said and ended the call.

Jules stood stock-still for a moment, her heart pounding faster and faster.

Jackson sighed, then turned to see her standing there. He could read her expression. He knew her well.

"You know this is about business," he said. "We make millions off this arse Kasagian, not to mention what he spends on his slag of a daughter."

"I know," she answered, not caring one whit. "Business comes first."

There was tension in the air that was palpable. It usually meant one thing: sex.

She brushed past him, gliding her hand across his crotch as she moved to the credenza in front of the window. She slipped the business card she'd just gotten into her pocket and leaned over seductively.

For a moment, he forgot about business. Jackson crossed to his office door and locked it, then loosened his Armani tie.

As Jules pulled the drapes closed, she could see down the forty-one floors to the street. From this height, she fixated on what looked like three ants crossing the street to their reasonably priced car. They were the investigators who'd given Financial Gaines Group, LLC, a clean bill of health. Why wouldn't they, since they had only seen the books in the front of the office? The only books Jackson knew existed.

Her hand rested on the drapery pull.

Jackson moved up behind her and placed his hand over hers, shutting the drapes with force. He cupped her breasts and drew her tightly against his body.

"Don't worry; I'll be back to London in a flash," he said, hiking up her skirt.

We'll see, she thought.

He thrust himself inside her.

Enjoy this one, Jackson! Her mind was whirling, and not from the sex. *It's the last time for both you and your dear old daddy.*

∞

Olivia and Charley were at the shop, selling ridiculously expensive last-minute frocks, belts, and bling to the celebs who'd popped over for the "Party of the century!" as Kasagian insisted on calling it. They had to be selective, though, as they didn't want to see any OMGs in the "Who Wore it Best?" columns in the tabloids.

As she led a pouty Megan Fox into one of the white leather dressing rooms, Olivia overheard Charley talking with her brother.

"They'd better not miss that plane," Olivia warned.

"They know better. They're Gaineses," Charley answered, hoisting her head high with a snobby tone.

Olivia laughed, then handed several high-end, low-cut garments to Ms. Fox. "No one could wear these like you, gorgeous."

Charley rolled her eyes at her mother, muttering, "Especially since Jessica Simpson has passed on them."

"It's all about salesmanship, sweet girl," Olivia reminded her daughter.

"I'm a Gaines, Mother. I know," Charley said reassuringly.

Olivia's platinum iPhone vibrated. "Don't tell me it's one of those tacky *Real Housewives* people." She grimaced. Her eyes widened as she saw the text.

"Favor?" She pouted to her daughter.

"Anything," Charley said, giving her standard reply.

"Joy Vella and Teddy have flown in from LA to do Gemma Kasagian," Olivia started. "They're two of the best hair people in Hollywood. And they can fit me in this morning at the house."

They, both in unison, said, "Could you cover here for me?"

Olivia cocked her eyebrow and laughed. "You know me too well. You know how I love them."

"You know I will, and you know how I love you," Charley assured her always–very-catered-to and always-very-spoiled mother. She also knew that Charley loved one-upping the mega-rich Gemma and would pay anything to get them to her first. Ah, Olivia…control, control, control.

Olivia's need to be in control was infamous. Which would have made her even more enraged if she had any idea that at that very moment, Richie was at the house, in bed with their sweet Portuguese housekeeper, Kelsey.

Olivia literally shoved Charley to the dressing-room door and knocked lightly. "How we are doing, darling?"

The door opened, and Megan Fox looked fabulous. Her curves filled out the white mini and low-cut chemise top beautifully.

"Stunning." Olivia gasped. "Charley's going to finish you up. I've had a family emergency, and she's the best."

"See you at the bash," Megan stated as she stared at her

image in the mirror. The mini clung perfectly to her highly publicized tush.

"The white thigh highs," Olivia suggested as she gave Charley a peck on the cheek and sailed out the door.

Entering as she swept by were Chelsea and Abby, trying to get a peek at the shop that currently catered to the crème de la crème in Monaco.

"*Un moment, s'il vous plait*," Charley called to them.

"No problem." Abby smiled. Then, under her breath to Chelsea, "Megan Fox. I thought that was her bodyguard out front."

"Right again," Chelsea said, impressed.

Charley returned, having delivered the boots to Megan. She couldn't help but notice Abby's camera.

"No cameras inside. I'm sure you understand our clients need privacy," Charley said nicely but firmly.

"I don't even have mine." Chelsea smiled in assurance.

Charley blanched, realizing Chelsea's smile and perfectly straight teeth were practically mirror images of her own.

"'Scuse me?" the famous customer called.

Charley gave the girls a "sorry 'bout that" look, and headed back to pamper her client.

"This makes it fun," Abby said under her breath to her buddy. And off Chelsea's quizzical look added, "The forbidden shots are the ones we die for."

She put her phone to her ear, aiming the camera directly at the dressing room. Abby was a pro at this and got a quick shot before Chelsea knew it.

"Still trying to figure out tonight, though," Abby added. "No unauthorized press on the yacht, and even then, no cameras, including mobiles, allowed."

As if in answer to her prayers, the door opened and a stunning, blond, and tanned thirty-year-old walked in. He looked as if he had stepped off the pages of a Tom Ford campaign.

"Hi." He grinned, nearly knocking Abby's socks off.

Charley returned and flashed a knowing smile. "Andy, here for the swag?"

"Thanks." He nodded.

Charley unlocked the cabinet under the counter and retrieved three white leather locked boxes and handed them to Andy with the keys. His gaze was fixated on Abby.

"Andy?" Charley interrupted.

"Ah, yeah?" he said, snapping back from his fascination with the all-American blonde.

"If there are any left, Mr. Kasagian can keep them. He's paid for them all," she said. "You handling security personally tonight?"

"I am," Andy responded.

"See you then." Charley smiled.

Andy hoisted the boxes of white gold OMG key chains and headed out of the shop, stopping to glance back at Abby.

"Too bad he's always had a thing for blondes," Charley said, looking to Chelsea.

"Too damn bad." Abby sighed with a Cheshire-cat grin.

Chelsea knew exactly what that meant.

10  *MARLENA AND JOHN*

IT NORMALLY TOOK MARLENA LESS THAN AN HOUR TO REACH the Geneva International Airport from Maison du Noir. It was a beautiful drive with the Swiss countryside on one side and views of Lake Geneva on the other. Today, however, the traffic was heavy.

August is the busiest month for tourism in most of Europe, and Switzerland is no exception. A fender bender in the fast lane of the thruway didn't help. European traffic was no better than that in the States; there are lookie loos in every country of the world.

On top of the frustrating traffic, the drive with Desiree was strained, and Desiree was visibly shaken.

What Marlena didn't know was that Desiree's father, Maurice Gauche, had been guiding his daughter's investments since she graduated from nursing school. And things were falling apart.

Dr. Gauche, because he was so well respected, had the ear of not only Desiree and her friends, but also dozens upon dozens of medical professionals from nurses' aides to heads of the medical boards across Europe.

Everyone trusted him completely.

In fact, Marlena had once been contacted by Dr. Gauche for a meeting, but John's condition had been so tenuous at the time that she passed.

Marlena pulled into the airport whose northern end runs along the Swiss-French border. Fortunately, travelers going to or from France didn't have to go through customs and immigration if they stayed in the French section of the airport, so Desiree would likely make it to the plane on time.

"I cannot thank you enough for this, *Docteur* Evans," Desiree said as she grabbed her overnight case from the Mercedes.

"Let us know if someone needs to pick you up," Marlena said.

"You are too kind," Desiree answered, then sprinted into the Air France Terminal for the two-o'clock flight.

Not too kind.

Marlena didn't want to admit it, even to herself, but she relished excuses to drive through the Swiss countryside. Not that she needed them, but with John growing more and more distant, she found herself welcoming time away from the estate.

She checked her rose gold Oyster Rolex that had been a gift from Salem Hospital's staff when she and John left.

It was 1:25.

Marlena checked her phone. There was no return text from Blake Masters.

When she had received his text that morning, Marlena had been interrupted by Desiree. Then, in her rush to leave, she had merely texted back that she could see the plastic surgeon today.

He could be in surgery, she thought. *For what other reason wouldn't he answer?*

Someone honked behind her and shouted something rude in French. Before she could put her foot to the floor, a burly Frenchman jumped out of his car, slamming his door.

It was times like this she appreciated John's insistence on the best for her. Her Mercedes, an S65 AMG, was not only the safest car on the road, but also the most agile. She was away from her pursuer in a flash and maneuvered quickly out of the airport and toward Blake Masters's four-story offices on Route de Chêne.

Her fingers tapped the steering wheel as she drove, and she became very aware of the diamond on her left hand.

After parking her car with the strapping young valet downstairs, she entered through the familiar pink door.

∞

"Dr. Evans," the receptionist said, perplexed. "Did you have an appointment?"

The receptionist remembered her after only one visit, and Marlena was once again impressed.

She stammered, "I–I'm not actually sure. Dr. Masters said he wanted to see me today…"

That's not exactly true, she realized.

"There must be some error. I am so sorry." The petite redhead frowned. "Dr. Masters isn't in the office today."

"Oh, it must be my mistake," Marlena said.

"He'll be in tomorrow, and we have a cancellation. Would you like me to put you in the book?"

"Tomorrow," she said. "Yes, please—" Marlena realized she'd never asked the receptionist's name. That was not like her.

"Lisa," the redhead answered, saving embarrassment. "Three o'clock?"

"Perfect," Marlena said, though she had no idea if it was. Feeling flushed, she just wanted to get out of there.

Taking the card from Lisa, she put it in her bag and quickly exited.

The afternoon air was balmy, and she drank it in. Without her even asking the valet, he brought her car.

What now?

Putting the car in drive, she headed for one of the parks. The Natural History Museum was a few blocks away, and she could clear her head.

Then the *ding!* of a text: "Perle du Lac. 5 p.m.?"

It was a lovely restaurant next to the Lake Geneva footpath.

Marlena hesitated. *A restaurant?*

After a two-second hesitation, she texted back: "See you then."

Marlena knew the shorthand text lingo, but it seemed so impersonal. She checked her watch again. Two hours to kill. Or should she go home? Now? Right now?

∞

She was sitting under a turquoise umbrella on the serene terrace of Perle du Lac overlooking the footpath and nursing a glass of Domaines Ott when she finally saw Blake headed toward her.

"Dr. Evans," he said shakily.

"Marlena," she corrected him, then quickly wished she hadn't. "Are you all right?"

"My son was playing baseball this morning and got hit in the face with a bat." He cleared his throat and signaled a nearby waiter. "He lost six of his permanent teeth and is a mess."

"My God."

"Bourbon on the rocks," he clipped. "Make it a double."

No need for translation. The staff in every restaurant and hotel spoke fluent English.

"A concussion?" she asked.

"Slight. He's going to be okay, but he'll have to have several sets of implants as he gets older."

Permanent teeth. Baseball. As he gets older. How old is he? What's more, how old are you?

"He's twelve."

That's right. He can read my mind.

"This is why all the confusion today," he said. "I stopped at the clinic, and Lisa said you'd been in. Checked my phone and realized…"

"As long as your son's going to be all right." She tried to comfort him. "And if there's anything I can do for him or you, I'm happy to."

"The doctor doctoring the doctor," he said, smiling that crooked and sexy smile.

The waiter set his bourbon on the table and also a fresh glass of rosé for Marlena.

"You needed to see me," Marlena said.

There was an odd mix of tension and guilt in the air. Blake had wanted to see her again, badly, having had dreams of his hands all over her body and knowing that for some reason John wasn't being honest about his own.

"Evelyne, my wife, has sent the samples from John's back to the lab," he answered. "She should have the results back in the next few days."

"Good."

"To his health," Blake said, raising his glass.

"And your son's," Marlena answered. The crystal glasses pinged as they toasted one another. Their hands briefly touched, and both reacted by pulling away. It was a familiar touch and made them instantly uncomfortable.

A moment lost, he thought.

A moment saved, she thought.

Adultery was something Marlena abhorred. She had only strayed once in her life, while she was married to Roman. But that had been a confusing time in her life in Salem. Salem, where life was never quite normal. Her lover then was John, and their encounter had caused her to become pregnant with Belle.

All those thoughts swam through her head as her eyes met Blake's.

If only she weren't so needy, and Dr. Masters so incredibly fascinating.

But vulnerability was no excuse, and she was as vulnerable as she'd ever been. She knew at that moment that she needed to steer clear, very clear, of this temptation.

11   *CHARLEY & OLIVIA*

THE SUN WAS SETTING OVER THE HILLS BEHIND THE GAINES Villa, streaking hues of peach and crimson across the crisp blue sky. The August night, as usual, was spectacular.

The engraved invitations for dumpy little Dalita's party stated that the festivities began at eight o'clock sharp and would last until a line of Swarovski crystal question marks. In other words, this party could go on forever.

Party wasn't just a word in the south of France; it was a lifestyle. But even those who regularly partied until dawn felt that for a sweet sixteen, the extravagance was a little much.

That didn't stop anyone from RSVP'ing, as much to see the obnoxious extravagance of offshore pharmaceutical king Serge Kasagian as to fete his daughter. Oh yes, and Gemma Kasagian.

It was rumored that Gemma owned three of the largest diamonds in the world and loved to pass them around for her friends to hold and drool over during dinner parties. Of course, the Kasagians didn't realize their blinding flash didn't stir up envy, but instead pity for a family who had wealth but no self-worth. They were an amusement and nothing more.

The Gaineses, while occasionally invited onto the yacht, weren't truly on that social level, as hard as that was to believe. As successful as Olivia was, she couldn't stop trying to compete with their socially ridiculed friends.

It was the one thing Charley didn't like about her mother.

It was after seven when Charley got home from the shop and flew up the stairs to get dressed.

Jackson and Chance hadn't arrived but were due any minute, and she had to be ready.

Charley's loo was a bit of a mess, but she knew exactly where everything was.

She threw on a big plastic shower cap covered with flamingos, then got in the shower. The water was tepid, as she liked it in summer, and jets from all sides cooled her.

"7:10," she muttered, looking at the clock embedded in the side of the marble shower. She began scrubbing quickly.

"Have you heard from Jackson?" Olivia said as she poked her head into the bathroom.

"Not yet," Charley answered.

"I told your father I'd meet him there. Why he likes to arrive on time is a mystery to me."

The truth was, Richard Gaines never wanted to make a big entrance, and it was impossible with Olivia on his arm. Even though he'd walk three paces behind her, he'd be caught by the cameras, and he didn't like it.

If Richard went on his own, he was just one more mega-multi-millionaire so no one cared.

It also meant he could have his daily tryst with one of the women he had in every port. Kelsey, his Jennifer Lopez look-alike housekeeper here in Monte Carlo. Jules in London, Mimi, Gayle, Robin...some with names he'd never bothered to ask.

Charley flipped off the shower and grabbed a plush towel from above the bidet.

"The party's all on a timed schedule, with guests arriving at fifteen-minute intervals," Charley reminded her.

"Gemma is such a control freak," Olivia responded, totally oblivious to this flaw in her own character.

"It makes sense when trying to get three hundred guests down that dock," Charley answered. "Is Garrison driving you?"

"He has the night off," she said gleefully. "I'm going to drive all of us. Won't that be fun?"

Charley pasted on a smile. "Fun," she answered.

Truth be told, her mother's driving made them all crazy. But Olivia loved her yellow DBS and loved seeing herself in the press described as "free-spirited, unpredictable, and carefree."

"Now hurry! And no yellow!"

While hot orange was *the* color this season, Olivia was known for always wearing shades of yellow to parties. She knew it made her stand out—as if she needed to—and matched her ridiculously expensive car.

Charley pulled a slim orange sheath from her closet as Olivia smiled and flitted out.

Charley wasn't like her mother. She could throw herself together and look fabulous. Her makeup routine was minimal, in part due to her flawless skin, lush lashes, and perfectly arched brows that framed those sensational blue eyes flecked with hazel and brown.

While orange wasn't known to complement brunettes, everything seemed to complement Charley's coloring beautifully. She slipped on a pair of five-inch OMG pumps, applied a few quick strokes of her favorite Bobbi Brown mascara, followed by rich salmon lip color, and ran a brush through her hair.

In twenty minutes total, she was ready.

∞

"Is this osetra?" Olivia said, curling up her nose in disappointment, looking at a silver tray full of canapés set on the bar downstairs near the foyer.

"I'm sorry, Mrs. Gaines, but with the Kasagians' party…" Kelsey's voice trailed off.

"I can't believe they bought up all the beluga in the area," Olivia answered.

"Mrs. Kasagian sent this to tide you over," Kelsey informed her.

"Typical of the bitch," Olivia said, scrunching her well-sculpted nose.

This was a routine they went through every time Olivia had a big night out. Whether in Monte Carlo, London, or the Hamptons, it was the same story.

Kelsey knew her boss would only take a nibble or two at the party. Olivia wanted everyone to believe she stayed thin through dieting, not liposuction at the bitty bulge of an extra pound.

She would have a drink or two, or three, maybe more, which is why she insisted on caviar before she went out. She'd been given a tip that eggs contain cysteine, the same nonessential amino acid that helps combat a hangover.

Olivia rationalized that if poultry eggs have it, certainly the crème de la crème of cysteine would be in caviar. Thus, she reasoned, a few ounces of caviar with blini and an egg-salad tea sandwich or two before a party would not only help keep her from chowing down in front of the crowd, but would also stave off a killer headache in the morning. She was such a fanatic that she'd also recently bought cysteine capsules that she'd down on her way out the door.

Olivia was a master at rationalization.

The silver tray with blini and caviar, cucumber tea sandwiches, and pâté with crackers was set on the bar that was just off the foyer in the villa. Within minutes, the caviar was nearly gone.

It was seven forty-five when Charley scurried down the massive staircase.

"Any word from Jackson, Mum?" Charley asked, trying to hide her concern.

"I spoke to your father, and he said the boys were running late," she answered. "Jules called from London saying they had been detained."

"I'm going to wring Jackson's neck when I see him." Charley scowled.

Charley scooped up a spoonful of caviar and popped it in her mouth.

"Well then, we need to go without them." Olivia grinned.

"Your vitamins, ma'am," Kelsey said. She offered Olivia two of the bright red capsules on a rectangular porcelain tray that was imprinted with the royal seal of Monaco. Her hands were a bit shaky. It had been a long day filled with arguments, and she had a headache.

"Thank you for remembering, Kelsey." Olivia smiled as she placed the capsules on her tongue. She took them with a sip of champagne. "And get two for Charley, Kelsey."

Charley held up her hand.

"I don't believe in supplements, Mummy, you know that," Charley answered.

"Humor me." Olivia pouted, giving her that look that only meant she'd never give up.

Kelsey hesitated, but Charley finally nodded in agreement. She knew if she didn't agree, they'd never get out the door on time.

Kelsey checked the bottle, but there were none left.

"Sorry, Mrs. Gaines. Those were the last two," she said somewhat shakily.

"Shucks." Charley smiled. "To a fabulous night," she added, then downed the last of her Dom Pérignon rosé.

12 IN AN INSTANT...

ABBY HAD APOLOGIZED TO CHELSEA FOR NOT TAKING HER TO the blast on the boat but knew she had to be able to maneuver solo.

"Any chance you have my camera, Shawn?" Chelsea said in a voice that meant she didn't think so.

"Your Nikon?" he said.

"I love you!" she squealed. Chelsea was on her cell, wandering the beautiful streets of Monaco as she looked out to the harbor. The party was definitely under way.

"The camera's not that expensive, but I have so many memories on it."

"Not to mention that Robert Pattinson thing," Shawn added.

"How humiliating." Chelsea laughed. "Don't know if you can see the party from your boat, but all I can say is, wow."

She could indeed see paparazzi swarming the docks as celebrities arrived one by one in chauffeured Bentleys, Lamborghinis, and Maseratis, having been picked up from the gem of Monte Carlo, the Hôtel de Paris.

Dropped at the easternmost dock of the most beautiful and

infamous harbor in the world, they were escorted a few steps to four suited, immaculately groomed men armed with earpieces.

Andy, whom she and Abby had met at OMG, was one of them, and even from a distance, Chelsea could see he was in charge.

Ivanka Trump, Kate Moss, Emma Roberts, and Katy Perry and Russell Brand were greeted by name and given a personal escort to the ship. In fact, one of the jobs of this security detail was to have visuals on all the guests who'd been invited. They had to recognize by sight everyone from the most popular stars in the world to Serge Kasagian's most boring friends.

There was also a high-def security camera trained on the entrance, recording everyone's moves.

Flashbulbs popped, and the night air was charged as if it had been hit by lightning. Abby was amid the banned reporters.

The celebs and glitterati kept arriving, and Richard Gaines was among them. As he'd wanted, no one from the press paid the least attention to him.

"Are you guys still in town?" Chelsea asked hopefully.

"Nope."

Shawn and Belle were back in the main cabin of the *Fancy Face IV*, Belle cradling a very tired little girl.

"Oh…" Chelsea replied, unable to hide the disappointment in her voice.

"Maybe we can hook up tomorrow?" Shawn asked.

Belle signaled him. "Meet her tonight."

"Really?" he replied.

"I'm exhausted, and Claire won't know you're gone," Belle said, gesturing to their conked-out three-year-old.

"Want me to come in to meet you now?" Shawn asked.

"Really?" she answered, echoing her brother.

"Where do want to meet?" Shawn asked, appreciating Belle's offer.

"We're staying at the Monte Carlo Beach Hotel," she said, then quickly added, "Not the heart of Monte Carlo, but we didn't have reservations, and apparently, Kasagian—"

Shawn cut her off. "Booked out the entire city."

"Pretty much."

Seeing Belle wave him off, he said, "I can meet you in twenty."

"Heaven," Chelsea replied.

Shawn hung up and turned to his wife. "You're the best."

"Have fun. But don't wake me when you get back. I am just—"

"Exhausted," he said, finishing her sentence.

Giving Belle a quick kiss, Shawn disappeared up the steps of the galley.

Belle cradled her sleeping daughter.

What's wrong with me? she wondered. *Why don't I want Shawn to touch me?*

Deep in her heart, she knew.

∞

It took less than thirty minutes for Shawn to take the dinghy past the yachts, sailboats, and launches into dock, and within five, he saw his half sister.

The night was so beautiful that they decided to have drinks on the hotel's terrace. The views were calming, and most of the tourists were out on the town, so it was quiet enough to talk.

SHERI ANDERSON

They took a seat and ordered drinks. Chelsea asked for a lemon drop, and Shawn an Amstel.

"Abby at the party?" he asked as the waiter served them.

"Yes. Well, not sure, but knowing her, she definitely will be."

"You're looking good."

"You too," Chelsea stated. Then she wondered aloud, "Have you talked to Dad lately?"

"Texted a few times," Shawn said. "But you know him. Not that great a communicator."

Chelsea envied that Shawn knew Bo that well. She was a daughter Bo hadn't even known he had until she was well into her teens, and she had caused plenty of grief for him and Shawn's mom, Hope, when she landed in Salem.

"I heard he and Hope have had problems lately," she said carefully. "Not that it's any of my business."

"You love him and want him to be happy. That makes it your business."

She clinked her glass to his. "Thanks."

He took a swig from his beer.

"You know, I bet he'd love a picture of us together. What do you say?"

Chelsea smiled at the idea. She liked being a part of Shawn's family.

Shawn flagged down the waiter. "Could you take our picture?" The waiter feigned being busy and dismissed the request from the American tourists.

There was a young, honeymooning couple at the next table. They looked American.

"Think you could give us a hand?" Shawn asked. "You take our picture, we'll take one of you."

The handsome young groom took Shawn up on the offer.

Chelsea and Shawn glanced around for the most appealing backdrop. After several tries, they realized shooting with the harbor as a backdrop just didn't work. The lights were indistinguishable.

"How about there?" Chelsea suggested. The jagged hills behind the hotel were lush and beautiful.

Shawn and Chelsea took their positions, and after several tries, he linked his arm around her waist.

They heard the hum of the camera's motor and then—*click!*

"One more for safety," their amateur photographer suggested. "Hold that!" he added.

All of a sudden, they heard screaming and a deafening crash high above them. Trees were being sawed in half as a car careened down the steep hillside.

"Oh my God!" the young bride wailed.

Click.

Click.

Click.

Now it was the silence that was deafening.

∞

The bright yellow of the DBS complemented what Olivia and Charley were both wearing for the gala. Olivia had a way of orchestrating every appearance she made as though it was part of OMGs marketing campaign.

As Olivia slid behind the wheel and onto the soft leather seats, she was exhilarated.

"If Gemma sees the two of us arriving, she'll be green with envy. And green's definitely not her color."

"We'll make a statement, that's for sure," Charley said in agreement.

Charley snapped her seat belt and urged Olivia to do the same.

Kelsey watched from the front door as Olivia wrapped her head with a pale gold scarf that matched the highlights Joy had given her, and then started the engine of the immaculate yellow Aston Martin.

The scrolled gates opened on cue, and the women drove out onto the spectacular drive that would take them to the beach several miles below.

The night was indeed gorgeous, and there were very few cars on the road. Stars illuminated the sky, and it was a full moon to boot.

Cool jazz filled the air as they listened to Thelonious Monk on their drive. Jazz always put Olivia in a sexy, cheeky, and, sometimes, raunchy mood.

After she navigated about half a mile, Olivia started trying to gulp in air.

"I'm more excited about this than I thought," Olivia said, gasping for air. "Do not tell Gemma. You promise me?"

Charley nodded, then noticed her mother's hand go to her tiny waist as she grimaced.

"You okay?" Charley asked.

Olivia nodded, but weakly.

"Mum?"

"The caviar," she said over the jazz and wind. "Probably American sturgeon. Ugh."

Olivia tried to keep steady on the road, but it was getting increasingly more difficult. The car swayed, and Charley had to steady the wheel.

"Mummy, pull over and let me drive," Charley insisted. She was feeling absolutely fine. If it was bad caviar, it certainly hadn't affected her.

"No, silly, I'm—" Olivia's voice was barely a whisper.

By now the car was beginning to swerve badly. Although they were on the treacherous Route de la Grande Corniche, Olivia was able to keep it under control.

Then a bicyclist appeared as if out of nowhere and stopped directly in their path. There was no way to avoid hitting him.

"Mummy!" Charley screamed.

The timing couldn't have been worse, as Olivia passed out, releasing the steering wheel from her grip.

Horrified, Charley grabbed the wheel with one hand and yanked it to the right to avoid hitting the bicyclist, while desperately trying to steady her mother with the other.

She missed him within inches, but the car slammed into the side railing.

It didn't stop them, however. Because of their speed, the DBS smashed the guardrail to bits and went airborne.

A streak of bright yellow, Charley's piercing scream, and the sound of splintering trees caught the attention of the tourists below as the gleaming Aston Martin plummeted to the street.

To those watching in shock, it was as if it were all happening in slow motion.

The car hit the pavement on the driver's side, then rolled twice before it landed upright.

A light hissing sound emanated from the engine. Then silence.

Charley was groggy in the passenger seat, strapped in and bleeding badly from a gash in her neck. She groaned softly and reached for her mother.

The driver's seat was empty. Olivia had been thrown from the car.

Charley slumped back in her seat as she lost consciousness.

Lying on the side of the road, twenty feet away, was Olivia. Her soft, shimmering, lemonade-colored dress was splattered with blood, and there was no sign of her breathing. The side of her beautifully sculpted face was crushed in.

She had died on impact.

13   *THE PARTY*

ONCE ON THE MAIN DECK OF *K*, SERGE KASAGIAN'S MEGAYACHT, guests were escorted to the first upper deck by white-mini-skirted waitresses and tanned shirtless waiters. With guests from all over the world, the waitstaff had been scrupulously vetted. Virtually every language was covered, so every guest would be royally taken care of.

Since no paparazzi were allowed on the ship, the blinding flash of cameras ceased once the guests made it inside—Richie Gaines among them.

Amid the gaggle of Euro-trash tweens, paid famous faces, and sycophant business associates, Serge made his way to Richie immediately and personally escorted him to the first of dozens of bars that peppered all three decks of the ship. With fifty bartenders, there was one for every six guests.

Cristal champagne flowed freely, as did the most expensive liquors in the world. Evan Williams bourbon, 1926 Macallan Fine and Rare scotch. For those who favored beer, one-hundred-dollar bottles of Sam Adams Utopia were on ice. For those who sipped cognac, they were offered Louis XIII Black Pearl.

"Your wish is her command," Serge said to Richie as he nodded to the blonde, well-endowed teenage bartender. The bar was lined with the finest crystal, including colorful Murano Carlo Moretti flutes.

"Vodka martini, straight up," Richie requested.

Serge nodded, and the seventeen-year-old retrieved a four-thousand-dollar bottle of Diva. Richie appreciated that. Each bottle contained real gemstones like the hidden jewels in Olivia's early designs.

She poured the liquid platinum into a silver shaker, chilling it to perfection.

"Sorry about all those cameras out there," Serge offered.

"I'll bill you if I need new glasses," Richie joked.

"Damn Fortunatov," Serge growled. "Did you hear about the *Elite*? That so-called boat has lasers that shoot right back in paparazzi's lenses. No one can get a good shot!"

Richie took the stemmed glass with slivered ice crystals from the beauty, who batted her eyes at the man old enough to be her grandfather.

"Where is your gorgeous wife?" Serge interrupted with a hint of jealousy. "And little Charley? What a stunner!"

"Should be here in about thirty minutes in all her glory, I assume. And she would not like those camera-blocking lasers." Richie smiled.

"The boys?" Serge asked.

"Running late too, but they wouldn't miss it."

"Gemma is not going to be happy if her schedule gets fucked up." Serge scowled. "And there's nothing else to buy her to keep her happy."

"Serge!"

Russian billionaire Alexei Fortunatov interrupted them. "What a nice little boat you have here," Fortunatov sneered. He was known for owning the Chelsea Football Club in the United Kingdom—and the most expensive yacht in the world. With its lasers.

"Serge was just showing me around, Alexei," Richie said, pasting on a sincere but firm smile. "Perhaps we'll chat later."

With that, Richie led Serge away from Serge's nemesis. One thing Richie knew was which side his bread was buttered on.

≈

"When will Da be home?" Claire yawned to her mother as the two sat in the cockpit of the *Fancy Face IV*.

"Probably not for a while, sweet pea," Belle answered. "He and Chelsea haven't seen each other for a long time."

"Will you read to me?" Claire asked.

"Why don't you run down and get your pj's on, and I'll be there in a few," Belle said gently. "I just want to finish up here." Claire tottered down the steps into the main cabin.

Belle was sitting at the small teak table, poring over the sketches she'd been working on for months. If she indeed managed to get a meeting with Olivia Gaines, she wanted them to be perfect.

Belle's career as a designer with her father's company, Basic Black, had been short-lived, but not because of her talent. She relished the idea of working for someone other than family, and the quality of the fabrics Olivia used complemented Belle's simple draped designs

Belle sat alone, nursing a Campari and soda to settle her

stomach, watching the beauty that surrounded her. The night was indeed stunning, and there was activity throughout the glittering harbor, hotels, and casino, and it spilled onto the jubilant streets of Monte Carlo.

Shawn and Belle's boat was moored a ways out from the main harbor, but from this vantage point, she could hear and see it all. The most activity obviously surrounded *K,* with the flashes of paparazzi on the dock and music pouring from every deck of the floating estate.

She wondered what had happened with Abby, and if she had been able to get into the soiree.

"Mommy!" She heard Claire call from below.

Shaking off her reverie, she called down to her daughter, "Right there, sweet pea."

Gathering up her sketches, she went to mark the upper corner of her revisions. She'd lost track of the date, which she'd often done on their remarkable journey, so she checked her iPhone.

August 16.

With her charcoal pencil, she scrawled the date on the three sketches she'd revised.

"August 16?" she thought aloud.

She was five days late.

"Must be all the excitement," she added.

Putting away the sketches in a watertight sleeve, she started making her way to Claire. But before she reached her daughter, something caught her eye in the distance.

Through binoculars, she could see the flashing of white police cars hurtling toward the base of the hills. A huge red fire truck behind them. The sounds barely audible over the cacophony of Dalita Kasagian's party.

Little did she know, Shawn was in the midst of the action.

∞

The Aston Martin sat teetering on its passenger side and looked as if it had been put through a vise. Every one of the aluminum panels were crumpled, the hood twisted like a piece of used foil.

Shawn was first on the scene and horrified by what he saw. Charley was strapped in her seat, blood spurting from a massive slice in her neck, but at least she was breathing.

"Call 911," he shouted to Chelsea.

"Do they have that here?" she blurted as she frantically dialed the number. "Hello! Hello!"

Before she could finish, she heard sirens in the distance.

"Mummy?" Charley groaned softly as she began to regain consciousness.

"Stay quiet," Shawn said, avoiding her question. "Help's on the way."

To stanch the flow of blood, he pulled off his T-shirt and pressed it firmly to her neck.

By now, Chelsea had reached Olivia's limp body and was checking her vitals. She'd been a candy striper at Salem University Hospital and knew to check Olivia's neck for a pulse. Even though she didn't feel one, she tried to administer CPR.

It was just too late.

Olivia had been thrown from the car because she wasn't wearing a seat belt. She always refused to do so when going to an event in which she would be photographed. She knew how everyone loved to see even the slightest flaw in celebrities, and she thought she was one. So no seat belt for her.

Now she was dead, the left side of her stunning face caved in. She would not look her best in the pictures soon to be taken.

A crowd was gathering, and there were gasps of horror and disbelief. The paparazzi from Dalita Kasagian's party were already on their way.

From high above the scene, on the Route de le Grande Corniche, the bicyclist watched the chaos below, then casually rode away.

∞

"There's been an accident. Bright yellow Aston Martin," the German photographer whispered to his partner excitedly. "Gotta be something good there!"

The news spread like a wildfire in a parched forest, and the paparazzi scrambled to their scooters, vans, and cars to be first on the scene.

The majority of the well-heeled partyers had arrived on Kasagian's yacht, and with no access inside the event, the paps were hungry for scoops.

Abby stayed put and sidled up to the hottie Andy, who'd flirted with her at the boutique. He had no idea who she was.

"Vultures," she said, cringing. She was grazed by one of the desperate parasites and feigned nearly falling at Andy's feet.

Andy had not seen the disturbance in the hills, so he opted not to notify Serge Kasagian that something had distracted the paparazzi and they'd left. The music was so loud inside the yacht that no one would have heard an atomic bomb. And if it was nothing, there'd be hell to pay and a job to lose.

"This is too dangerous," Andy said. "Get her inside," he instructed one of his other security guys.

Abby dashed up the gangplank and into the party. No one checked to see if she had a camera.

∞

For the moment, the party seemed to be wilder than ever. Abby took a lobster roll from the tray of a passing waiter, who asked, "What's going on out there?"

Abby shrugged. "Just some paparazzi climbing all over each other."

Abby took a glass of Cristal in one of the brightly colored hand-blown champagne flutes and headed to the upper deck.

Knowing how to blend in or stand out were tricks of Abby's trade. She'd learned from her father that the best journalists were the best observers. Like John Black had learned in the ISA, Abby had learned by working side by side with her parents just what was important to take in.

She passed the elite partygoers who had pasted-on smiles and chattered endlessly one-on-one, group-on-group as they scoured the room for more important guests to talk to. Dalita, the gnome, was in the midst of it all.

The ship was indeed mind-blowing, and the largest Abby had ever been on. Three decks, a ballroom, two massive dining rooms large enough to feed hundreds, a cinema, a disco, and who-knew-how-many cabins.

She headed up a winding Plexiglas staircase and noticed Serge Kasagian was not happy. She floated past him inconspicuously and heard him growl, "Emilio was not to leave this ship, in case Gemma needed him."

"I saw him on the lower deck, sir," answered one of the crew, who was nearly shaking in his boots. "Just before I came up."

Kasagian turned without seeing Abby and went a few feet to a wall panel that slid open in front of him. It was a private elevator, and in a second, he was gone.

Just after he disappeared, a furious Dalita came running up the stairs screaming, "Daddy! Daddy!!" Gemma, decked out in all her ostentatious jewels, appeared from the ballroom, a trail of syco-phants behind her.

"Precious girl, what's wrong?" she asked.

"That bitch just ruined my party!"

"Who?" Gemma sneered.

"Charley Gaines, that's who," Dalita wailed. "She and her fucking mother just had an accident, and no one's left outside to cover my party!"

Abby was in shock. So that's where they all went.

"I'm sorry, Dali," Gemma cooed. "So Olivia won't be here?" she added, more of a statement than a question.

"Any word on their condition?" Abby asked, out of true con-cern. Although she had only had that brief encounter with her earlier, she truly liked Charley.

"No. The police just came and took Mr. Gaines to the hospital." Dalita scowled. "Why do you care, anyway?"

"Don't worry, baby," Dalita's bitch of a mother said, taking her chin and disavowing Abby's existence. "All the fabulous people are still here."

Abby was dumbstruck by Gemma's monumental insensitivity. Her reporter instincts kicked in; she knew she was at the epicenter of one damn good story.

She flew down the stairs and made her way through the jabbering guests. In the corridor, she saw Dalita's father reading the riot act to another male employee in front of the partyer, the employee hastily buttoning his crew jacket.

Abby shuddered at the guy's humiliation. "Ah, the lives of the rich and famous…"

14   *THE HOSPITAL*

THE PAPARAZZI WERE SWARMING LIKE FLIES AROUND THE entrance to Princess Grace Hospital Centre. Considered the best hospital in Monaco, it was also the hospital where Princess Grace had died after her crash in the early '80s. They were falling all over each other to get shots of Richard Gaines's arrival.

This was one time he couldn't escape the cameras.

Monaco has the largest police force per capita in the world, and they flanked Richie as he entered the hospital. A dozen other officers remained outside to control the crowd.

Once inside the vestibule, Chief of Staff Roisten met Richie in the lobby. The moment Richie saw him, he knew it was bad news—horrible news. He learned that Olivia had died on impact from a crushed skull and internal injuries and that Charley was in surgery.

Uncharacteristically, Richie broke down in tears.

Shawn and Chelsea were just inside the door of the hospital, as they had been detained by the police. They were being questioned about the accident. They gave details about the sound of the crash and their rushing to the mangled Aston Martin.

Chelsea was shakily recalling how she had checked Olivia's vital signs and given CPR.

"You are sure there was no pulse," she was asked.

"Definitely," she said.

"Then why administer CPR?"

Chelsea knew that in the States a lot of medical professionals no longer administered lifesaving techniques at the scene of an accident, for fear of a lawsuit.

"If there was a breath of a chance, I wanted to give it to her," was Chelsea's shaky answer. She held back tears. This experience was bringing up memories of a disastrous time in her life when she'd been involved in a hit-and-run. The child she had hit—her own half brother—had died.

There was the sound of a text alert on her phone.

"May I?" she asked. The officer nodded.

The text was from Abby: "All hell broke loose. Where r u?"

"My best friend," she told the officer. "I need to let her know where I am."

The officer looked at the text and again nodded in agreement.

Chelsea texted: "Pr Grace Hsptl."

Abby's response: "U OK?! I'm outside."

Chelsea showed the officer the text. Her hands were starting to shake badly.

"Could they let her in, please?" Chelsea said, nearly pleading. "I really need her," she added.

"Of course," the officer answered. "Show me who she is."

The two of them headed to the door, passing Shawn, who was just completing his report to another officer.

"That pressure on her neck probably saved Charley Gaines's life," the officer said. "Somebody find this guy a shirt."

In the middle of the madness swirling around them, a nurse rushed in from the surgical ward.

"Mr. Gaines," she blurted, "your daughter's blood type is rare, and we're low. Do you know if you're a match?"

"Is she going to die?" was his first thought.

"Only if she loses too much blood," she answered.

"I think I'm type O," he said. "Would that make sense?"

"She's B negative," she answered. "One of the rarest. You're not a match. Neither was your wife."

"I'm B negative." It was Shawn. "I used to donate at University Hospital. Let's go."

Without a second thought, Shawn headed toward the lab.

∞

Abby was let in by the officers at the front door, and Chelsea went into her arms. They were given a moment alone.

"You're a wreck," Abby said. "What are you guys doing here?"

"Charley, the girl we met this afternoon," she stammered. "She and her mother were in a horrible accident. Shawn and I were the first ones there."

"You witnessed it all?" Abby said incredulously.

"It happened right behind us…" Her voice trailed off. "This nice guy was taking our picture, and…"

"Picture?" Abby gasped.

Chelsea could only nod, wrapping her arms around herself.

Sympathetic as Abby was, the journalist in her kicked in. "With your camera?"

Chelsea immediately understood the implication and gave Abby a withering look.

"This is international news, Chels," Abby reminded her.

Chelsea started to reach into her purse, but Abby stopped her.

"Is it all right if we go to the ladies' room?" Abby asked the policeman, who was going over his notes.

"Just don't leave the building," he answered.

"Not a problem," Abby said.

There was a woman in the handicap stall who was grunting and groaning. Chelsea asked if she needed help, but the woman said no.

Abby was on pins and needles until the woman opened the door with her foot and wheeled herself out to the sink and washed her hands slowly. She stared at the two girls, who'd done nothing since they entered ten minutes earlier.

"Let me help," Abby said, opening the exit door.

The woman exited without a word.

"Thank you too" Chelsea said, shaking her head.

"The camera?" Abby demanded. "In here."

The girls ducked into the handicap stall, and Chelsea retrieved her camera. She handed it over a bit reluctantly.

Abby clicked through the digital shots and nearly fainted.

"Take that TMZ," she squealed. "World exclusive."

∞

Charley's surgery had been going on for two hours.

Shawn and Chelsea were in the waiting room. He'd been given a lavender shirt by one of the interns, who had it in his locker. The sleeves were rolled up, and his arm bandaged from where the nurse had drawn his blood.

Abby was with them, taking notes as she clicked through the images of the accident, one by one. She would have to get to her computer to upload them.

The door opened, and one of the OR nurses entered.

"Mr. Gaines would like to see you," she said. "He's on the VIP floor and asked if I'd find you."

"His daughter?" Shawn asked.

"Still in ICU," she told him. "The transfusion should take a few hours. Your boyfriend's a hero," the nurse said addressing Chelsea.

"He's my brother, and yes, he is," Chelsea responded proudly.

The elevator to the VIP floor was large and less practical than those in the rest of the hospital. There were actual mirrors and wainscoting and rich wood floors.

Richie had sequestered himself in the private area to avoid heading out into the melee outside the hospital. There were reporters and police and tourists all wanting to see his grief.

He was alone on his mobile when the door opened. Shawn, Chelsea, and Abby were escorted in by one of the volunteers, a striking woman in her seventies with better jewelry than most of the female doctors.

"Shawn and Chelsea Brady?" he said, already knowing.

"Half brother and sister," Chelsea said immediately, to avoid the confusion.

"And you?" he asked Abby.

"Abigail," she said, omitting her last name. If he heard "Deveraux," he might have connected her to the press.

"Have we met?"

"No, sir," Abby answered, though she hoped he wouldn't remember seeing her at the party. "We're all family," she added, hoping to divert him from any more questions. "I'm actually Shawn's cousin…It's, um, complicated."

"We can all use family," he said. "Can't believe my own sons aren't here." Then, shaking it off, he asked, "Did Olivia suffer?"

He looked directly at Chelsea. "I hear you were the last…"

"No, Mr. Gaines. I'm sure she didn't." Chelsea expressed what she believed to be true.

"I owe you my daughter's life," he said to Shawn. "I must find some way to repay you."

"Not necessary, Mr. Gaines," he said.

"Necessary," Richie insisted. "Did you see the fireworks tonight? I saw them out this window," he said, looking out to the harbor. "Austria won last year, and France was determined to take home the prize this year."

Spectacular fireworks displays happened every night at nine thirty in August. The International Fireworks Festival was fierce and made every day even more of a party. Shawn realized they were making small talk to avoid the realities of a desperate and grim situation. Abby was taking notes in her head. Such personal insights would be fascinating to her readers.

They suddenly were distracted by the sounds of arguing in the hallway.

The door opened, and Richie was alarmed to see the chief of staff once more.

"So sorry about this, Richard," he apologized. "It's not Charley; she's actually doing fine."

"Then what?" Richie asked.

Four men in dark suits entered. Their expressions were serious and delighted at the same time. The oldest, a balding man with steel gray eyes pulled out handcuffs.

"Richard Gaines," he said, "Securities Division of the ISA. You're under arrest for securities fraud, investment fraud, and money laundering."

Richie's shoulders drooped, and he had nothing to say. Not one word. He extended his arms, and the cuffs were snapped on his wrists.

Click.

Click.

And the third *click* was from Chelsea's camera. Abby had just won the megamillion-dollar jackpot.

15 JACK AND JENNIFER

JACK DEVERAUX WAS STARING OUT HIS OFFICE WINDOW ON THE
tenth floor of Eight Canada Square in the Wapping area of London,
when his phone rang.

He was watching the activity at the building across the street
so intently that he didn't hear it. It was One Canary Wharf
Tower, and he could see people carrying things out of Financial
Gaines Group.

The door to his massive office was shoved open as Jennifer, his
beautiful blonde wife, entered. Although now in her forties, she
still had the luminescence of the guileless young woman he'd fallen
in love with.

"Jack, that's Abby!" she said, recognizing their daughter's
ringtone.

Jack snapped out of his reverie. "What are you doing back?"

Jennifer worked only part-time at the paper while she raised
their son J. J., With the newspaper business in the toilet, the
Spectator had been having such a difficult time that she was pitching
in when she could to cut costs. When Jack called and told her he'd

be late, she left J. J. with the nanny and decided to bring him a late dinner. Fortunately for them both.

"Jack! Get that!"

"Ohh!" He answered, "Abs."

"Dad, I know you've just closed the presses, but—" Abby said.

Jack interrupted, "In fact, we're holding them. There was late-breaking news about that designer Olivia Gaines and an accident in Monte Carlo. But there's been a media blackout and a lot of activity over at her husband's building today. I tried to reach you—"

"I couldn't use my phone! Then the reception was terrible. But you're not going to believe what I have," she rattled on.

From the tone of her voice, Jack knew it was huge.

"You got into the party?" he asked, expecting that she had a celebrity scoop for her site online.

"Oh yeah. But this is much bigger than that, Dad. I'm sending you photos in a few seconds."

Abby's heart was beating faster than a hummingbird's. She was back in her Monaco hotel room at her laptop. Chelsea's Nikon was connected and downloading the unfathomable.

"You can have them all; I have plenty of dirt for Spectator.com."

She quickly typed in Jack's email address and hit Send. "I'm forwarding them small, but I have them all in high-res."

By now, Jennifer was at Jack's side. She had been both a television and newspaper reporter for years and knew how to smell a scoop if there was one.

"What is it?" Jennifer pleaded with her husband, who was an amazing publisher but could be a bit of a goof.

"Let's see…they're coming in now," he said as he indicated for Jennifer to sit in front of the computer.

"Holy shit," they both said in unison.

Jack hit a button on the phone on the desk. "Print room, we've got something."

Jennifer grabbed the cell phone from Jack's hand. "Sweetie, it's Mom. Where, how?" She stopped. "Wait! Is that Shawn with Chelsea?"

"And they got the whole thing, Mom. But there's more, so very much more. Keep looking."

Jack was still on the line with the print room. "Make room on page 1," he said, then added, "Jennifer and Abby'll write the copy."

Jennifer was nearly weak with shock. "Jack?"

Jack took another look and saw Richard Gaines in handcuffs.

"Richard Gaines, Mom?"

"Was he driving?" Jennifer asked, totally confused.

"Nope. Arrested at the hospital for securities fraud, investment fraud, and money laundering. We were there when it happened."

"Another Madoff?" Jennifer said incongruously.

The couple stared at one another, and Jack lit up for the first time in months.

"Get us what you've got ASAP, Abs," Jack said.

"I'm madly typing."

Abby hung up, leaving her parents stunned.

"Woo-hoo!" Jack yelped and started a silly dance. Even though he was tall, lean, and handsome, Jack was always unpredictable in the best ways.

"I don't know what to say," Jennifer said, shaking her head.

"How'd she do it?"

"She learned from the best," he said as he pulled Jennifer to her feet and kissed her. "But I'd say the *Spectator*'s troubles may be over."

Jennifer tried to match his enthusiasm, but it was hard for her to put her emotions on hold. While she relished the idea of eviscerating a financial piranha, from what she saw in the photos, Richie's wife was dead, and their daughter seriously injured.

"I think we'd better call Bo," she said. "And Hope," she added. "Before they read about all this in the paper."

❧

Belle was awakened when she felt the boat rock as Shawn returned from his emotionally exhausting evening. She heard him climb down the stairs and inched herself off the queen-size platform bed in the front cabin.

Shawn was washing his face in the galley as she opened the hand-carved teak door and watched him a moment.

"Hi," she said softly.

"Sorry I woke you," Shawn answered.

"You and Chelsea have a good time?"

"There was an accident," he started carefully.

"Up in the hills? I saw something going on through the binoculars," she said, then realized he was wearing a shirt she'd never seen before. "Whose shirt are you wearing?"

"One of the hospital interns'."

"Are you all right?" she asked, alarmed.

"Physically, oh yeah, I'm fine. We both are," he said. "And

we weren't in the accident actually…but there's something you should know."

Shawn's phone vibrated. It was late, and he hesitated but saw it was Bo, calling from Salem.

"Dad," Shawn said, heaving a sigh of relief. It was good to hear from him.

"I know it's late there, but your mom and I each got a call from Jack."

"Leave it to Abby," Shawn said, shaking his head.

Belle was totally confused.

"They said you're a hero."

"Hero? I only did what I knew you'd do," Shawn said.

"You're your own man, Son," Bo replied.

This was a big moment between the two, and both of them knew it.

"Chelsea was great too," Shawn said, deflecting too much emotion. "If they didn't call her mom, will you?"

"Sure thing."

"Dad, I hope this doesn't become a big deal," Shawn said. "Keep it on the down low around Salem, okay?"

"I get it," Bo said. He was never one for wanting to be the center of attention either. "I will if I can. Give my love to Belle and the little one. I really am proud of you, Shawn."

"Thanks, Dad," Shawn said, clearing his voice as it began to crack.

Belle was full of questions when Shawn hung up the phone, and although Shawn was totally drained from the events of this evening, he knew he had to give her the details. Most important to her was the fact that Olivia Gaines, Belle's icon and the woman she had hoped to meet in the next few days, was dead.

"I know meeting her was important to you," Shawn said.

"Shawn, that's the last thing to worry about. But thank you."

"Your dreams are important to me."

"You're all that's important to me. You and Claire," she answered. "And you really were a hero."

"And women all love heroes, don't you?" Shawn answered.

"What do you mean?" she said with a twinge of guilt.

Shawn realized he'd hit a sore spot totally unintentionally.

"Nothing, truly," Shawn replied and meant it. "The past is the past."

Philip, who Belle'd once not only loved, but also briefly married, had been a war hero in Iraq. It was one thing Shawn could never compete with.

Until now.

"I need some sleep," he said, gently changing the subject.

"Maybe we can just hang out on the boat tomorrow." She sighed. "Really take it easy."

"I want to be back at the hospital by eight."

"Why?" Belle asked.

"Charley Gaines should be conscious by then," he answered. "She doesn't know that she lost her mother and that her father's been arrested. I was there for it all. Do you understand?"

"Sure," Belle replied.

Shawn took her in his arms and held her a long moment. Then he gave her a peck on the forehead and headed back to their cabin.

Belle stood silently for a moment, her hand going to her stomach. The only noise was coming from the partyers still reveling in the wee hours.

I understand, she thought. *But will you?*

16   *THE MORNING AFTER*

When copies of the *Spectator* hit the stands, they caused an international uproar. "ILL-GOTTEN GAINES LOSES" was the headline splashed across the front page.

Photos taken by Chelsea's camera covered the top half of the paper: Shawn and Chelsea in the foreground with the Aston Martin hitting the ground behind them, and Richard Gaines being handcuffed by the ISA agents at the hospital.

Jennifer Horton Deveraux's byline accompanied the heartbreaking story of Olivia's accident, while Abby's detail of Richie's scandalous arrest had her name firmly under the subhead.

Media from around the globe were outside Princess Grace Hospital.

"There he is," screamed a producer from Argentina as Shawn was dropped by taxi at the front door.

Police were quick to surround him as he entered the building with reporters shouting questions to him in various languages.

An equal number of rabid reporters were outside the Monte Carlo Police Department as Jackson and Chance Gaines headed into the station. Their father had been arrested on securities fraud, and they were his business partners. They had not been arrested, however, as authorities quickly believed they had no knowledge of their father's despicable crimes.

Led to Richard Gaines's cell, the boys were stoic, but devastated by the revelations. Their glorious, larger-than-life mother had also just been stolen from them in a horrific crash that nearly has taken their sister. And if the charges were true, they had been lied to for years by the father they adored.

Chance, the twenty-six-year-old graduate of Harvard Law, was representing his father. Prematurely silver-haired with piercing gray eyes, he had often been compared to Anderson Cooper, for more reasons than one.

When his sons arrived, Richie was lying on a cot, his right arm covering his eyes.

A guard opened the cell.

"Dad," Chance said simply.

"It's all true," was Richie's equally simple reply. "All lies all these years."

"We've posted your bail," Jackson said. "Five million euros."

"The house in London as collateral," Chance added.

"Let's get out of here." Richie sighed heavily.

"There is a stipulation," Chance told him.

"You're released on bail, but under house arrest at the villa."

"Could be worse," Richie said blankly. "Can we see Charley first?"

"We'll check with the court," Chance said.

The atmosphere was cold, clinical, and distant. Chance nodded to a guard outside the cell, and he entered.

"What's this?" Richie asked as the guard asked him to pull up the cuff of his thousand-euro slacks. It became immediately clear as the guard pulled an ankle monitor from a small case.

"Sorry," Chance said, steadying his father as the ankle bracelet was strapped on.

"Jules plea-bargained a deal," Jackson added matter-of-factly. In certain ways, he was so much like his father.

"Pity," Richie said. "I guess our dicks are what did us in."

"Our?" Jackson blanched. He should have known she was one of Richie's girls all along.

The ankle bracelet was locked into place.

"When they're that hot and smart, you've gotta be extra careful," Richie warned. "I always told you that."

"Guess I just didn't listen."

"As if any of that matters now," Chance said, shaking his head. "Come on, let's get out of here."

Richie took a long beat. "I am sorry, guys."

Chance and Jackson just nodded. No way they could forgive him right now.

Jackson led the way as the three headed out together, Richie fully aware of the monitoring device that would be a part of him for who-knew-how-long.

None of them mentioned the devastating loss of the boys' mother.

John had been watching CNN on the plasma flat-screen in his room as the remarkable events of the last twelve hours unfolded.

John had been through the tortures of the damned over the last few years, and his paralysis wasn't the worst of it. His mind had been wiped clean, and he spent over a year as an emotionless robot.

Time and experimental underground treatments had returned his memories. His mind was functioning again, with the intelligence that allowed him to be a human chameleon.

During the months and months of grueling physical therapy, his only salvation was television and his computer. He refused to let his brain and imagination die, especially if that's all he would have left.

"You're watching it too," Marlena said as she quickly entered in her silk robe.

John was so focused on the screen that he didn't hear her enter.

"What are you doing here?" he said, startled.

"It's just unbelievably sad," she answered. "I didn't think to knock. I'm sorry."

She truly was sorry. They had agreed she would never enter without knocking.

If he knew that I'd climbed into his bed the other night, he wouldn't be happy, Marlena thought. No, she knew.

If she climbs into my bed like she did the other night, I may have to make love to her, John thought. It's why he made the rule about knocking. He had to steel himself from her touch, her smile, and her smell. He could not make love to her yet. Not now. Maybe not ever.

"Another Princess Grace tragedy and Bernie Madoff debacle," she said to avoid more discussion. "To one family, all in less than an hour."

"Is that Shawn?" she asked as her son-in-law's face splashed across the TV screen.

"You haven't been watching," John mocked.

Marlena shook her head and watched in disbelief as the story unfolded as a CNN field reporter from France was in front of Princess Grace Hospital thrusting a mic in front of Shawn's face.

"Mr. Brady, could we speak to you for a moment?" she asked. "CNN. We understand you were not only at the accident site, but in the room when Mr. Gaines was arrested."

"Only speaking to the *Spectator,* sorry." He tossed off as he passed. "You can read everything there."

"He's certainly matured," Marlena said. "Where's Belle?"

As if on cue, her phone rang. She pulled it from the pocket in her robe.

"We're on the same wavelength, sweetie," Marlena said.

"You've seen the news," Belle stated.

"It's everywhere," Marlena answered. "How are you? How is Claire? I'm sure you know it's all very confusing."

"For all of us," Belle said. "We're fine, really. I just didn't want you to worry."

"We always do," Marlena said. "From one mother to another, I'm sure you understand."

Belle glanced at Claire. Yes, now she truly understood the bond of a mother and daughter.

John signaled for Marlena to let him talk to her.

"Dad wants to speak to you," Marlena told her and held the phone up to his ear.

"Hey, baby girl," John said.

"Hi, Daddy," Belle said warmly. "Can't wait to see you."

"You too. When?"

"We were supposed to drive up there tomorrow," she answered. "But now I don't know. How are you, Dad?"

"A bit better than when we last saw you," he answered. "Even though that was almost two years ago, don't expect miracles."

"I'm Mom's daughter," she replied. "I always do."

"Keep us posted, and let us know when to expect you," John said. "Kiss little Claire Black for me."

Marlena stared at John. He caught her gaze.

"Sorry. I should have let you say good-bye," he said and then turned back to the news.

"I'll speak to her later," Marlena replied. She couldn't take her gaze off him. She had seen a glimpse of the man she loved when he was talking to their daughter.

Why couldn't he respond like that to her?

∞

"Can she have visitors?" Shawn asked the volunteer outside of Charley's private room in the ICU. He could see a glimpse of her, hooked up to tubes and catheters, with electrodes monitoring her.

Charley had a large bandage covering her neck where Shawn had applied pressure to keep her from bleeding out. Her dark hair was pulled up behind her, and she was sleeping.

"Are you family?" the efficient but gentle woman asked.

"No, I'm—"

Before he could finish, Esther, the nurse who'd taken his blood donation, appeared from the other side of the nurses' station.

"Mr. Brady," she said.

"You remember." Shawn smiled.

"He's the gentleman who donated the B negative for Miss Gaines," she told her co-worker, then addressed Shawn apologetically. "Are you here to give more?"

"How is she?" he asked.

"She's been heavily medicated since the surgery," she answered. "But she's expected to make a full recovery."

"Good." Shawn sighed.

An alarm went off from the monitors, which had been steadily beeping softly. There was a flurry of activity as two nurses came from opposite directions and made a beeline into Charley's room. Shawn jumped aside as one of the doctors rushed past him at a clip.

The volunteer strained to see inside, but they'd pulled the curtain closed.

"If you'd like to donate, the clinic is on the second floor," she said to Shawn.

He hesitated, not wanting to leave.

Before he had to answer, the doctor emerged. "She's awake and talking," he reported.

"Great." Shawn smiled.

"Could you call the chaplain?" the doctor asked the volunteer. "We need to inform her about her mother."

The doctor moved behind the nurses' station to complete his report, and one of the nurses got on the phone to the chaplain.

Shawn had spent a lot of time in and around the hospitals of Salem. His great-grandfather, Tom Horton, had been the chief of staff at one time, and hence, a number of his relatives had become doctors or nurses. It still amazed him at how they could be so compassionate and clinical at the same time. His own parents, both cops, had also instilled in him the belief that life had to be fair and balanced. Sometimes he didn't feel like either a Horton or a Brady.

His reverie was broken when the gentle nurse, Esther, emerged from Charley's room.

"She'd like to see you," Esther said.

"Now?" Shawn asked.

"She saw you out here and wanted to say thank you."

Shawn moved into her room, and he was struck again by her natural beauty. She was a bit groggy, but her eyes widened when she saw him.

"Thank you," she said softly. "If not for you, my mother and I wouldn't have made it."

Shawn tried to not react, but his expression betrayed him.

There was no need for the chaplain to deliver the news.

Charley grabbed his hand and squeezed it like a vise, her breathing getting deeper and deeper, until she was gulping in the dead air that filled the room.

"I'm so sorry," was all Shawn could offer.

Charley let out a mournful, empty wail that sliced into his heart like a knife, then collapsed into his arms, sobbing uncontrollably.

The mother she adored was gone.

17   *RICHIE*

"NEVER THOUGHT I'D LOVE TO SEE THE HOUSE THIS MUCH," Richie said as he pulled aside the privacy curtain in the backseat of his shiny new graphite Bentley Mulsanne.

Jackson was at the wheel of the car his father had purchased less than a month ago for nearly $400,000 (and which now was certainly in jeopardy if the charges against him were true). He and Chance both wanted to believe the charges were bogus, but Richie had already admitted to the ISA that the Financial Gaines Group was one big fat scam.

The door opened, and Richie stepped out of the car, catching the ankle monitor on the running board.

"Damn," he said.

"Going to have to get used to that, Dad," was all Chance could say. Both the boys were angry. Their father had lied to them for over a decade.

As the three approached, Kelsey opened the front door to the villa. They brushed past her without so much as a hello.

The emotional toil was getting to them. They moved into the

living room and sank into the large down-filled couches.

"Give me all you've got," Richie threw at his sons. "I have no excuses for what I've done."

"Monaco extradites," Chance started. "If you'd bought the villa in France—"

Richie cut him off. "Wouldn't make a damn bit of difference. I deserve whatever I'm handed."

"Jeez, Dad, thanks," Jackson spit. "Do you know what we had to go through yesterday? We were grilled for four hours."

"Mr. Gaines?" Kelsey said meekly as she approached. "I'm so sorry to hear about, well, everything."

"I need a drink," was Richie's response.

Kelsey had hoped she could take the man she loved in her arms and comfort him, but in front of his sons, she knew better.

"Scotch, neat," he barked.

"Same," Jackson added.

"One of us has to be sober," Chance said, refusing the alcohol. "And it's time we discussed Mom."

They didn't see Kelsey cringe as she headed to make the drinks. The room fell eerily silent for a moment.

"I don't want to believe she's gone," Richie said, choking back emotion. "Maybe with this, it's better," he added, pointing to the ankle monitor.

"Don't even think that," Jackson said harshly.

"They said her gorgeous face was crushed," Richie said, trying to shake it off. Whatever he had done over the years, he had always and always would love her. "We need to make sure she looks her best, you know?"

Chance knew what he was saying.

"We'll call her personal physician," Chance replied. "If he's unavailable, we'll call Sharon Osbourne's guy. He's amazing."

"Whatever it costs," Richie said.

"They've frozen all our bank accounts, Dad," Chance reminded him. "But we'll make it work somehow."

Kelsey finished pouring the Macallan into Baccarat snifters and set them on a sterling silver tray. Next to the tray was a beautifully framed photo of Olivia with Charley, smiling and laughing. It was a portrait Charley had done, and it was one of Richie's favorites. She put it facedown and then delivered the drinks.

Jackson took his glass first, and then Kelsey served Richie. She gave him a sympathetic look that the boys didn't catch. Neither did he.

Richie raised his snifter to Jackson.

"To your mother," he said. "No one will ever replace her."

Kelsey's back went up, but she knew she'd forgive him. She knew all this was for show, and there was no way he could reach out to her yet.

"Why'd you do it, Dad?" Jackson asked.

"For all of you. Because I wanted you to have the best, and I love you," Richie said with conviction.

Chance's phone rang. It was the hospital.

"Yes?" Chance answered. He listened a moment. "We'll be there as soon as we can."

He hung up and half smiled. "There's good news and bad."

"Bad?" Jackson said, concerned.

"Charley's awake and now she's stable, but she found out about Mum, and she's devastated."

"I have to go with you," Richie said.

"Can't."

"She's my little girl," Richie added as a demand.

"And the press will have a field day with you," Jackson reminded him. "We'll fill her in."

Richie was like a racehorse at the gate, he was so anxious to join them. "Please."

"Sorry, but no," Jackson added firmly.

"Tell her I love her," Richie answered, knowing they were right.

"What you've done for love," Jackson said, shaking his head.

"Let's go," Chance said, not wanting to argue.

The two boys headed out through the massive foyer. Richie sat nursing his drink.

Kelsey waited until she heard the smooth sound of the Bentley as it drove away, then moved to the man she had been having an affair with for over two years.

"It will all be fine, *papi*," she said and attempted to wipe his hair from his face.

Richie brushed her hand away sharply.

"Olivia's dead," he said with an anguished tone that surprised her. "And I'm going to prison."

"I'll wait for you," she said with a seductive smile that only made him angrier.

"You're fired," he snapped. "Get your things and get out."

Richie pulled away from her and stormed through the doors leading to the back patio. The last thing he needed right now was a clingy mistress.

Kelsey sat numbly; then she started to weep.

She was jolted out of her shock as police sirens blared.

Richie had accidentally pierced the perimeter of the rolling grass lawn, and the ankle monitor had tripped the alarm. Within seconds, the police were heading in his direction.

He smashed the Baccarat snifter against one of the massive trees that lined the property.

No matter how gorgeous it was, he was in a prison of his own making. Until he got sent to a true prison forever.

18 *SHAWN AND CHARLEY*

CHARLEY HAD BEEN SEDATED AN HOUR AGO, YET SHAWN WAITED patiently outside the ICU. He was inexplicably drawn to this girl, and he didn't know why.

The chaplain assured Shawn he had done nothing wrong. Shawn knew that, but it didn't make him feel any better. Charley was suffering, and she had no idea the mess her father was in.

Shawn's phone rang, and the nurse at the desk coughed to get his attention. She pointed to the sign that said "*TÉLÉPHONES PORTABLES INTERDITS*" with the translation "No Mobiles Allowed" below it.

He pressed the button on the upper–right-hand edge of the phone, sending the caller to voice mail. He did see that it was Belle, and he realized he hadn't checked in since he'd left the *Fancy Face IV* that morning. He needed to call her but didn't want to leave Charley alone, in case she needed him.

When Shawn saw two men in their twenties exit the private elevator, he had no idea who they were. He was never one to read the gossip columns or tabloids, although it was a favorite guilty pleasure of Belle's. If he had, he would have recognized them from their various escapades.

"We're here to see our sister," Chance told the nurse in perfect French. "Charley Gaines. How is she?"

"Resting, but doing well," the nurse assured him in French. "I'll let Dr. Bonnet know you're here."

"Thanks," Jackson said in English. He too spoke fluent French but preferred using English since it had become the international language.

"How much do we tell her?" Jackson asked his brother as the nurse turned to call Charley's doctor.

"Just that Dad's dealing with some financial issues at the moment?" Chance answered, unsure.

"She'll see right through that, bruv," Jackson cautioned. "Best to say he's taking care of things for Mum."

Chance nodded. They didn't like lying to her but feared another shock could send Charley over the edge. "I wonder how much she remembers about the accident."

"She remembers the car sailing over the railing," Shawn said, interrupting.

"Who're you?" Jackson asked.

"Shawn Brady."

"The guy who saved her life," Jackson said, recognizing the name.

"Whatever," Shawn said modestly. "Now that you guys are here, I'm going to go call my wife."

Shawn headed out, and Jackson and Chance steeled themselves, then went in to see their beautiful little sister.

∞

Charley was thrilled to see Jackson and Chance.

"Hey," Jackson said sweetly.

"Hey," Charley answered, managing a smile.

"Someone needs to bring you a hot orange robe, Sis," Chance teased, pointing at her hospital gown.

"How's Dad?" she asked with sincere concern. Others were always her first priority.

"A wreck," Jackson said. He knew that was truer than she could imagine. The emotions were too raw to dive into immediately.

"I'm sure."

There was an awkward silence.

"Whew," she said, breaking the tension.

"Whew," Jackson echoed, arching his eyebrows.

"Whew," Chance added, quickly completing a familiar ritual the siblings had.

All three managed to smile.

"For someone who lost over two pints of blood, you look pretty good," Jackson said. "Sorry we weren't here."

"Let's not get into that now," Charley said, staring into his dark brown eyes. Unsaid was the fact that if Jackson and Chance had gotten to Monte Carlo on time, everything might have been different.

Dr. Bonnet entered and shook both of their hands. He was clinical but also kind as he gave them all details of both Charley's condition and Olivia's injuries.

The three were relieved to learn that Charley's only major injury was the gash on her neck, which appeared to be from a branch she hit on the car's trajectory through the trees. It was also a mixed blessing that Olivia had died. The injury to her skull had damaged her brain and spinal cord so badly that she would have surely spent the rest of her life as a vegetable.

"I was lucky," Charley told them as she touched the abrasions on her chest.

"We spoke to the mortuary and think we can have Mum's funeral at the end of the week," Chance ventured. "Only if you're out of the hospital by then, of course."

Dr. Bonnet let them know it was likely that Charley would be in the hospital only a few days.

"I'm anxious to get home," she said.

Jackson and Chance exchanged a look. At some point they'd have to let her know about their father.

"I'll check in on you in a while," Dr. Bonnet said warmly. "And whatever you need, let the nurses know. They'll be in soon with your meds," he added as he left for rounds.

Charley nodded as she watched him go. Shawn had returned from his call and was outside the door. Something was forming in her mind.

"We should let you rest, Sis," Jackson said.

"Try to forget everything that happened," Chance added.

They kissed her on both cheeks simultaneously from each side of the bed. As they headed toward the door, Charley tried to clear her head, but her mind was reeling.

"Guys," she called out. Her tone was serious, and they stopped. "Mummy was...incredibly dizzy before the crash."

"Had she had champagne?" Jackson said. They all knew their mother's habits.

"I know her when she's tipsy, and that wasn't it," Charley said, straining to remember. Her eyes widened. "She was dead before the accident."

"What?" Chance sputtered.

"Before?" Jackson said.

Both brothers were stunned.

"What are you saying?" Chance asked, as only a lawyer could.

Even from outside the room, Shawn heard the conviction in Charley's voice.

"I spent nearly the entire day with Mummy, and she was fine. Better than fine, she was at the top of her form because of that ridiculous party," Charley said, gaining steam. "She wasn't sick, she wasn't tired; she had even had a physical two weeks ago, and her test results were normal."

"Charley, you've been through a lot and—"

She cut her brother off. "I reached over to help her when she passed out, Jackson, and I can't tell you why, but I realize now, at that very moment, I knew Mummy was dead."

"But you said she was fine before you got in the car," Jackson demanded.

"She was…" Charley insisted. "Which means one thing." She took a long breath, barely able to say the words. "I think she may have been murdered."

19   *ABBY AND CHELSEA &*
BELLE AND CLAIRE

"Auntie Chelsea!" Claire squealed as she and Belle walked onto the terrace of the Monte Carlo Beach Hotel.

The day was a sunny, balmy seventy-eight degrees, and Belle enjoyed being on solid ground. Her months on the boat were exhilarating, but exhausting, and the firmness beneath her was welcome.

"Is there anywhere around here that's not gorgeous?" Belle asked.

She heard, "Belle, is that you?" coming from Abby's MacBook Air.

It was Jennifer, who was iChatting with Abby from her home office in the upscale section of London's Notting Hill.

"Jennifer?" Belle smiled. "Hi! Claire, say hi to Abby's mommy."

"Hi," Claire chirped and leaned into the camera.

"You are so pretty!" Jennifer said.

"I know." Claire giggled and started making funny faces.

"Claire!" Belle chastised her.

"It has to be true. Everybody tells me," Claire said matter-of-factly.

"It's great to see so many people from home." Belle laughed. "Is anyone left in Salem?"

"Give your mom my love, will you?" Jennifer smiled. "Tell her and John we miss them."

"I will," Belle answered. "You guys are obviously working. Sorry to bother you. But good for you with the exclusive."

"Thanks to your husband and Chelsea," Jennifer answered.

Chelsea waved her off. Yes, she and Shawn had been integral to all this, but there was something about it all that made her uneasy.

"We'll be another twenty minutes or so," Abby told Belle, Chelsea, and Claire.

"This is boring, Mommy," Claire piped in. "Let's go."

"Ah, motherhood." Jennifer laughed with a look to her daughter.

Chelsea came to the rescue. "Why don't we get you some gum? They have it in the hotel gift shop."

"Yum!" Claire said, throwing her hands in the air. "I love gum."

"And me?" Chelsea scowled.

"Yup," Claire said as she grabbed Chelsea's hand and pulled her toward the doorway. "Come on!"

The three of them exited as Abby continued her work with Jennifer.

"Let me show you the accident site," Abby said. She got up from the table with her computer and aimed the built-in camera toward the street, which had been totally cleaned up. The detritus in the hills was still evident. Tourists were taking photos.

"Tilt up the camera," Jennifer requested.

Abby moved her computer so her mother could see the street to the broken railing on the Route de la Grand Corniche marked with yellow police tape.

"Honey?" Jennifer asked quietly.

Abby turned the computer back to her own image.

"What's the image in the upper–right-hand corner of the photos?"

"Where?" Abby asked.

"Is that someone looking over the guardrail?"

Abby studied the photos that were downloaded on her desktop.

"Poor guy." She shuddered. "Whoever it is, he must have seen the whole thing happen. How awful."

❧

Chelsea was leading Belle and the antsy Claire through the hotel lobby when Shawn called.

"Stop, baby girl, stop," Belle instructed her daughter. "It's Da."

"Tell him I'm getting gum!" Claire said, tugging at her mother.

"Tell him *we're* getting gum." Chelsea took Claire's hand. "See you inside," she added to Belle.

"How's Charley Gaines?" Belle asked.

"As good as can be expected, I guess," Shawn responded. "Are you okay if I stick around?"

"Sure," Belle assured him. "Claire and I haven't had a day together for a while. You're always showing her the sights."

"Thanks. How're you feeling?" he asked.

"Great." She lied. In fact she was feeling queasy.

"You sure Claire's not too much for you?" he chided.

"As my mom just reminded me, there's no stronger bond than between a mother and daughter."

"True. No insult intended," he teased.

"You know what I mean," Belle said.

"I do, and frankly, you're right. Your mom is one smart cookie."

"Text me later," Belle said.

"Love you," Shawn said.

"Same back." Belle hung up. *I do love you, Shawn, I really do*, she thought. *Then why won't I tell him about Philip?*

Shaking it off, Belle headed into the hotel gift shop and found Chelsea and Claire at the cash register. Claire had five packs of gum, every flavor and color, and already had a purple tongue from the three grape sticks she'd popped in her mouth.

"Yum!" Claire smiled. A purple, drooly smile.

"You are getting spoiled!" Belle teased her daughter.

"I love Auntie Chelsea," Claire mumbled through the wad in her mouth.

Chelsea signed the bill to her room as Claire jiggled around excitedly. The little girl bumped into the counter, jarring it.

"Claire!" Belle scolded as several things fell from a display. Belle scooped them up. They were pregnancy tests.

Belle dropped them as if they were hot potatoes.

Chelsea noticed.

"Belle?" Chelsea questioned.

"I'm on the pill," Belle said, defending herself way too much.

Chelsea gave her another look that only said *So?*

Chelsea grabbed Claire's hand and swung her around. "Wanna see the pool?"

"Yup!" Claire said, oblivious to the tension bubbling beneath the surface.

"I'll race you!" Chelsea said, pretending to run.

Claire bolted past her.

Belle stood stock-still for a minute that seemed like an eternity.

She wondered, *Could I be pregnant?* then shouted in her mind, *But I'm on the pill!*

Belle started out but stopped in the open doorway and returned to the salesgirl. She put one of the pregnancy tests on the counter.

"How much?" she asked, handing the beaming teenager a stack of colorful notes.

"Fifteen euros," she was told as the girl took a ten and a five.

"Why?" Belle muttered to herself.

"Because that's what they cost." The clerk grinned.

Belle simply smiled but inside was torn apart.

Why now, you idiot? she thought. *Why is this happening now?*

20  *THE GAINESES*

"THERE WILL NOT BE AN AUTOPSY!" RICHIE BELLOWED, SLAMMING his pool cue into the rack of balls on the antique pool table.

Jackson and Chance stood in front of him in the den where they'd played so many games since he'd bought the house when they were teenagers.

Richie had purchased the six-million-dollar villa on the edge of Monaco as the family's base to avoid taxes. Truth was, it was their vacation home, but they spent exactly the minimum amount of time there to be considered permanent residents. There is no doubt that the Riviera is a playground, but Richard Gaines's best game was finance, and he loved duping the stuffed shirts in London.

The balls scattered, two landing in side pockets from the force of his break.

"Charley's insisting, Dad," Jackson said.

"Your mother died from her lousy driving and refusal to wear a seat belt. I won't have her carved up because Charley has a hair up her bum," Richie sputtered.

"She is dead, Dad; she won't feel a thing." Chance glared.

"Funny."

"Not meant to be."

"Who'd want her dead?" Richie asked incongruously. "Whatever she thought, she really wasn't that important."

Maybe the twenty-four hours of incarceration were already getting to Richie, but Jackson and Chance did not like what they saw in their father.

Richie hit an intercom on the side table.

"Sophia, we need drinks," he barked.

"Sophia?" Jackson asked.

"I fired Kelsey. Don't ask."

Jackson and Chance never asked their father questions. They learned from observing. It was how Jackson had become such a smooth womanizer; he had observed the best.

Richie took another angry shot, the eight ball careening off the side of the table and landing in a side pocket.

"Don't say it," he said, throwing the cue on the table.

"Mr. Gaines, you called?" It was an unfamiliar voice to Jackson and Chance. A pale, average-looking girl in her midtwenties appeared in the doorway. Tall with slim hips and only the hint of breasts, unlike Kelsey, she was not Richie's normal type.

"Drinks in the bar, please," he said, and the girl slipped away. "Your mother hired her last week. She'll cover Kelsey's shift until you can find me someone better."

Richie strode out of the room, and his sons followed.

Sophia had scooted ahead of him and was at the bar.

She began pouring a double Macallan into a snifter and handed it to her boss. She already knew his likes, but it didn't matter a whit to him—she wasn't pretty, so she wouldn't last.

Richie took the drink. "Make it three," he ordered, and she started to pour.

"None for me," Chance said and pulled out a joint from his breast pocket.

Richie went to his perch on the sofa overlooking the patio. He swirled the snifter with his palm under the bowl. The heat released the pungent bouquet.

Jackson took the golden nectar from Sophia and noticed a picture frame had been turned over. He looked at the images of his sister and mother in goofier, lovelier times.

"Dad," Jackson said. "Charley deserves our respect. If she thinks something's fishy, we need to listen."

Richie sat quietly for a long moment, then indicated for Chance to pass him the joint.

He took a long hit from the indica marijuana, held it in his lungs just long enough, and released it slowly.

"No autopsy," Richie said with an expression they knew all too well. "And that's final."

∽

Several hours later, Jackson and Chance returned to the hospital. Charley was sitting up in bed, her hair combed beautifully, and she was picking at food from a silver tray. Poached eggs, fresh fruit, and scones were served on Hermès porcelain dinnerware. VIPs were treated very well at Princess Grace Hospital.

The color was returning to her cheeks, and she looked

amazingly radiant for a woman who had plummeted down an embankment less than twenty-four hours before. Her brow, however, was furrowed, as she was deep in thought about all that day had brought her.

"Hope this fits," Chance said as he put a bag from Hôtel de Paris on her bed.

Inside was a luxurious burnt orange Chinese silk robe.

"I'm a J.Crew kind of girl, you've forgotten," she said with a voice devoid of emotion. "But it's beautiful. Thanks."

Although the three were thicker than thieves, there was uncharacteristically not much being said between them.

"Dad said no," Jackson said, unable to avoid the obvious. "No autopsy."

Charley's back went up, and her eyes widened.

"Something's not right," she said. "Did you tell him what I saw?"

Her blood pressure was rising, and the beep of the monitors reflected it.

"Calm down, Sis, please," Chance cautioned. "Besides, I think we can have it done without him. If you're sure."

"I'm sure, dammit!" she insisted. She had just lost her mother in the worst way and all this was unimaginable.

A nurse appeared in the doorway.

"We're sorry," Jackson apologized as the nurse checked Charley's vital signs.

Charley took a couple of deep, cleansing breaths. From all her visits to spas with her mother, she knew the art of relaxation, even at times of crisis. The last thing she wanted now was for the staff to send her brothers away.

"She needs to rest, gentlemen," the nurse ordered.

"Promise me you'll find a way, Jackson…" she said with the plaintive voice her brother couldn't resist. "I need answers. I just feel so empty."

He nodded, holding back tears.

"We love you, squirt," Chance said as he kissed her on the forehead. He motioned to the new robe. "We'll get an aide to help you put that on."

Charley managed a smile, and the boys exited into the hall.

"You think we can do this?" Jackson asked as soon as they were out of earshot.

"Dad's been arrested, and he loses that privilege," Chance stated. "As his sons, we can do whatever the hell we want."

Jackson fist-bumped his little brother.

"It's going to open a barrelful of worms, bruv," Chance said. "The officials are going to need Charley's statement. And once the press gets hold of it…"

"Do you think he did it?" Jackson said, clearing his throat.

"I don't know. Did we think he was a scumbag?" Chance answered.

The sad truth was, they realized, did anyone ever really know their father?

∞

The Monaco medical examiner was busy when Jackson and Chance entered his office. It had been a busy month with several suicides, ODs, and a boat accident or two. The playgrounds of the rich and famous are also rife with drama.

"Are you the next of kin?" he asked them as if they were one. He was a well-built man of about forty who had a pleasant face, short-cropped hair, and a professional demeanor.

"Sons," Chance nodded.

"From the police report, it looks pretty cut-and-dried as to what happened," he said. "No pun intended."

"We're not sure the accident was an accident," Jackson offered, ignoring him.

He cocked his head and looked to Chance. "Criminal circumstances?"

"Our sister, who was in the car with her, said Mum passed out just before she lost control. Our mother may have seemed fragile, but she had the constitution of a horse."

"What'll it take us to get this done?" Jackson said, noticing the examiner checking out his brother.

"You need to sign the authorization papers and guarantee the cost," he said.

"That's it?" Jackson asked.

"That's it," he answered.

"How much?" Chance wondered.

Looking at their John Varvatos shoes and Jaeger-LeCoultre watches, he smiled. "I'm sure you can afford it."

Chance returned the smile. The examiner was actually warm and engaging, which they needed under the circumstances.

"You understand the procedure?" he added. "Some like to know the details of how it works; others would rather believe it's just magic."

Both guys shook their heads. No need for the gruesome details. They'd rather think of their mother as whole.

He pushed a letter of authorization in front of Chance.

"A full autopsy?" he asked.

"Whatever will find out what killed her," Jackson said.

"If something killed her," the examiner reminded them.

"How quickly will we get results?" Chance asked.

"It could be several weeks to a month," the examiner said, tapping his pencil idly as he stared directly into Chance's eyes.

"Any way to hurry it up?" Chance asked.

"I've got two corpses in front of your mother—"

Chance slipped off his $39,000 chronograph. "Are you sure it'll take that long?"

"I can't take a bribe, Mr. Gaines," the examiner stated coolly.

"Chance," Chance offered. "And Jackson."

"William," the examiner offered.

"Consider it a gift, Willy," Jackson said as Chance laid the exquisite Swiss watch on the desk.

"It'll help you keep track of the time." Chance smiled.

Willy was taken by the man in expensive accessories and 501 jeans that fit like a glove.

"We need to keep this under wraps," Chance added. "No pun intended."

"I'll do my best," Willy said, lost in Chance's eyes.

"Call me directly when you're done."

Chance handed Willy a business card with one hand and adjusted his crotch with the other.

"I'll get on it as fast as I can," Willy said with a tone that was an obvious double entendre.

Jackson and Chance headed out.

"And I thought Dad taught me well," Jackson said once they were out of earshot.

They both chuckled, although the laughter soon faded.

21 *MARLENA AND JOHN &*
   SHAWN AND BELLE

"Om...Om...Om..."

Since leaving Salem, Marlena had returned to practicing meditation. Used for centuries to ease tension and open the mind, she had come to crave the stillness and peace it offered her at a time when her life was so confusing.

She had used different meditation techniques in her practice for years and now could truly appreciate how they opened her mind.

If they saw me in Salem, they'd think I'd lost my mind, she thought, and a smile crossed her face. *They might be right.*

"Om...Om...Om..." she repeated. Sitting on the floor of their gym, she had perfect posture, the soles of her feet touching and her hands resting gently on her knees. New age music wafted through the speakers, and her breathing slowed. The tension left her face. Until suddenly she felt as if she'd been hit by a cattle prod.

"Oh!" She gasped. Looking at herself in the floor-to-ceiling mirrors, she studied her face as if looking for answers.

"One of the girls," she said softly.

Over the years, when she'd had a feeling like this, it nearly always had to do with one of her daughters. That connection was so strong that she knew someone was in trouble.

There was a message on her voice mail from Blake Masters who wanted to see her tomorrow. So far, she hadn't answered.

"Docteur Evans," she heard coming from the doorway.

It was Desiree back from the trip to see her father.

Momentarily distracted from her worries, Marlena rose from her position.

"Your tone isn't good, Desiree."

"I'm not," the normally poised nurse rambled. "Did you hear about the Gaines Financial Group, or whatever they're called?"

Marlena had not only heard about them, but her family was tangled in the midst of the drama.

"Of course, it's international news," Marlena said.

"My father—he was a major investor with that charlatan," Desiree said, near tears. "He got me and my best friends involved, and now we've lost everything."

"I'm so sorry." Marlena could feel Desiree's anguish.

"Bernie Madoff?" Desiree scoffed. "At least he targeted people with tons of money, who can make it back somehow. Gaines?" she spit. "He stole our future."

"If you need a loan…" Marlena offered sincerely.

"I don't know *what* I need, Docteur Evans," Desiree answered. "But thank you for the offer."

"Your job is safe. I hope you know that."

"Thank you," Desiree said. She liked Marlena and felt guilty for keeping John's secret. "It's time for Mr. Black's evening medication."

"You pull yourself together. I can bring his meds," Marlena said.

Normally, Desiree wouldn't have let her, but Marlena was right. Desiree could see herself in the floor-to-ceiling mirrors, and she was a wreck.

∽

Marlena knocked softly, and John answered, "Come on in."

He was once again watching CNN and surprised to see Marlena with his meds.

"I thought I saw Desiree was back," John said.

"She is, but she needs some time. She's one of Gaines's victims," Marlena said sadly. "Your meds?"

John slowly lifted a glass of water from the tray Marlena carried, and swallowed a handful of pills.

She loved even just watching the cut of his arms as he placed the glass back on the tray. Although his movements were unsteady, his hands were still strong, with long, masculine fingers.

"Can we talk?" she asked hesitantly.

"Sure, Doc."

He didn't want to. He didn't want to be this close to her for this long.

She turned off the TV and set the tray next to his bed, and as she did, he could see the soft curve of her back beneath the formfitting leotard she was wearing. If she had seen the desire in his eyes, she would have kissed him gently and mounted him. Satisfied both of them in ways they haven't felt in so long.

But she didn't see his desire, and he didn't feel her longing.

"Have you heard anything from Sami?" she asked.

"No, why?" Then he saw her expression. "One of those pre-monitions of yours?"

"Carrie seemed fine when I spoke to her yesterday, and if it's trouble, it usually involves Sami," she said, tilting her head.

He loved when she did that. He also loved what he called her "smiling eyes." Every emotion was in those hazel beauties.

"Could be the Belle thing," John reminded her.

"It doesn't feel like it is, but I've been wrong before," she said.

"When?" he said, and it was as if he was teasing.

"When I thought I was wrong, and I wasn't."

They shared a smile.

"Let me see," John said, taking her hand.

Marlena's fists were clenched, as they always were when she felt tense, and boy, was she feeling tense now.

He massaged them gently for a moment. His hands weren't as agile as they once had been, but she welcomed his touch. Like old times. Good times.

Are we connecting, John? Actually connecting? she thought.

The moment was broken by John's cell phone ringing. It was Belle.

"Belle," he said as he answered by speakerphone.

"Dad, I'm trying to reach Mom, but she's not answering her phone. Do you know where she is?" Belle asked.

"I'm right here," Marlena said, adding, "Belle, are you sure you're all right?"

"Another of your premonitions, Mom?" Belle said gently.

"Yeah, yeah," Marlena answered, realizing they all knew her too well.

"I'm fine," Belle said, Marlena not believing her for a minute. Marlena nodded to John.

"But that's not why I'm calling."

"Talk to me," Marlena said.

"It's a favor for Shawn, really," Belle said, glancing to Shawn, who was sitting in the *Fancy Face IV* galley. "He's right here."

"Marlena," Shawn said.

"You know you've made us very proud, Shawn. And don't say we shouldn't be," Marlena scolded lightly.

"Thanks, but this isn't about me; it's about Charley Gaines."

"Oh?"

"I know it's weird, but I have this need to help her somehow," Shawn said.

"It's actually a typical reaction for someone to connect to a person they've literally saved," Marlena said, putting on her psychiatric hat without even realizing it.

"But I need to be spending time with my own wife and daughter," Shawn said, warmly stroking Belle's arm. "Charley's a total wreck right now, and I thought if anyone can help her through this, it's you."

"Oh."

"I know it's asking a lot, but could you leave John for a few days and come down here to see her?"

Marlena was torn. She didn't want to leave John, but if she did, she could see Belle and Claire. She would also have an excuse to avoid Blake Masters.

"If it's all right with your father-in-law," she said, looking to John. "A few days in Monaco to help a friend of theirs?"

John nodded. In fact, he was happy to see her go.

"I'll be there tomorrow?" Marlena offered.

"Thanks. We'll pick you up at the Nice airport. There's an Air France flight that comes just before noon."

"I'll be the one with the pink rose in my hair," she said lightly.

"Belle says good-bye too," Shawn said as he disconnected the call.

"Bye," Marlena said, but he was gone. "You sure?" she said to John.

"I'll be fine, Doc," he said firmly.

"Guess I'd better let the nurses know," Marlena said.

John nodded again in that silent, sure way that always made her feel safe.

Once Marlena was gone, John snapped on the TV again. When he was sure she was long out of earshot, he dialed a number on his cell phone.

"Donovan, it's John," he said. On the other end was Shane Donovan, one of John's closest friends and a bigwig in the ISA.

"Is it time?" Shane answered.

"Doc's going to be gone for a few days," John said, swinging his muscular legs over the side of the bed. "I've got to prove to myself I'm ready."

∞

Several hours later, Marlena was in her bedroom, packing.

She'd only be gone for a few days, so she didn't need to bring much in the way of clothing. A few crisp white cotton blouses, lightweight tailored slacks, and a beige linen jacket. The monochromatic tones complemented her blonde hair perfectly.

It was August and beautiful in Monte Carlo this time of year, but there could be a few scattered thundershowers, so she threw a small umbrella and a cashmere sweater into her carry-on. She zipped her cream-colored Tumi and set it by the door.

Her cell phone was on the desk by the window, and she stood gazing out while she texted Blake Masters.

"Out of town a few days. Sorry."

Simple. Direct. Send.

Sorry? she thought. *Should I have said sorry? Am I?*

Before she could put the phone down, it dinged! It was a text from Blake: "Should hav bio report on ur return. C U then."

Marlena stared at it a long moment. His response was simple and direct too.

Good, she thought.

Right now she just didn't want to see him.

She slipped out of her clothes and into a lounging robe, then sat at her desk to read. She'd spent hours reading since she and John moved to Lausanne, but this time she couldn't concentrate.

The late-summer sun was setting, and the view from Marlena's bedroom was beautiful.

The Swiss Alps were on one side of Maison du Noir, and while known for their snowcapped glory in winter, they were equally stunning all year long, on account of their craggy, jutting peaks. Lake Geneva was in the distance, seen over the fields of grapes that were just about ready for harvest.

She put her elbows on the desk and leaned on her clasped hands. Rubbing her palms together slowly, she felt the spot John had massaged so tenderly. It was as if he were touching her again, and she gasped.

Had she known John was standing at the matching window in his room, just across the hall, staring out at the same magnificent landscape and rubbing his palms in the exact same way, she would have flown to his side.

But she didn't. So she didn't. Instead, she was leaving town in the morning.

22  *CHARLEY*

"Ow," Charley yelped as an Italian male nurse firmly pumped up the collar on her arm to take her blood pressure. "Too tight," she scolded in perfect Italian.

Esther scurried in and shooed the scowling thirty-year-old out of the room.

"*Ptiu*," he spit silently through pursed lips. This guy had a problem.

"I am so sorry, Miss Gaines," Esther apologized. "Let's try this again, and I'll surely report him."

"Thank you," Charley said, confused. "If he's having a bad day, he doesn't know what a bad day is," she added.

"Beautiful robe." Esther smiled, trying to change the subject.

"From my brother," Charley answered. "He's always had the best taste in the family.

Esther completed the blood pressure test and found that Charley was 140/70. It was an excellent reading for someone who'd been through such physical and emotional trauma.

"I guess we won't need any more blood donations from your friend," Esther offered.

"My friend?" Charley questioned.

"Mr. Brady," Esther answered. "The young man who donated blood. So lucky you share B negative. Very rare."

"Lucky," Charley said.

"Especially since neither your father or mother, God rest her soul, were a match," Esther said gently.

"Lucky," Charley replied.

Wait, what?

"Your brother called, and they're on their way up with your father," Esther said.

Charley was so deep in thought that she didn't answer.

"Miss Gaines?"

"Yes?"

"Your brothers and father. You are up to visitors, aren't you?" she asked.

"Of course, why?" Charley asked.

"I can tell Mario upset you," Esther answered warmly.

Little did she realize it was her comment about the blood match that had Charley's head spinning.

"And there they are," Esther said, noticing Richie, Jackson, and Chance coming down the hall from the elevators.

Charley was in a state, and her heart monitor showed it. The *beep, beep, beep* of the machine was getting faster.

"Let me give you something to relax," Esther said.

"No, I'm fine," Charley lied. Right now she didn't want to be sedated; she wanted answers.

Esther gently touched her hand, then headed out to the nurses' station, scowling at Mario, who was glaring at Richie.

Richie walked straight past him and into his daughter's room. Jackson and Chance were behind him.

"Sugar," Richie said, taking her hand and giving her a kiss. "Sorry I couldn't be here sooner."

"I understand," she answered, studying his face.

"I'm pleased to see you're doing so well," Richie said with true fatherly concern.

"Dad wanted to stop and see Mum, but we don't think that's a good idea," Chance said to her pointedly.

"Too soon," Jackson added, looking to his sister for support. The last thing they wanted was for Richie to hear about the autopsy.

They could hear a loud disagreement from the nurses' station and saw Mario slam down a file and storm off in a huff.

Jackson closed the drapes to give them privacy. They were unaware that Mario was one of the thousands of healthcare professionals who'd just lost their savings due to the Financial Gaines Group's collapse. The Hippocratic oath or Nightingale pledge notwithstanding, no one named Gaines was a popular patient with him.

"There's something you need to know, sugar, and I wanted you to hear it from me," Richie said, taking her hand. For some reason, his touch felt different to her.

Charley steeled herself. She had seen enough medical shows in her life that she knew a child would have at least one parent as a compatible blood type

"Yes?" she said with no emotion.

"You may wonder why you've not had access to any media," Richie said. "No television, radio, computer."

"I'm in ICU—" She faltered. She couldn't call him Dad.

"It's why you were kept here instead of recovery," he explained.

Charley was more puzzled by the second.

"I'm not the man you've thought I was all these years," he said.

I know! Charley thought.

"My financial empire has been a sham since before you were all born," he stated.

"What?" she said, glancing to Jackson.

"Your brothers weren't involved, just me. I've ruined a lot of people's lives, sugar, and I'll be going to prison. I am so, so sorry."

Charley was stunned.

Richie continued on with details of his house arrest, the restrictions, and what this disaster would mean to them financially.

Charley didn't hear a word. Her shock wasn't about their whole lives being a charade.

You're not my real father? she thought. *Isn't that something you'd like to tell me?*

The heart monitor began to beep faster, faster.

"Nurse!" she called. "I need that sedative!"

23 *MARLENA AND MONTE CARLO*

"GiGi!" Claire giggled as she ran at top speed toward Marlena.

Marlena scooped up her granddaughter and hugged her tightly as Belle and Shawn caught up. Some of the sexiest women in the world now were grandmothers, and Marlena was proud to be one of them.

"You are soooo big!" Marlena laughed. "And just—"

"Adorable!" Claire giggled back, plucking the pink rose from behind Marlena's ear. "I know!"

"And heavy," Marlena said, putting her down next to her carry-on and teasingly groaning.

"You look fabulous, Mom," Belle said, going into her mother's arms. "I've missed you so much."

"You have no idea how much I've missed all you guys." Marlena beamed.

John was right. When Marlena smiled, she had smiling eyes.

Shawn gave her a kiss on the cheek and took the handle of the carry-on. "How was the flight?"

"Short and sweet, thank God," Marlena answered. "The man next to me was desperate for a cigarette from the moment he sat down."

"French?"

"Could be." She smiled.

Smiling. She was doing it again, and it felt so good. The last few years had been especially grueling for her. Not only had she had to watch the despair John had been going through, she was in a new country far from the family she adored. Since she'd come through the French side of the Geneva airport, she didn't have to go through customs, so they headed straight for the exit.

"I need to make a quick stop, Mom," Belle said. She needed to get to the little girls' room and fast.

"I could use it too," Marlena said.

"You go with them, Clairebear," Shawn suggested. "I'll get the car."

Shawn headed to get their rental car as his three girls ducked into the ladies' room. Belle grabbed the first stall and threw up immediately.

"You all right, baby girl?" Marlena asked through the stall.

"She does that a lot, GiGi," Claire reported.

Belle flushed the toilet and opened the door. One look between mother and daughter, and Marlena knew.

"Does Shawn know?" Marlena beamed. She was thrilled at the thought of another grandchild.

"Know what?" Claire asked with her wide-eyed innocence.

"Hurry up, baby doll. We don't want to keep Da waiting," Belle said, dodging the question.

Claire scooted into the handicap stall with Marlena, and Belle splashed cold water on her face. When the two emerged, Belle caught her mother's reflection in the mirror.

"I guess we have a lot to catch up on," Marlena said as she helped Claire wash her hands.

"I guess we do," Belle answered.

The airport was a madhouse. It was August, after all, and the girls dodged tourists from around the world as they made their way to the bright blue Peugeot convertible with Shawn in the driver's seat.

"A convertible," Marlena said, complimenting Shawn.

"We wanted you to see everything." Shawn smiled. "Sit in the front."

"I want to sit with Claire," Marlena said as she climbed in the backseat. She also knew that Belle could get carsick, and if she was right, and her daughter was pregnant, the winding roads could be miserable.

"Here we go!" Shawn said, putting his foot to the floor. They sped out of the airport, and Claire thrust her hands in the air.

"Whee!" Claire laughed.

"Whee!" Marlena said, throwing her hands in the air and laughing with her.

The feeling of freedom was something she'd desperately missed.

The eighteen-mile drive along the Côte d'Azur to Monte Carlo was always spectacular. Marlena had done it before a number of times but didn't mention that to Shawn as he pointed out sights along the way.

She was confused when they drove into the Place du Casino, and Shawn pulled up to the magnificent Hôtel de Paris.

"Shawn, this isn't my hotel," she said.

"It is, Mom," Belle said. "Dad asked us to change your reservation. He wanted you—"

"To have the best," Marlena said, completing the sentence.

John knew her very well. Even though she often protested extravagance, when it came to a hotel, there was nothing like it.

The palace hotel, built in 1864, was elegant and grand and sat next to Casino de Monte-Carlo, which was made internationally more popular by the James Bond 007 films. The domed lobby of the palace was gorgeous with its inlaid marble floors and polished wood ceilings, plus the bronze statue of Louis XIV on horseback in its center.

"I need the ladies room." Belle smiled halfheartedly.

The concierge directed her through the massive arched columns that lined the foyer, while Shawn took Claire's hand and they escorted Marlena to check-in.

Marlena was drinking in the peace she felt in this exciting, glamorous environment. She handed her platinum credit card to the elegantly suited gentleman behind the desk.

"Marlena Evans," she said.

"Your suite is not quite ready, Madame," he said in French-accented English.

"Suite?" she said, inwardly pleased.

"It's a junior suite, facing the Mediterranean."

"Lovely, thank you."

"Sounds like Dad," Belle said, returning.

"Marlena?"

She heard a man call to her from the next check-in.

"Blake?"

Yes, indeed, Blake. The man checking in next to her was the one man she'd been avoiding: Blake Masters.

∞

Le Côté Jardin was the lovely terrace restaurant overlooking the immaculately manicured gardens of the Hôtel de Paris. There were three distinctively different dining rooms, but this was the best spot for lunch with a nearly four-year-old.

Marlena sat at the skirted table with her fidgety granddaughter on one side and Belle on the other. Shawn was next to Claire, which put Blake directly across from Marlena.

Shawn, ever the gentleman, had invited Blake to join them. She'd called him by his first name, so they assumed he was her colleague. Little did they know, it was an awkward situation.

"I didn't expect to see you here," Blake said to Marlena as perfect medium-rare hamburgers were served.

"Likewise," she offered. "Shawn asked me to consult with a friend of theirs."

"Charley Gaines," Shawn said. "I don't know if you're familiar with all that's been going on."

"Who isn't?" Blake said.

"Shawn's the one who was on the scene of the accident," Belle said.

"Wow," Blake said.

"It's how I know Charley," Shawn told him. "And she's obviously having a hard time. I asked my mother-in-law to talk with her. There's no better psychiatrist than Marlena."

"I'm sure." Blake smiled.

Marlena looked away, which only Belle noticed.

"Pommes frites!" Claire squealed as she popped several in her mouth. "Yum."

"We never have them when we're out at sea, so she's all over them when we're in port," Shawn said to Blake.

He could see Blake's confusion, so he went on to describe the voyage he and Belle had been taking, about John's generosity, and the last six months of the trip that Shawn had been dreaming about since they left the United States.

Marlena caught Belle's expression as she shrugged lightly.

It must be about the timing, Marlena thought. *Belle doesn't want to ruin Shawn's dream.*

"And what's the dream?" Blake asked.

"Deep sea fishing in Trinidad." Shawn beamed.

Belle began to turn green.

"Terrific there; I've done it," Blake said with enthusiasm. "And oysters?" He continued, "they like to say they grow on trees there. You like oysters, Claire?"

"Yum!" Claire declared. "I want oysters!"

As if on cue, Belle bolted from the table.

∞

"Olivia Gaines would have probably loved this," Belle commented as they entered Marlena's suite, which, as to be expected, was beautiful.

Facing the Mediterranean, it had deep mahogany empire furniture accented by the finest fabrics in shades of yellow.

The bellman opened the drapes and doors to the terrace, and Claire ran right to the edge.

"Hey, hey," Shawn cautioned as he went right after her.

"Shawn's become a very good man, sweetheart," Marlena said to her daughter.

"The best, Mom," Belle agreed. "That's why I so don't want to disappoint him."

"He loves kids."

"I know. But you heard him at lunch. This trip was his dream, and my throwing up all over the place is a nightmare. And we'd have to forget that trip to Trinidad because of the timing." Belle was rambling a bit, and Marlena knew it.

"This is about timing?" Marlena asked, suspecting different.

"Gonna getcha." Shawn laughed, chasing Claire back into the room.

"Timing," Belle said quietly.

"Whee!" Claire squealed as she jumped on the king-size bed, her dad jumping on top of her and tickling her madly. A tickle fight ensued. Then Shawn grabbed Claire's hands and slyly asked her, "Mommy?"

Before Belle knew it, they jumped from the bed and pulled her onto it with them. She melted into the fun and put her queasiness aside, thoroughly enjoying her family.

The phone rang.

"Hello?" Marlena said.

"How's your suite?" Blake joked.

"Lovely," Marlena answered.

"I hear the kids are still there," he said.

"For a while."

"If you're free later, we could have dinner. Le Louis XV is an Alain Ducasse restaurant," he said.

He knows his chefs? Marlena thought.

"Cooking's a hobby," he added.

Oh, right, he reads minds.

To her surprise, the other line rang.

"Could you hold on a minute?" Marlena said.

"I could hold on two," he said with a smile in his voice as she clicked over.

"Marlena Evans," she answered.

"Doc, how's the hotel?"

It was John.

"Gorgeous, thank you so much," she said, fully aware of the blinking light on the other line. "I miss you."

"I'm fine, really," John said.

He couldn't say I miss you too? she thought.

"Doc, you there?" he asked.

"Yes."

"Say hi to the kids for me," he said. "Tell 'em I love them."

"Will do," she said as she heard him hang up.

❧

John sat with his phone in his hand.

"Ladies and gentlemen, please get ready for takeoff," came over the speakers. "And please turn off all electronic devices."

John buckled his seat belt as a slim, statuesque flight attendant passed through the first-class cabin.

"Are you sure you are all right with this?" the female voice with a Dutch accent in the seat next to him asked, as her slender hand touched John's.

"We'll see, won't we?" he answered.

"I guess we will," said Tara, patting his hand and turning to look out the window.

24   *JACK AND JENNIFER*

JENNIFER WAS PROOFING THE GALLEYS FOR THE *SPECTATOR*'S print edition at her computer when Jack came bounding in, carrying something behind his back.

"Jen!" he called as he leaped to the mezzanine level of the house, where she had her desk.

"Jack!" she wailed as he spun her around to face him. "I've told you not to do that!"

"Can't help it, you hot mama, sexy lady, sensational journalist. Because of you," he said, kissing her, "and Abby"—he kissed her again—"we have quadrupled sales of the *Spectator* in two days!" He plopped a bottle of Cristal next to her computer, pulled her out of her chair, and planted the biggest, wettest kiss on her that she'd had in ages.

"Honey, that's fantastic," she beamed, hugging him.

"We're not going to lose the house," he exalted. "Not gonna lose it, never gonna lose it..." He swung her around, and they started dancing around the room Fred-and-Ginger style.

Jennifer couldn't help but laugh at his joy, but still said, "Jack! Jack, stop it."

He gave her one last twirl and sank into a chair.

"I know. Isn't it unbelievable?"

"Yeah…"

"But?" he said.

"Were we really going to lose the house?" she asked weakly.

Jack hadn't said a word. He was a man with a tremendous sense of pride, and once upon a time, he'd been her unemployed house-husband and had not handled it well.

"I didn't want you to know, Jen," Jack answered. "We've been uprooted so much, and I know how you love it here. But yeah, we moved here at the top of the market, and with the economy and the state of the newspaper business and—well, it was almost a goner."

Jennifer let out a huge sigh of relief, tinged with annoyance. They had indeed had a rocky path stemming back to their times in Salem, once having to go on the run from police and then living in Africa for a while. The denizens of Salem all had remarkable stories.

"I love you, Jack." She beamed. "But don't ever keep something like that from me again!" she added, hitting him lightly.

"Ow!" He feigned injury, rubbing his arm. "You may have to kiss that—and a few other things."

Jennifer hit him again. "Tonight, that," she said, indicating toward the champagne. "Then it's all about you," she added seductively.

The first time they'd ever made love was after Jack had saved Jennifer's life. Now she, with their daughter, Abby, had saved his.

"Now all we have to do is keep the scoops coming," he said ruefully.

"We know what that means," she said, picking up her cell and dialing. "Abby?" Jennifer said.

"Mom, hi, I was just about to call you," Abby said. She was sunbathing in an OMG bikini and looking through binoculars as she spoke.

"Shawn and Belle are spending the day with Marlena, so Chels and I are on the boat. She wanted to avoid being hounded, and I had a hunch, so…" She couldn't finish her sentence.

"Your dad's with me, wait," Jennifer said as she put Abby on speakerphone.

"We all know the funeral's the day after tomorrow," Abby said.

"Just not the final location."

"St. Nicholas Cathedral," Abby said with conviction.

"Are you 100 percent positive sure?" Jack asked. "Isn't Richard Gaines Episcopalian?"

"I'm looking at Jackson Gaines right now, Dad, and he's in the back of the cathedral with the priest. They're shaking hands… and…yes, he's saying it's at five p.m." Abby had long ago learned the value of reading lips.

"Abby," Chelsea interrupted, signaling to Abby's laptop. "Olivia Gaines was brought up Catholic."

"It'll get out faster on Spectator.com, Dad," Abby reminded him.

"Go for it, baby!" Jack said excitedly.

Jack took the phone from Jennifer's hand as their daughter hung up. "Where's J. J.?" he asked.

"At Theatreland with his friend Reggie from Notting Hill Prep," she reminded him. "Then Reggie's parents are taking them to dinner." Noticing the gleam in his eye, she added, "Why?"

"Press time's not for three hours," he said, gallantly scooping Jen up in his arms.

"Jack Deveraux!" she scolded, knowing exactly where this was headed.

"Get that, woman," he added wryly, nodding to the champagne before burying his head in her neck.

Caught up in the moment, Jennifer grabbed for the icy bottle. "What the heck?" She laughed as Jack whisked her up to their bedroom.

25 MARLENA

THE NIGHT WAS SUPERB AND THE VIEW YET AGAIN BEAUTIFUL AS Marlena sat alone having room service on her terrace , which overlooked the Mediterranean. While she truly loved Maison du Noir, with its views of Lake Geneva, there was nothing like the sound of the ocean waves in the distance and the freshness of salt air.

She understood the unmatched appeal of the city carved out of the rocky hillsides of Italy and France. The host to royalty and the brightest stars of painting, music, film, and dance, Monte Carlo was like a fairy tale. It was Disneyland for fabulously wealthy adults.

Shawn and Belle had taken Claire back to the boat. Marlena had wanted them to spend the night, but they hadn't brought extra clothes, so she understood. Besides, she could get a good night's sleep, which she hadn't truly experienced for years, when there was always a chance that John would need her in the middle of the night.

The city was coming alive, and Marlena was antsy.

She opened the leather-bound folder on the desk and perused the city guide that listed, in several languages, all the festivities Monte Carlo had in August.

She had missed Elton John's summer concert performance at the Prince's Palace, which she would have loved. She was a huge fan of the fabulous work he'd done for over forty years with his writing partner, Bernie Taupin. OMG's styles were a bit tame for the flamboyant performer, but she wondered if he'd return for the funeral.

There was a jazz concert at Square Théodore Gastaud, which was less than a ten-minute walk from the hotel. With the security cameras scouring the city, plus the size of the police force, she felt safe walking there alone.

After slipping on her linen jacket and throwing the cashmere sweater over her shoulders, Marlena headed out of her room.

In the lobby, there he was again. Blake Masters.

"We've got to stop meeting like this." He smiled.

It was a good smile, a warm smile, and the lines around his eyes crinkled just a bit. So many plastic surgeons Marlena knew were victims of their own profession, but not Blake.

"How old are you?"

"Forty-five," he said.

"Did I say that out loud?" She grimaced, embarrassed.

"No, I read your mind," he joked.

"I'm sorry I never called you back," she apologized.

"That's okay, I assumed you made other plans for dinner," he added casually.

"I, um, I did," Marlena stammered. "I had room service."

"Well, you missed a terrific dinner," he said. "Le Grill? Don't miss it."

"You didn't try Le Louis XV?"

"Not the place for a meal solo," he admitted. "You want to share that kind of experience with someone."

"Well, nice to see you again," she said in a tone she hoped he could only interpret as friendly.

"You too," he said.

After an awkward moment, they each headed for the hotel exit. They stopped. Shared a look.

"The jazz concert?" Blake said.

Marlena could only nod, chuckling.

The doorman stepped forward. "I'm sorry for eavesdropping, but there are no more tickets for tonight's concert."

So much for that.

"You up for a walk?" Blake asked.

Marlena hesitated a moment, then answered, "Sure."

The night air was more invigorating outside than in. The mood was festive and glamorous in Casino Square. Vacationers and summer residents filled the streets, and the yachts were party central.

They chatted about nothing terribly important—the yachts, the weather, and the extravagance surrounding them, which was mind-boggling.

On their way back to the hotel, they strolled past the designer boutiques, including Chanel, Cartier, and OMG. The OMG shop, unlike the others, was closed, and there were flowers and candles, mostly in yellow, in front of the door.

"I'm here for her, you know," Blake said simply.

"Olivia Gaines?" Marlena was surprised.

"She was a client for years, having the most minuscule tweaks you could imagine."

"You are good."

"So they tell me," he said. "The family knew how important it would be for her to look perfect in her casket. Not like Princess Grace's fiasco."

Princess Grace, the actress turned royalty, had been buried in a bad blonde wig to cover the scars from her fatal accident. Olivia had often joked that she would never let that happen to her. Now it didn't seem quite so funny.

"Her face, yes," Marlena remembered.

"They're also performing an autopsy," he added.

"They are?" Marlena asked, puzzled.

"That's all highly confidential, of course," he said, adding, "I really shouldn't have even told you."

"Of course," Marlena assured him.

"She was really a piece of work, that one," Blake said.

"Tragic really," she said gently. "Makes you realize you have to live every day as if it's your last."

Pheromones were flying. He wanted to kiss her. She knew it. She also knew she couldn't let him.

"Time to par-tay!" they heard, breaking the moment as two young women came flying past them.

"Par-tay on," Marlena called to them, relieved for the interruption.

They stopped in their tracks.

"Marlena?" Abby said.

"Hi," Chelsea added, thrown to see Marlena.

"What are you doing here?" Abby said. She was intrigued that Marlena was with a very handsome younger man. "I thought Belle and Shawn were going up to see you."

"Plans changed, so here I am." Marlena smiled, not wanting to betray any patient-doctor confidentiality. She felt guilty and hated herself for it.

"Dr. Masters, these are friends of my daughter Belle," she said. "Chelsea and Abby." Going into all the connections would be too much. "Girls, Dr. Masters is a colleague."

Why she was explaining to them, she had no idea. Overexplaining anything was always a bad sign.

"Nice to meet you both." He nodded. "Going to the casino?"

"It's been a long couple of days," Abby said. "Girls gotta have some fun."

"Why don't you join them, Blake?" Marlena asked, her voice cracking. She realized she suddenly sounded too familiar.

"Not my thing, and I have an early day tomorrow," he answered. "I'll just walk you back to the elevator," he said, more as a question than a statement, "and we'll catch up tomorrow."

Now he's overexplaining, Marlena thought. *This isn't good.*

They headed to the hotel entrance as Abby and Chelsea exchanged glances.

"You don't think…" Chelsea said, leaving the question in the air.

"Nah…" Abby said, adding, "but he sure is hot."

Chelsea hit her on the shoulder.

"Let's go have some fun," Abby said brightly, heading toward the gleaming Lamborghinis, Maseratis, and Bentleys lined up outside the most famous casino in the world.

∞

Blake's room looked over the courtyard and was much smaller

than Marlena's. In deep red tones, with fabric wall coverings and white-leaded furniture, it was more masculine, but still beautiful and featured a luxurious king-size bed.

The bathroom had exquisite faience tiles, rich enamels, and the same plush towels and robes as in Marlena's junior suite.

Ten minutes after Blake left Marlena at the elevators, he was in a much-needed cold, cold shower.

∽

Marlena slipped into her bed. Settling against the down pillows, she felt good about herself.

She opened a novel she'd been reading off and on for several months. It was Dominick Dunne's *Justice*. Crime novels were a guilty pleasure of hers, and she loved his writing.

After a few moments, something dawned on her.

Autopsy? Why would Olivia Gaines be having an autopsy?

She pondered that for a long moment.

Blake said it was strictly confidential. Why?

Marlena was drawn back to thoughts of him. She knew what he wanted and still wants, and the Hôtel de Paris could surely lure even the most loyal spouse into an indiscretion.

But she wouldn't.

She couldn't.

John Black was the only man she wanted.

And if she knew he was at a hotel in London at that moment, with another woman, it would have broken her heart.

26   *CHARLEY*

"Thank God they're not here," Charley said as she walked out of Princess Grace Hospital on Chance's arm.

There were no paparazzi outside when Chance picked up his sister. The city was buzzing with even more celebrities than ever, after Dalita Kasagian's embarrassing, overblown bash and Olivia's upcoming funeral. "Your accident is already old news," he said.

"To everyone but us," she said sadly.

Chance opened the door of his silver ice Maserati and helped her in. Charley had always been the bright light of the family. She was the one who cheered everyone up when they were down and who had an inner strength they admired. For him to see her so emotionless was especially painful.

"Right now that's probably best," he said. "The last thing we need is someone following our every move."

"Is the autopsy—" she said, faltering.

"It's done," Chance said. "Now we just have to wait." Chance punched the Start button, the engine hummed, and they headed to the villa.

When Chance turned left instead of right, Charley gave him a look.

"Thought we'd go the back way," Chance offered.

"No," Charley said. "It'll take forever. I'm okay, really."

Hoping she was telling him the truth, Chance flipped a U-turn and headed back up the road Charley and Olivia had been on when the accident happened.

Chance turned up the volume on the sound system. Listening to Katy Perry always cheered her up, and "California Gurls" was Charley's favorite song. Well, before the accident, that is. He hoped it would distract her.

It didn't.

The turn where they had had the accident was coming up, and Chance didn't know if he should ignore it. There was still caution tape across the broken rail, and yellow candles and flowers similar to the ones in front of the boutique.

"If that guy on the bicycle hadn't been there, maybe I could have done something," she said and softly began to cry.

Chance took her hand and opted not to question her.

∞

There were indeed paparazzi in front of the gates to the villa. A few stragglers were fascinated with the investment scandal.

Chance activated the remote, and the gates opened.

"We're going to lose the villa, aren't we?" Charley asked.

"My guess is yes," Chance offered. "Dad screwed over the investors to the tune of 1 billion euros."

Charley flinched. She knew it was bad, but not that bad.

"We always liked camping," he said, trying to lighten the moment.

The front door opened as they drove in. Richie was in the doorway, and the paps got a shot or two of the man reviled for his actions.

Charley was a mess. Not only had she lost her mother, but her father was a felon. Truth was, she loved him anyway. She just no longer trusted him.

Chance got Charley's belongings out of the car as Richie took her in his arms. It was a long and awkward hug.

"You look good," Richie said, brushing back her hair. The bandage on her neck was more evident.

They moved into the house.

"I have to check with the doctors tomorrow," she said.

"The funeral's at five," Richie said. "And if you're not up to going…"

"I have to be there—"

Charley stopped again. She wanted to call him Dad but couldn't. "I need to go up to my room," she added.

Charley made her way through the home she loved, up the stairs to her bedroom, which had a panoramic view of the sea in the distance.

∞

"We have a court date next Tuesday," Chance told his father.

The proceedings were all going as planned.

"You really should plead innocent," Chance advised.

"I'm guilty as sin, Chance," Richie replied. "Why drag this out?"

"To buy us some time," Chance said.

"After Madoff, it's all pretty cut-and-dried," Richie said as he poured himself a scotch from the bar. "Anything?" he added, motioning to the bar.

"Still recovering," Chance said.

"I heard you come in at five a.m.," Richie said, raising his glass.

"We're still in Monte Carlo," Chance answered. It helped that he was in his midtwenties.

"You should take three aspirin when you hit the sack," Richie said. "Never a hangover."

"What about those pills Mom got into?" Chance asked.

Richie's stare softened. "None left."

Richie didn't even look for them.

Suddenly, a buzzer went off.

"If it's another of those damn reporters..." Richie scowled.

"Yes?" Chance said, looking at the security monitor.

"This is Shawn Brady." Shawn was at the gate with Marlena in the passenger seat.

"Charley's expecting me," he said. "I just spoke with her."

"Give me a minute," Chance said.

He checked with his sister, and yes, she had spoken with Shawn and wanted to see him and Marlena.

Richie wasn't sure this was a good idea. He loved his daughter and knew she'd been hit hard by the accident and the incredible shame he'd brought to the family, but he had no idea who this woman was who would be talking to his daughter.

"She trusts this guy for whatever reason, Dad," Chance said. "Maybe because she has his blood flowing through her veins."

When Chance opened the door, and Richie saw Marlena standing there, he changed his mind. Not only was she beautiful, but he sensed a warmth and kindness he'd never seen in Olivia. While Olivia had always pictured herself as the epitome of class, he realized Marlena had it in spades.

"Richard Gaines," he said, extending his hand as Marlena entered with Shawn. "And I have no excuses for the chaos I've wrought."

"I'm here to neither judge nor treat you, Mr. Gaines," she said, not taking his hand. "Just here to see if I can help a friend of my son-in-law's."

"No harm, no foul." Richie smiled.

My God, she's beautiful, he thought. *If only I weren't such a scumbag and felon.*

"Char said she'd meet you in the sunroom," Chance interrupted. "Right this way."

◈

Charley was in one of the overstuffed chairs in the room that opened to the rose gardens and tennis court, and she was staring at a framed photo when Chance entered with Shawn and Marlena.

"Sugar?" Chance said.

"Oh, hi, Shawn," she said softly. "And Dr. Evans?"

"Why don't you call me Marlena?" Marlena said warmly. For some reason, she felt formality would have been totally inappropriate.

"I'm headed to meet Jackson about Mum's funeral," Chance explained. "Don't you worry about a thing," he added to his little sister.

"I trust you, Big Brother," Charley said with a hint of sadness. "I always have."

"Mind if I take a look around?" Shawn asked, wanting to give Charley some time alone with Marlena.

"There's an incredible view just beyond the courts," Charley told him. "You can see them readying for tomorrow's race."

The Palermo–Monte Carlo yacht races were all the next week. She knew that would fascinate Shawn, and it did.

"Thanks," he said warmly.

Shawn headed out, and Marlena observed how Charley watched him. The two had a connection that was immediately comfortable and caring.

"He's a great guy," Charley said warmly.

"And a great son-in-law," Marlena added.

Charley managed to smile. She was well aware he was married, and actually appreciated Marlena being protective of her daughter.

"I like you," Charley said.

"Same back," Marlena responded. "And I'm so sorry for what you must be feeling."

"You have no idea," Charley said, her shoulders sagging as she looked at the photo in her hand.

"Disneyland Paris," she said, showing Marlena the image.

"I was five. The guys were just teenagers and wanted nothing to do with me."

The photo was Charley with Olivia and Richie on either side of her. She was wearing a pink princess dress, and they were in front of Le Château de la Belle au Bois Dormant—Sleeping Beauty's Castle. They were flanked by all the costumed princesses,

Mickey, Minnie, Goofy, and Pluto. She had been one spoiled little girl.

Charley chuckled sadly. "I never noticed before. Look how my…dad…was staring at Princess Aurora."

Indeed, Richie's eyes were glued to Aurora's chest.

"Look at your mother, though. She obviously adored you," Marlena said reassuringly.

Charley sighed. Silently, she rose from the chair and placed the framed photo amid a dozen or so elegantly framed family photos from their trips around the world.

"If you want to talk about her…"

After what seemed like an eternity, Charley said, "She wasn't my mother." The disbelief in her voice was palpable. "I'm not their daughter."

Marlena could tell she wasn't being flippant.

"Neither one had my blood type, and no one's ever said a word about it," she wailed.

She grabbed a beautiful photo of herself as a baby in Olivia's arms and slammed it against the marble-topped credenza, the glass shattering in a thousand pieces.

"Who am I?" she wailed. "Who am I really?"

Charley started to sob.

Marlena wrapped her arms around the desolate creature and cradled her gently.

27  *THE ISA*

THE INTERNATIONAL SECURITY ALLIANCE OPERATED IN CON-junction with numerous branches of law enforcement throughout the world. While their main headquarters were in Washington, D.C., they also had bases in London, Rio, and Hong Kong. The UK headquarters for the ISA were located just down Vauxhall Cross from Britain's Secret Intelligence Service.

John Black had been recruited through Washington because of his intelligence, physical prowess, and incredible charm. A major aspect of infiltrating dangerous and often-unpredictable situations was the ability to fit into most any environment from blue-collar to white-tie. John was exactly that man.

Until the paralysis that had felled him.

It had been nearly two years since that fateful moment when he had tried to save Marlena from a maniac and ended up taking the shot that had been meant for her. He had saved her and lost her in one fell swoop.

Though he'd been to hell and back with her over the years, he'd finally hit rock bottom. He wanted to believe that their love could survive this seemingly insurmountable obstacle, but as time went on, he doubted it was possible.

Not because he loved her any less; in fact, seeing the sacrifices she had made for him made him love her even more.

No, he believed in his heart that she deserved a whole man. A hero.

Men raised when he was were taught that men were the hunter-gatherers and providers. The protectors and confidants. Lovers and friends. It was not just enough for John to be there for Marlena and love her. He had to feel worthy of that love, and he hadn't for some time.

In his eyes, he was no longer a man. Not worthy of Marlena or even worthy of the woman who accompanied him to London— Tara, the gentle soul with the strong hands and caring heart.

∞

Tara had no idea what to expect when they arrived at ISA headquarters. The building was not as impressive as the behemoth M16 fortress, which had been nicknamed Legoland because of its massive stacked-brick architecture.

John brought Tara through the back entrance, where they were greeted by black-suited men and women who were cheerful and meticulously groomed.

"John Black, welcome." The girl smiled.

"Laney," John said. "And Mac, good to see you," he added to the middle-aged mustachioed man who operated the phones next to her.

"Mr. Black," Mac said. "Mr. Donovan's waiting for you."

"Second floor," John remembered. He turned to see Shane getting off the steel-plated elevator.

"John," Shane said warmly as he gave him a manly hug. "It is so good to see you."

"Same here," John said.

"You must be Tara," Shane offered. "John's told me a lot about you. It's nice to meet you."

"You too, thanks." Tara smiled. The Dutch lilt in her voice was charming.

"You want to show her around?" Shane asked.

"It's a pretty big place," John answered. "And I'd like to get to this. That okay with you, Tara?"

"Absolutely," she said, touching his arm. "This is all about you."

"We've got formal gardens, if you'd like to take a stroll, and a museum with fine art from around the world," Shane said. "We like our guys to be comfortable in any environment, so there's plenty to do and see here. This is going to take a while."

"I'm ready for that," she said. "I'd like to stick close to John, if you don't mind."

"I like that," Shane told her. "You've both eaten?"

"Breakfast at the hotel."

"Then let's get started," Shane said, pushing the Down elevator button.

John was in for a grueling day, but he hoped it was worth it.

⚭

Over the years, John had periodically revisited both the ISA in

Washington and the headquarters in London. Like Don Corleone in *The Godfather*, somehow he was always pulled back in.

Today was different. He was not only going to take the psychological exams that would show his intelligence, judgment, and mental stability, but the grueling physical tests that would determine his viability.

Tara watched behind two-way mirrors as a panel of experts threw him current-events questions about Afghanistan, the Vancouver Olympics, *American Idol*, Barack Obama's healthcare plan, the Madoff scandal.

His brain, it was obvious, was working just fine.

Tara joined him as he went up to Shane's office, which overlooked the Thames.

"Passed that leg with flying colors, my friend," Shane said in that mellifluous voice with the high British accent.

"You sure you want to do more today?" Tara asked, concerned as John rubbed his forehead.

"Gotta be today," John said. "Gotta be ready."

"We're running the American army fitness test this afternoon," Shane said.

"Hand to hand?" John asked, adding, "Defensive driving? Jump school?"

"John," Shane replied, "if you can pass the fitness test, you're ready for anything."

The months of his incapacity had eaten away at John's confidence. Today's hours of intense scrutiny were changing all that.

Tara was pleased.

∞

It was nearly 11 p.m. when John and Tara arrived at Cecconi's in Mayfair. Although it was late, the place was buzzing. The classic Italian restaurant had once been owned by the manager of Cipriani in Venice and had been reinvented to become the hottest dining spot in London.

John and Tara opted to sit at a table rather than one of the coveted barreled high stools at the classic bar.

John ordered martinis and a rare steak for himself and grilled sea bass for Tara. They'd had a long, difficult day, and it was time to relax.

The drinks came perfectly iced, and John raised his glass to the woman who'd seen him through one of the most grueling days of his life.

"To me," he said. His hand was a bit shaky, but with all he'd been through, it was to be expected.

"To you," she responded as they clinked their crystal-stemmed martini glasses and sipped the cold, crisp Grey Goose with a lemon twist. "I'm ready," he said.

"I'm glad," she replied. "More than you know."

"You knew it was only a matter of time, didn't you?" he asked.

"You are one of the—no, let me correct that—you are the most perfect male specimen I've ever known."

Tara looked at him with the admiration he used to get from Marlena.

He felt like a man again.

28   *SHAWN, BELLE, AND MARLENA*

"MOMMY!" CLAIRE SAID, POUNDING ON THE DOOR OF Marlena's bathroom. She wasn't used to her mother locking her out.

Belle needed total privacy and not the prying eyes and questions of her nearly four-year-old. She was peeing on the pregnancy test she'd dared not use for fear of the answer.

Not to her surprise, the test was positive. Belle was pregnant, and an avalanche of emotion hit her. What actually was a surprise were the tears that sprang to her eyes as both the joy and complications this would bring washed over her.

"Mommy!" Claire repeated.

Belle took a deep breath as she dabbed at her eyes.

"What are you doing in there?"

Belle steeled herself and unlocked the door. "Hey, lovely girl."

"Were you puking again?" Claire asked.

"No, but I probably will be for a while," Belle said to her precocious daughter.

"Okay!" Claire beamed. "Can I order more frites?"

Belle couldn't help but smile. Her daughter had no idea what the implications of her condition were—all she wanted were more of the most delicious french fries she'd ever eaten.

"Maybe at the pool!" Claire said, her eyes wide. She loved to swim, and because of Marlena's room, they had access to the aquafitness center, with its pool and solarium that overlooked the Mediterranean.

Belle really wasn't in the mood, but pleasing Claire was important to her. She'd learned the value of good parenting from Marlena, but it seemed that Shawn had been the one truly excelling in this area lately, since she'd not only been obsessed with her fashion ideas, but feeling consistently lousy.

"You got it," Belle said.

There was no doubt that a father's love was incomparable, but the bond between mother and daughter, with their hormonal similarities and emotional needs, was indescribable.

"I love you, Mommy." Claire smiled.

"I love you too, pud," Belle responded.

By the time Shawn and Marlena returned to the hotel, Belle and Claire had spent hours just being girls. They had laughed and splashed in the pool, had ice cream on the beach, and had manicures and pedicures at Les Thermes Marins de Monte-Carlo, the hotel's spa and beauty center.

Belle gave Claire a bubble bath in Marlena's tub and asked, "Would you like a little brother or sister?"

"A sister!" Claire giggled. "No boys, Mommy. Uh-uh."

Belle understood. If they had a boy, it would be wonderful for Shawn, but Belle had always wanted a little sister of her own.

Someone who would look up to her and be her very best friend, not how she had been treated by her half sister, Sami.

"Where's my CB?" they heard as Shawn and Marlena returned.

"Da!" Claire squealed as she jumped out of the bathtub, covered with bubbles.

He scooped her up in his arms and gave her a big kiss.

"Am I really getting a baby sister?" Claire spurted.

Shawn was thrown. "No." Then he caught a glimpse of Belle in the doorway to the bath. "Yes?"

Belle nodded.

Shawn swung Claire around. "Yes!" He laughed. "Isn't that great?"

Claire giggled, and Belle smiled with relief. But as soon as Shawn looked away, her expression sank.

Marlena saw Belle's concern. There was more to this than her daughter was admitting.

29  *THE FUNERAL*

OLIVIA MARINI GAINES COULD NOT HAVE PICKED A MORE beautiful day for her funeral. It was seventy-eight degrees in one of the most special places on the planet, and crowds were gathering.

The paparazzi had all been invited to this one. Like Princess Grace's funeral or Princess Diana's or the service for revered Italian designer Gianni Versace, who had been gunned down in front of his home, it was a veritable who's who.

While most funerals were seas of black, this one was a sea of black and yellow. Those who hardly knew Olivia, or the hangers-on to the celebrity aspect, were in respectable black. Those who knew Olivia personally wore her favorite shades of yellow. From the air, it must have looked like a swarm of bumblebees had landed.

The cars and the stars were flash-photo worthy. Diddy was still in the south of France, and Madonna had flown in for the occasion. Princesses Caroline and Stéphanie were both there, and Prince Albert had returned from a publicity junket for the occasion.

The front of the cathedral was adorned with a crown of yellow and cream roses, which was a perfect photo op for all who entered.

The majority of the guests were already seated, when two white limos pulled up in front of St. Nicholas Cathedral.

The door to the first limo opened, and Richie stepped out, his ankle monitor fully visible above his handmade John Lobb St. James's Street shoes.

Jackson and Chance exited the limo next, dressed in smart slate gray suits with pale yellow shirts and Hermès ties.

They made their way through the paparazzi, who paid little attention to them. Their lenses were directed to the second limo, which contained a stoic Charley, who was escorted by a beautiful blonde in a simple black dress.

The cameras went wild taking photos of Charley and Marlena.

Shawn had opted not to attend, even though Charley had asked him to join them. With the news of Belle's pregnancy, he felt it would be wrong of him to leave her at the *Fancy Face IV* with Claire, and a funeral was no place for a nearly four-year-old.

Charley respected him for that. If she'd admit it to herself, it made him even more attracted to her.

The cathedral itself was overflowing, and there was a buzz as the Gaineses entered and took their seats in the second pew. There was a mixture of deep sympathy for the children, who'd lost their mother, but disdain for their once-revered patriarch, who had just destroyed the lives of so many in the solemn chamber with his egregious scam.

Marlena opted to sit directly behind Charley. She turned and found herself sitting next to Blake. Again.

Was it fate?

She nodded a pleasant hello, and he nodded back, smiling.

Abby and Chelsea were several rows back. Abby poked her friend in the ribs as she noticed the exchange between Marlena and Blake.

"No," Chelsea whispered firmly.

"No?" Abby asked. She then changed the subject with a "yes?" as she pointed in the direction of Jackson Gaines. True, he was known as a rogue who'd dated and dumped most of the celebutantes in Hollywood, but he was one hot number.

"Hardly the time to hook up," Chelsea admonished her friend.

Samuel Barber's "Adagio for Strings" resonated throughout the cathedral from the bows of Yo-Yo Ma, Joshua Bell, and Itzhak Perlman.

"Taken too soon" was the theme of the funeral that lasted just over an hour.

Alison Krauss ended the service at the piano with her rendition of "I'll Fly Away," and the assembled guests were caught up in the shock and awe of the Baptist hymn being performed in a cathedral. Southern Baptist song or not, Olivia had always said that she wanted that sung at her funeral, and her sons were respecting her wishes. She hadn't expected they would have to be fulfilled so soon.

The family filed out to pass the flower-laden casket. There were few tears at this point; they were all still in shock. Charley stopped. She just stared. She then bent over and kissed on the cheek the woman she had believed was her natural mother.

Charley made her way out of the cathedral on the arm of Jackson. Her brothers were both amazingly protective.

Once the family exited, the rest of the assembly passed by the open casket. Some cried, others threw kisses, and several crossed themselves. It wasn't a particularly religious crowd, but moments like this always seemed to bring out one's spiritual side.

Richie's driver, Garrison, was waiting with the door open to the first stretch limo.

"Sorry I can't be there," Richie told his kids, lying. While he would have welcomed getting out of his home prison, he'd have to face dozens, if not hundreds, of former friends he'd screwed. Often not only financially, but physically.

Jackson, Chance, and Charley all just nodded as Richie got into the limo. After the door closed, Richie glanced out the window in time to see their former staff member and his former lover Kelsey in the crowd of mourners. Her expression was blank. He turned away, rolling up the window to avoid her.

∞

"Where's your brother?" Gemma Kasagian demanded to the new girl, the one she'd hired the same day the girl had been fired by Richie. Whenever Gemma caught wind that experienced help was available, she hired them before anyone else could get to them.

"Your car's across the street, Ms. Kasagian," Kelsey answered sweetly through gritted teeth. While she hated the way Gemma spoke to her, she knew it was best not to show she was perturbed.

"He couldn't have parked on this side?" Gemma snapped, rolling her eyes. "Dalita, come," she called to her daughter. "Serge!"

Serge Kasagian maneuvered his way to his wife. "I've invited a few friends to meet me at the casino, then back to the yacht at midnight." He directed his remarks to Kelsey.

Gemma's eyes lit up. "They're fun, I hope."

"Make sure the majordomo's on top of it," he said to Kelsey.

"Yes, sir, of course," Kelsey answered.

Serge waved her off with one hand and patted her behind with the other. "So, go!" he added as he guided Gemma and Dalita to the waiting Rolls-Royce Phantom stretch limo.

"Lovely man," Abby said from behind Kelsey.

"Pardon?" Kelsey asked.

"You work for him?" Abby replied.

Kelsey nodded.

"If you ever have any info, call me," Abby said, handing Kelsey her Spectator.com business card. "Sources are strictly protected, and you could make some money."

Abby winked as Chelsea joined her. "Sorry, but I had to go bad," Chelsea apologized.

"No problem, Chels," Abby said. "Nice to meet you—"

"Kelsey Silviera," Kelsey answered. "Nice to meet you too."

Kelsey slipped Abby's card in her pocket and headed toward the docks.

"Need you ask?" Abby responded to Chelsea's quizzical look. "She works for the Kasagians, and she doesn't look happy."

Serge Kasagian's limo, the most expensive in the world, started the short, short trip to the Hôtel de Paris.

Abby caught sight of the driver of the frighteningly ostentatious car as it passed in front of the cathedral. For a second, she felt like she'd seen him before.

30  THE RECEPTION

"So sorry you didn't let us host everyone on the yacht," Gemma Kasagian cooed as she kissed Chance on the cheek. Gemma was sure the rumors about Chance were true, but in case he could be turned straight, she felt he'd be a perfect match for her little Dali.

"Mum's fave room in town was this one," he said of La Salle Empire, the prestigious Renaissance banquet room overlooking Place du Casino. "Besides, she wouldn't have wanted you to be working while going through all your grief, Gemma," Chance said, pasting on the phoniest smile he could muster.

"Dali was so upset you couldn't be at her party," Gemma said, totally ignoring him and shoving Dalita toward him.

"Is that Prince Harry?" Chance said, glancing over their shoulder into the elegant room, which had been a historical site since the 1800s.

"Where?" Dalita and Gemma chorused in unison and snapped their heads. If Chance wasn't interested, there was always Harry. Who knew? Maybe his relationship with Ms. Davy was still rocky.

Chance took the moment to escape their despicable clutches.

Literally everyone who'd been at the funeral was at the reception following, except Richie. Under the terms of his house arrest, he's had to go straight to the villa once the funeral ended.

The gathering was costing Jackson and Chance the bulk of the cash they'd stashed at Credit Suisse bank in Zurich, but for them, it was a no-brainer. They had never anticipated their father's downfall and their plummet with him, but when it came to celebrating their mother, they had to be perfect sons. Whatever Olivia's faults, she had raised all her children beautifully.

Marlena was aware of Charley's fragile state and was concerned. She saw in this girl an earthiness and sensitivity that she related to.

"You don't need to stay the entire evening, Charley," Marlena said. "Everyone knows you're still on the mend."

"My head or my heart?" Charley asked.

"Both."

"Whenever you'd like to go, feel free," Marlena assured her. "Or if you want to go up to my room and rest, you could do that too."

"I didn't realize you were staying here," Charley said, changing the subject.

"My husband's choice," Marlena answered.

"I didn't even think of your being married."

"Do I give off that vibe?" Marlena said, a bit surprised.

"No, of course not," Charley said, uncomfortably.

Suddenly, a voice interrupted them. "It was a beautiful service, Charley."

She turned to see Blake Masters behind her. He was unaware she was in conversation with Marlena.

"Sorry," he said to Marlena. "I'm not stalking you. I promise."

Charley didn't even hear him.

"Thank you for all you did, Dr. Masters," she said. "Mummy looked beautiful."

Her voice choked.

"You okay?" he asked sincerely.

"I will be. For some reason, I have the stoic gene," Charley answered.

"From your dad," Blake said, unaware.

Charley nodded unsurely. "I think I could head out now, do you?" she asked them both.

"I can come with you." Marlena offered.

"No, I need to be alone." Charley sighed. "Dad's locked away in his den, so no worries. I'll be fine."

"You have my number," Marlena said directly.

"I do." Charley half smiled. "I guess I owe you both."

Marlena and Blake watched as Charley went to Jackson and Chance. They saw Jackson slip out with her.

"She's incredible," Marlena said.

"So unlike her father," Blake answered.

"I should probably go too," she said. "I was really here for her."

"There's something I need to tell you," he said. "Could we have a drink and talk?"

Marlena was torn, until he added, "It's about your husband."

They made their way through the room and through the massive golden silk drapes out onto the terrace. While the mourners paid their respects to the only Gaines left inside—Chance—Blake and Marlena took a table.

"I'm not sure how to say this," Blake said.

"We're doctors; we know how," Marlena answered.

"Evelyne's report confirmed what I already knew from my exam," Blake offered.

Marlena steeled herself for the grim news.

"John hasn't been paralyzed for at least several months now."

"So, the movement in his arms is all he'll ever have?" she asked.

"You're not hearing me, Marlena," Blake said. "The serum injected into his neck was a Botox derivative infused with curare. When it hit his spinal column, his muscles were frozen for a specific amount of time. That time has run out. He can move now."

"He's not been able to move, Blake," Marlena countered firmly.

"Yes, he has," Blake said. "But for some reason, he never told you."

Marlena felt numb.

"You're wrong," she insisted. "You have to be."

She pulled out her BlackBerry and dialed John's number.

It rang, but John didn't answer.

"Probably can't hear the phone," she said, defending him.

"I thought he always had it at his bedside," Blake said.

Marlena dialed another number. "His nurse."

"*Allo?*" the voice said on the other end. It was Desiree.

Blake snatched the phone from Marlena's hand. "This is Dr. Masters. Is John Black available? He gave me your number in case I couldn't reach him," he said. He was taking a risk, but his gut said this was right.

"I'm sorry, sir, but no," she said.

"I'm in Lausanne and was hoping to see him tonight, if possible. I have his test results."

"Ah yes. I believe he will be back the day after tomorrow," Desiree said.

"He's out of town?" Blake asked for Marlena to hear.

"Yes," Desiree answered.

Blake nodded to Marlena, who tried to cover her shock. "I'll check back then. Thank you."

Blake hung up the phone. "When are you expected back?"

"There has to be some logical explanation," she said.

"There is. You just don't want to hear it," Blake offered gently.

There were other guests nearby, regaling each other with wild stories about Olivia. Marlena felt hot all over, terribly out of place, and had a knot in her stomach.

"I'll walk you to your room," Blake said.

"No," Marlena told him. "I'm fine."

But in truth, she was anything but fine.

31 THE SEDUCTIONS

Marlena was quiet as Blake escorted her to her suite. Shawn, Belle, and Claire were on the boat, and she wished she'd asked them to say. It wasn't that she was weak or needed an excuse. It just would have made life easier.

"I'm going to have to process this," Marlena said. "I'm still not sure."

"Understandable." Blake nodded as Marlena inserted her key into the digital lock.

Marlena waited for the green light to open the door. It didn't appear. She reinserted the plastic card again. Red.

"Is Mercury in retrograde?" she asked wryly. "Nothing goes right when the planets aren't aligned."

"No, not until September," Blake answered.

Marlena couldn't help but laugh sardonically. Blake would know that. Seems he knew everything.

Blake took the card and tried it several times. Fast. Slow. Very fast. Excruciatingly slow, and then in and out, in and out, in and out.

The red light appeared every time.

4

0

"We can get another key from the front desk," Blake said. "Do you want me to do that?"

"I don't want to stand around here," Marlena answered and headed for the elevator.

⚯

A beautiful cream silk negligee was draped across the king-size bed. White lilacs with a cream ribbon lay across it.

John was in a tux.

Simple.

Elegant.

Handsome.

Masculine.

"How's my tie?" he asked.

"A bit wonky," Tara answered. She straightened it, smiling into his big, blue eyes.

"I wouldn't be here without you." He smiled. The deep affection between them was palpable. "Music?"

"Cool jazz?" she offered.

"Perfect," John answered.

The night was beautiful as John drank in the warm air filtering in through the floor-to-ceiling windows of the suite.

"I'm finally ready," he said and twirled a laughing Tara around the room.

⚯

"I am so sorry, Madame," the concierge told Marlena. "There was a flood in your lavatory, and we've had to change your room."

"How long should that take?" Marlena asked, unhappy with this turn of events. She was deeply confused and just wanted to climb into bed and crawl under the covers.

"Thirty minutes," the concierge told her. "If you'd like a drink at the bar, we'll call you when it's ready."

Marlena didn't want a drink. She wanted to be alone. Fate wasn't allowing that, however, so she nodded. "You know where to find me."

"One Campari and soda, and I'll go," Blake told her.

Marlena and Blake headed into Bar Américain. Elegant, with low-key ambience, soft lighting, and tables looking out to the sea, they settled into leather armchairs.

Doctor Gabs's fingers flitted across the ivories as he played a quiet collection of jazz accompanied by bass and drums.

"Campari and soda for me," Blake told the waiter.

"And for the lady?"

"Perrier with lime," Marlena said.

"Lillet on the rocks with orange," Blake told the waiter, changing Marlena's order. "With a splash of soda."

"A big splash," Marlena said. She hated to let him order for her, but maybe she did need a bit of alcohol after all.

The waiter left to get the drinks, and Blake took her hand.

"I owe you an apology," Blake said.

"That news about John was a bit of a shock," Marlena offered.

"Not about that," Blake said. "About my coming on to you."

Marlena was thrown. Her suspicions were confirmed; Blake had been coming on to her. While she was flattered, she knew both of them were married, and it was wrong.

"Evelyne's ill," he admitted. "She has a serious melanoma, and things don't look good."

"So you came on to me?" Marlena said with a tone that could only be perceived as disappointed.

"She's pulled away from me for months," he admitted. "I've felt less than a man, and I made a terrible mistake. I was using you to bolster my ego."

The seasoned waiter set down the drinks in front of them.

"I'm not that kind of guy," Blake said. "I hope you can forgive me."

Marlena's mind was whirling. She'd just been told that her husband had been lying to her, and the man who was flirting shamelessly with her was merely using her.

"Forgiven," she said with a half smile as she raised her glass to him. "We both know if things were different, things would be different."

Blake raised his glass to hers, and they toasted.

"To a long and beautiful friendship," he said.

They each took long sips from their fine crystal glasses as the concierge approached.

"Docteur Evans, we've found you a new room," he said. "Whenever you're ready?"

"I am exhausted," she said to Blake.

"Enough said," he countered.

"You're in the Churchill Suite, Madame," the concierge offered. "It's all that was available."

Marlena could only smile. This was ridiculous. She was going to be in the most exquisite suite in all of Monte Carlo, at least for the night. She'd have to invite Belle and Shawn over in the morning before they moved her.

"Charge these to my room," Blake told the concierge.

"On the house, sir," the concierge answered and handed Marlena her new key card. "May I accompany you?" he added.

Marlena stared across the table at the handsome doctor from Montana. She was spending the night in a suite fit for royalty and would be alone.

"I'd appreciate it," she told the concierge. "And thank you, Blake, for being so honest."

Marlena gave him a peck on the cheek and headed out with the concierge.

Blake stirred his cocktail. He was alone but knew it was right.

∞

"Oh my God," Marlena said as she got off the private elevator to the top floor of the hotel. "This is unbelievable."

"We hope you enjoy it, Dr. Evans," the concierge said.

Marlena dug in her purse for a tip.

"No, please," he said. "All's been taken care of. Enjoy your night." He smiled and winked.

Marlena had read that the suite had a round Jacuzzi tub, and that sounded like a wonderful way to spend time before climbing into bed.

She inserted her new key card. This one worked.

She entered the magnificent contemporary suite, which was nothing like the rich European decor of her other room.

Music was playing and candles were burning, which were lovely touches.

She placed her handbag on the glass-topped table. The living room was gorgeously decorated in creams and maroons, with contemporary art on the walls.

It was beautiful, serene, and lonely. She hesitated before moving into the bedroom, as she was sad at the thought of being there alone, but then steeled herself and entered.

Draped across the deep maroon silk bedspread was a cream silk negligee and lilacs with a cream ribbon. On the bedside table was a silver bowl with wild strawberries and crème fraîche.

"What took you so long, Doc?" she heard.

Standing next to the bed was John, in his tuxedo, holding two flutes of champagne.

"Do you know how much I love you?" he asked, cocking his eyebrow just that way.

"John, this is, I'm, uh"—she was in shock, thrilled, confused, delirious—"I knew something was happening, but this? What has been going on?"

"I had to be the man you need, Doc, the man you deserve," he said, staring into her smiling eyes. "I needed to be whole for you, and I know I am now."

"You always have been." She smiled with happy tears forming.

"If I hurt you…" he started.

"Oh, shut up," she cried and flew into his arms, knocking the champagne flutes to the floor.

The two melted into each other's arms.

John drank in Marlena's scent, then kissed the woman he loved so completely. It was a passionate, deep kiss that sent shock waves to her toes.

Marlena gasped, and John smiled. It was a gasp he knew well from all the delicious intimate times they'd shared.

Marlena studied his masculine, strong face, then reached for his tie and pulled it open.

The night had only begun.

32   *ROCK THE BOAT*

"THANKS FOR STAYING WITH US TODAY," BELLE SAID AS SHE leaned her head on Shawn's shoulder. "It meant a lot."

"You're my wife." Shawn smiled. "And you're carrying my baby. This is where I belong."

Claire had gone to sleep an hour ago, and Belle should have been relishing this time with Shawn. Instead, she was dreading it.

They sat on the prow of the boat, leaning against the window to the main cabin. They had done it many times since they had left Salem, and it was a place they both loved. Quiet. Calm. Removed.

Shawn tipped her chin and gave her a kiss.

"Boy or girl?" he asked.

"Healthy," she answered.

"Good answer, but a cop-out."

It was true. The general rule of thumb has always been that men want sons, and women want daughters. It's not because of some macho need or girlie-girl selfishness but comfort zones.

"Shawn, we need to talk," Belle said in a voice so serious that Shawn was thrown.

"You're all right?" he asked.

She sighed heavily.

"There's something you need to know," she said drily. "And you're kind of a captive audience."

The boat was rocking gently. Shawn was getting scared.

"Remember when we were in Egypt, and you took Claire for the day?" she said.

"And you went to the spa at the Four Seasons," he said.

"I did, yes," Belle answered. She was beginning to sweat. "I looked at it, anyway."

"What are you talking about?"

A 40-foot cruiser sailed passed them a bit too close. The residual crest rocked the *Fancy Face IV* harder.

"I ran into an old friend at the hotel," she admitted. "We had drinks. It was Philip."

Shawn's back went up. "Kiriakis."

Belle knew that any mention of her ex-boyfriend, ex-husband, and ex-friend was dangerous territory.

"It was nice to have a conversation with someone from home," she told him.

"Someone," he said flatly.

"We had a few drinks, and he had a business call. He was there for Titan Industries."

"Yeah."

"He said he wanted to check paperwork in his room," she said.

"So you joined him?" Shawn asked.

"I figured out pretty soon that he didn't need to get anything," she admitted.

"But you'd had a few drinks, and what the charming Philip Kiriakis, war hero, 'titan' of industry, wanted in his room was you."

Belle stared directly at the man she truly adored.

"Yes," she admitted. "I realized that when he kissed me."

"And you kissed him back," Shawn said and bolted to his feet. He hung on to the mast as though it was his savior.

"I did," she said guiltily. "Then I slapped the hell out of him."

Shawn took it in.

"You what?"

"When he kissed me, I was so caught off guard, that I was in shock. Then I slapped him so hard his teeth rattled. He's probably still bruised by now," she said. "I really clocked him."

"You what?" he repeated.

"I think I loosened two of his caps," Belle added.

"Really?" Shawn said, amused.

"Really." She smiled ruefully.

"So you didn't sleep with him?" Shawn said, beginning to chuckle.

"I didn't," she said, chuckling with him.

"So that's not his baby you're carrying?" Shawn was now starting to laugh.

"No! It's yours," she said, laughing even harder. "I just felt terribly guilty that I didn't tell you about Philip. It's been eating me alive."

"You loosened his teeth!" Shawn was hysterical now, and it was contagious.

"I did! Oh, I was afraid you'd hate me!" She laughed.

"I adore you!" Shawn howled as he pulled her up to face him.

"If I could, I'd sweep you up in my arms right now."

"We'd go overboard." She guffawed.

"You could follow me," he offered, still laughing as he headed toward the pilot wheel and jumped into the cockpit.

Belle did exactly that. On more solid footing, Shawn gave her a deep, thorough kiss through their laughter.

"I love you, Shawn Brady." She smiled with relief. "I really do."

"I know," Shawn assured her.

"Can I show you how much?" she asked.

Shawn drew her to him again and hugged her tightly. It was a long and meaningful hug.

He took her hand and guided her down into the boat and into their cabin.

Their lovemaking was just that. Pure love.

It was also the best sex they'd had since the baby growing inside her was conceived.

Shawn rested his hand on Belle's stomach, and she wrapped him in her arms. Content. Happy.

∞

"Should I put that on?" Marlena hummed as she indicated the luscious La Perla negligee laid out on the bed.

"Maybe take this off," John said as he slowly pulled the belt off her Diane von Furstenberg black wrap dress, which she'd bought that afternoon for the funeral.

One by one, Marlena unbuttoned the stubs on John's pleated white tux shirt, exposing his well-defined chest.

She kissed the base of his neck softly, and he responded by inserting his hands into her dress and slipping it to the floor.

Under the dress, Marlena wore a black lace bra and high-cut lace panties that sculpted her body perfectly.

The moon filtered in through the massive windows overlooking the harbor sending glints of highlights through her already flaxen hair.

Copying John's moves, Marlena put her hands under his jacket and removed it, letting it slip to the floor behind him. His Brioni shirt followed.

Marlena bent over to help take off his dress slippers. John traced the curve in her back with his fingers.

She shuddered.

Rising, there were no words as she unhooked his pants and unzipped his fly. The fine fabric trousers dropped to the floor, and he was totally naked.

John pulled back the plush comforter, which had been turned down for the night and took in the sight of his wife in black lingerie and high heels.

He sat on the edge of the bed and unhooked her bra, then slid her silk panties down her long, beautiful legs.

Marlena stepped out of them and then slipped off her heels.

Cupping her familiar flesh gently from behind, John drew Marlena onto his lap and rested his head between her breasts. This was territory they hadn't explored for more than two years, and they were savoring every moment.

Their bodies were trembling, responding to the touch, scent, and feel of each other's flesh.

John lifted her with his powerful arms and gracefully placed her in bed; her head sank into the down pillows. He kissed her neck, her breasts, and moved his tongue slowly down her taut stomach.

Marlena groaned.

She wrapped her arms around his back and drew him to her for a long and passionate kiss.

Spreading her legs gently, lovingly, hungrily, John guided himself inside her.

For what seemed like an eternity, their bodies moved in a rhythm they knew so very, very well. Two parts of one, both flushed with lust and love until they exploded simultaneously.

Marlena wept silent tears of joy.

John kissed them away.

They lay in each other's arms, drinking in the enormity of their reunion. They had been torn apart many times since they'd fallen madly, deeply in love, but this separation had been the most excruciating of them all.

"I love you, John," Marlena whispered.

"I love you, Doc," John answered.

"Don't ever go away again," she said, resting her head on his shoulder. "Emotionally, physically, spiritually," she continued.

His answer was a deep and thorough kiss. Marlena gasped.

It was a kiss that led to another.

And another.

33 AFTER MIDNIGHT

SOME CITIES ROLL UP THEIR STREETS AT TEN, BUT IN MONACO, life was just getting started.

Olivia's funeral had ended before sundown, and the reception that followed lasted until eleven. Some of the guests, the partyers who were invited to the Kasagians' for dancing and debauchery, had headed to the yacht.

Others who had tired of the superficiality of it all opted to stay in the heart of Monte Carlo, and for them, Jimmy'z was *the* place to be.

Chance and Jackson had opted to stay out for a while. They weren't being insensitive—just the thought of heading back to the villa and watching their father drink himself into a stupor wasn't the least bit appealing.

Charley wanted to be alone, and they respected her wishes.

Jackson was on the dance floor with Nikki Reed from *Twilight* as Abby and Chelsea entered amid a well-heeled group of smashed partyers.

"Don't know about you, but I could use a drink," Abby said above the noise. The room was crowded with international models, jet-setters, and twentysomething millionaires. "Thanks for the entree," she said, blowing a kiss to one of the twentysomethings who was just up for a good time.

Chelsea nodded as they peeled away from the group. "This mean you're done working for the night?"

"Never." She smiled ruefully. "But I got the shots from the funeral uploaded, so until dawn, I guess I'm good."

What no one had noticed earlier was the mini–spy cam embedded in Abby's yellow butterfly pin, which she had worn to the funeral.

"The shot I got of the casket is going to freak people out," she yelled into Chelsea's ear.

"What?" Chelsea said, straining to hear.

The music stopped.

"Nothing." Abby smiled, not about to repeat that bit of news.

Jackson dipped his celeb of the moment on the dance floor, then twirled her toward the table of eager partyers and headed to the bar.

"You throw girls away that easily?" Abby flirted as he brushed past her.

"The last one got me in a bit of trouble," Jackson said with a slur in his voice.

Jules had indeed screwed over him and his family. She had turned over the keys to the kingdom he hadn't even known existed. He didn't really blame her, though, when he realized she'd also been literally screwing his father.

Chance was at the bar refilling his martini glass from one of the thousand-dollar bottles of vodka that were not only de rigueur, but the price of admission at Jimmy'z.

"Hi," a voice said next to him.

With the flash of the disco lights, it wasn't easy to recognize anyone, but the guy had a friendly face and looked familiar.

"Hi," Chance said in a tone that gave away his confusion.

"I think this is yours," the classically hip man said, dangling Chance's Jaeger-LeCoultre in front of him.

"Willy?" Chance asked, surprised. "You clean up well."

"I try." Willy smiled.

Chance hadn't realized it when he and Jackson were in Willy's office, but the medical examiner was actually strikingly good-looking. He was masculine, but not macho, and dressed in a crisp white shirt and beige linen slacks with expensive loafers.

"I hope today wasn't too tough," Willy said sympathetically.

"Thanks," Chance answered. "And we gave that to you."

"I know," Willy said warmly. "But the last thing you need is someone using you. At a time like this, anyway."

It was said with definite double entendre, but not in any way salacious. It made Chance smile for the first time that night.

"Thanks," Chance said as he took the precious timepiece and slipped it back on his wrist where it belonged.

"I should get your mum's results back tomorrow. Yeah, I sped them up."

"Thanks again," Chance responded.

Rick Astley's "Never Gonna Give You Up" blared from the speakers. "You like to dance?"

"To this? Disco's not my style," Willy said. "But in your case, I'll make an exception."

The two headed past Jackson and Abby out to the dance floor, where their moves complemented each other *perfectly*.

"You were at the funeral," Jackson said as the disco lights flashed over Abby's face.

"Chelsea was at the scene of your mother's accident," Abby said, trying to talk over the music. She couldn't take her eyes off him.

"Sorry, what?" Jackson said, leaning close to hear. In the process, he knocked the bottle of vodka all over her leather handbag.

"I'll get you a new one," he apologized as he yanked it out of the spill. "Really sorry," he added as the contents tumbled out.

Abby's Spectator.com business cards fluttered onto the bar.

"Abigail Deveraux, Spectator.com?" Jackson said as he read it. "You're a reporter."

"Nice to meet you?" she said cautiously.

"Your site and your paper ran that exposé on my father," Jackson said, incensed.

This is not going well, Abby thought. *And tomorrow it'll be even worse.*

∞

Marlena had fallen asleep, her head resting on the sumptuous pillows. There was a contented smile on her face as she reached over to John.

He wasn't there.

Marlena bolted upright, her heart pounding. Had this all been a dream? Or was it a nightmare?

"Doc?" she heard coming from the open doorway to the bathroom. "You okay?"

She shuddered as waves of relief washed over her. John was there, and this was all real.

"Join me?" he asked.

It was then that she noticed the sound of the Jacuzzi gurgling.

The negligee was still draped over the end of the massive bed, and she reached for the robe as she climbed out of bed.

"Doc?" he said, cocking that eyebrow again.

"Isn't a little mystery more sensual?" she asked, slipping it on.

John could see how the silk draped over her breasts, and the soft light from outside formed a gauzy outline of her trim figure.

She moved toward him, causing the front of the robe to slide through her legs and then glide over the soft flesh John had tasted for the first time in years.

"Why are you always right, Doc?" he said, gazing at her hungrily.

Marlena picked up the bowl of tiny wild strawberries and cream and, without a word, entered the chamber that held the bubbling tub.

She set the plate of temptations on the edge of the tub and dropped the robe seductively. Then she slowly slipped into the heated water.

"Any more champagne?" she asked throatily.

"Enough for two," John answered.

He retrieved the crystal glasses from the ice bucket, and they were half-full.

"Should I order another bottle?" he asked.

"Doubt we'll have the time to drink it." She smiled.

John handed her the flutes and joined her in the tub.

In a ritual they'd performed so many, many times in their lives, Marlena dipped one of the perfect little strawberries in the rich cream and placed it in John's waiting mouth. He sucked the tips of her fingers slowly.

Another strawberry was swirled in the cream, and John brushed it against the perfect tip of Marlena's nose before popping it in her mouth. He licked off the sweet cream and moved his tongue over her lips and then slid it inside them.

Their lips and tongues were together again in seductive exploration.

The temperature of the water was heating up from their passion.

"If this is a dream," she whispered, "don't ever wake me."

∞

It was nearly three a.m., and the casino was buzzing. Not buzzing the way American casinos do, but the European roulette, craps, blackjack, and baccarat tables were filled as jet-setters and tourists alike tried their hands in the elegant setting.

Blake was at a fifty-euro-minimum blackjack table as a twenty-something girl slid into the seat next to him.

"Good or bad idea?" the girl asked with a slight Dutch accent. It was Tara.

"I'm up six hundred," Blake said.

"Fantastic!" Tara boomed.

"Mademoiselle, quiet please," the tuxedoed dealer warned. In the most famous casino in the world, chatter was not only discouraged, it was forbidden.

The dealer tapped the felt, then dealt two cards to each player with bets on the table.

Blake and Tara were each dealt an ace and a ten.

"Yes!" she said, fist pumping. "Oh, sorry," she apologized to the dealer.

A gasp went up from a nearby table. Blake and Tara turned to look. The table had been roped off, and a crowd had gathered.

"You're a lucky girl," Blake said quietly, turning back. "That's the first blackjack I've had all night. What's a pretty girl like you doing here all alone?"

"Just finished a job. I'm a physical therapist, and my patient just graduated with flying colors." She smiled. "And if you're hitting on me, I don't swing your way. I have a girlfriend. But that brunette's hot," Tara added, indicating a striking socialite at the next table.

Blake smiled as they each won another hand.

"Good for you," he said. "And I wasn't hitting on you. I'm actually more happily married than I thought."

Interesting, Tara thought. *This guy may not give the best first impression, but he isn't a bad guy after all.*

A loud wail was heard coming from a roped-off roulette table nearby, and the crowd began to disperse. Chief of Staff Roisten, from Princess Grace Hospital, came storming past them, swearing profusely in Afrikaans.

"Wow," Tara said as the man sailed by them, still sputtering, his face red with anger and despair. "He just blew over two hundred thousand euros."

Blake drew a pair of aces.

"Too bad he didn't have your luck at his table."

34  *CHARLEY*

L IGHT WAS STREAMING IN THROUGH THE PALE SHEERS THAT covered Charley's bedroom windows, when a tap came at her door.

She didn't answer.

"Lovely girl," she heard. "I'm coming in."

It was Richie, and she was not in the mood to see him.

Before she could protest, the door opened, and Richie entered. He was wearing lightweight white cotton drawstring pants and a lavender fine linen shirt rolled up at the sleeves.

He carried a bed tray with yellow roses and a glass of orange juice, toast, and an egg in a porcelain coddler.

"Sophia doesn't quite have Kelsey's cooking skills, but she'll learn," he said as he brought Charley the tray. "If the egg's done a little too much, she can do it again."

In the old days, he would have bellowed about that.

"I'm not hungry," she faltered. "But thank you."

Richie didn't notice she hadn't called him Dad, which stuck in her throat every time she even thought it.

"A girl needs to eat," he said.

Charley could feel him trying too hard, and she liked that even less.

"I'm not sure if I should eat before going to the hospital," she said.

"Ah yes, you have a checkup today," he remembered.

"Chance is taking me," she said.

"He never came home last night," Richie offered. "I'll have the driver take you."

There was a long moment of silence. Finally, she decided to speak.

"Is there something you and Mum should have told me?" she asked simply.

"Why do you think so?" Richie asked. He did not want to offer anything he might not have to. "Is it about her will?" he said.

"God no," Charley spouted.

"You up?" Chance suddenly called from the hallway.

"Oh yeah," Charley called back.

Chance entered still wearing his gray suit pants. His pale yellow shirt was untucked, with the sleeves rolled up. He was wearing his Jaeger-LeCoultre.

"Dad."

That's right, Charley thought. *Richie still is his dad. At least I think so, but what do I know?*

"Have fun last night, Son?" Richie threw at him lightly.

"Actually, I did," Chance admitted. "But not for the reasons you obviously think."

"You're here to take me to the hospital," Charley said appreciatively. "I knew you would be."

"We're supposed to be there at nine," he reminded her. "You might want to get ready."

Charley climbed out of bed and made her way into the bathroom, closing the door behind her.

Richie and Chance heard the water turn on in the shower.

"We should hear this afternoon when your arraignment will be, Dad," Chance said.

"One step at a time, I suppose," Richie answered. "One step restricted by this damned thing," he said, pointing to the ankle monitor. "Sorry for what this is doing to you kids."

By now they had realized that until it was all sorted out, they wouldn't be allowed to sell, leverage, or move any of their belongings or property that was worth more than $1,000.

Like the Madoff sons, they could wear their existing personal clothing and jewelry deemed normal. By whose standards, though? Chance doubted his watch would count in bloody Birmingham. But for the time being, he was pleased to have it back. It wasn't about the money; it was about the goodness of Willy's heart.

"For what it's worth, Dad, I wasn't out whoring around last night," Chance said. "Yes, I was with someone, but all he did was be there for me through a pretty tearful night."

"Will you be seeing him again?" Richie asked. He had long ago accepted Chance's homosexuality and truly wanted his son to be happy.

"This evening, actually," Chance said simply.

∞

Jackson was in Richie's office on his iPad, and he was livid.

He scrolled down the page and was horrified at each new image he saw. It was Spectator.com, and Abby's pictures from the funeral, both in the cathedral and outside, kept coming. The last was the close-up of Olivia in the casket.

Blake had indeed done a spectacular repair job on the face that had been shattered on one side, and Olivia looked as though she was having the most serene dream.

It gave him a weird feeling of solace to remember his mother this way, looking so free of pain. He still wanted to wring Abigail Deveraux' neck.

Jackson had heard Chance return to the house a short while ago.

"Chance?" he called out.

"Up here, bruv," Chance answered. It was coming from Charley's room.

"Need to see you now," Jackson said. "In the den. Alone."

Chance appeared upstairs on the landing, with Richie behind him.

"Alone, he said, Dad," Chance told his father firmly.

Richie didn't like it, but at this point he had no bargaining power.

Jackson was pacing, running his hand through his thick chestnut brown hair when Chance entered.

"What now?" Chance asked.

"Take a look."

Jackson presented his little brother with the image of Olivia in the casket.

"How…?" Chance was gobsmacked.

"That cute blonde at Jimmy'z last night?" Jackson answered. Chance looked confused. "Oh right, you were a little distracted. She runs the Spectator.com website and sneaked a camera into the funeral."

"Holy shit." Chance winced.

"Can we sue her ass?" Jackson was steaming.

"For being an insensitive twit? I don't see how."

"This has to be illegal!" Jackson railed.

"Immoral, maybe, but illegal, no," Chance answered.

"Someone's got to at least tell Dad and Charley," Jackson said. "I don't want Sis seeing it by accident. Him, I really don't care."

"We can tell her together," Chance offered. "I'm about to take her over to the hospital. Why don't you come with us?"

"Glad I got you, bruv," Jackson said.

"It's what family's for," Chance answered. "Let me get dressed, and we can go."

Jackson nodded.

"Oh, and my date last night?" Chance said. "Willy."

"The medical examiner?" Jackson said, floored.

"Pretty nice guy, actually. The toxicology reports are in, and I'm seeing him later. Want to be there?" Chance asked.

"I would," Jackson said, steeling himself. "For now, let's not tell Charley."

Chance nodded in agreement. Until they had answers, they didn't want to further upset Charley.

And tonight they would have answers.

35 MARLENA AND JOHN

MARLENA'S TOUSLED HEAD RESTED AGAINST JOHN'S STRONG chest as they held one another in the bed where they had reconsummated their unbridled love.

The phone on the bedside table rang, and John reached over to answer.

"Must be Tara," John said apologetically as he picked up the receiver. "My physical therapist," he explained.

"Tell her she did a very, very good job," Marlena smiled.

"Very good morning," John said into the phone.

"Oh, I'm sorry, I must have the wrong room," the voice said, startled.

"Belle?" John said.

"Dad?" Belle answered in total shock. "I, well, I was calling Mom at the hotel. I must have dialed wrong."

"Did the operator connect you to this room?" he asked.

"What is going on?" Belle sputtered.

Marlena took the phone from John. "Sweetie?"

"Mom...?" Belle said weakly, more confused than ever.

"Come on over to the hotel." Marlena smiled. "Your dad's here, and he's just plain fabulous."

"Things are fabulous here too, Mom," Belle said, smiling to a very confused Shawn. "Give us a little over an hour, and we'll be there."

Marlena handed John the phone, and he hung it up.

"They'll be here in—" Her sentence was silenced by John's kiss.

"A little over an hour," he said and kissed her again. "I heard."

He kissed her neck and then her shoulder, and Marlena melted once again.

"John?" she warned. "I need to shower and wash my hair."

His answer was to kiss her stomach.

"What the heck?" Marlena laughed and pulled the man she craved on top of her.

∞

Marlena had just finished blow-drying her hair when she heard a loud squeal coming from the living room. In a flash, Claire was bounding in to see her.

"GiGi!" Claire roared. "Grandpa's in there. Come in and see!"

Claire grabbed Marlena and started tugging, then stopped, wide-eyed. "Strawberries!"

It was easy for the nearly four-year-old to be distracted, and she grabbed the few red gems left and popped them in her mouth before tugging at Marlena again.

"Come on!"

The living room of the suite was not nearly as raucous. Marlena and Claire entered to find Belle wrapped in her father's arms, neither saying a word.

Shawn stood by, smiling.

John's incapacity had affected the entire family who prayed daily for his recovery while not quite believing it would ever happen. But there he was, strong, healthy, and the man who had promised to protect them all forever.

"Does Sami know and Brady? Did you call Eric?" Belle was overcome.

"You're the first, baby girl," John said warmly.

"I'm glad," she admitted guiltily. In her heart, she always relished that she was a composite of two of the best and most admired people she knew. She only hoped she was somehow like them.

"They like strawberries too," Claire chirped from a mouth red with the evidence. "They were by the bathtub."

The adults all shared knowing glances. Although kids never like to think of their parents having sex, this time Belle was thrilled.

The moment was interrupted by the ring of Belle's phone.

"Abby, hi," she answered.

"Chelsea Brady and Abby Deveraux are in town too," Marlena explained to John.

"We've got to head back to London today," Abby informed her. "Any time Chels and I can see you?"

"If I told you who I'm staring at right now, you wouldn't believe it," Belle said. "My dad."

"Huh?"

"He's surprised us all, and he's just, well, perfect."

Even Abby was dumbfounded. John's condition might not have been worldwide news, but in the world of extended Salem, this was bigger than global warming.

"When do you leave?" Belle asked.

"I think we may have to stay a little bit longer," Abby replied. She recognized a good scoop when she heard it.

36  *CHARLEY*

THE DRIVE TO THE HOSPITAL WAS EXHILARATING FOR CHARLEY. She had forgotten how lovely it felt to have fresh air rushing through her hair.

Chance drove, while Jackson sat in the backseat with his iPad, answering email. With all the chaos swirling around them in the last week, he was back-loaded.

Charley could see Jackson reflected in the mirror on her visor. She was fixated on his image and turned to look at Chance. Chance had a more refined nose and ears that hugged his head, but they were perfectly formed liked Jackson's. Now that she thought of it, they were also like Olivia's.

They also had the same square jaw and cleft in their chin as Richie. There was no doubt that they were brothers and shared the same parents.

She, on the other hand, was more fair than either of them, had a pointed chin, and nearly black hair with a slight widow's peak. Why had she never noticed those things before? Was it because they were boys and she a girl?

Since the revelation in the hospital about neither parent being a match for blood donation, Charley's mind had been spinning. On the few moments she had had alone at the villa, she sat in the sunroom and went through all the family photos.

Obvious now. So obvious. She was adopted.

Chance put his hand on her knee, pulling her out of her reverie.

"We're here, Charley," he said.

Chance pulled up to the back of the hospital at the private entrance. He had made arrangements for them to enter that way, in case there were any reporters. Like Abby Deveraux.

Chance stopped the Maserati and then walked around the car and opened the door for his sister. Charley smiled. Whatever else they did, the couple who had raised her had taught manners to all three children.

They made their way through the maze of hallways and were aware of a buzz among the nurses and volunteers.

"Tragic," one of the nurses said to another as they passed.

"I don't know if I could work in a hospital, dealing with tragedy on a daily basis," Charley said.

Then a young couple passed them with a newborn in the mother's arms. They were full of life and hope.

"Then again, maybe I could." Charley smiled softly.

They took the elevator, and Jackson punched the button for the second floor, where Chief of Staff Roisten had his office. Roisten had agreed to see Charley personally since he was a friend of Richie's. There were times that connections paid off.

When they turned the corner, they were stunned to see police making notes and a gurney being wheeled out of the chief of staff's office. It was a male form with a sheet draped over it.

"What happened?" Jackson asked a passing officer.

"Poor guy blew his brains out," the officer said. "Lost nearly everything he had in that bloody Ponzi scheme. Then put whatever he had left on his favorite number. You'd think a guy like him'd be smarter."

Chance and Jackson froze in their tracks as the officer moved on.

Charley was in shock. "This was because of Dad?"

Jackson grimaced at the realization. "He was one of Dad's first investors."

"And had a wife dying of terminal cancer," Chance added grimly.

"Sorry you had to see this," Jackson said, turning to Charley.

Devastated, Charley couldn't utter another sound.

Instead, she fainted.

⸺∞⸺

When Charley came to, she was in a private room on the VIP floor.

Esther, the warm and caring nurse she'd had before, was at her side. "Have a sip of water, love," Esther said. "Let me get the doctor."

Not Chief of Staff Roisten, Charley thought. *He killed himself because of my father.*

A handsome young Nigerian internist entered.

"Dr. Abani," he said, introducing himself. "How are you feeling, on a scale of one to ten?"

"Nine," Charley said.

"Really," he said, knowing full well it was a lie.

"Maybe a six," Charley admitted. "But I want to go home. I need to."

"Your vitals are actually in line, and the stitches don't come out until next week. Your brothers assured me you have someone there," he said. "So I can release you, but I think you might want to talk with someone."

"I will." She nodded.

"Call my mobile if you have any problems." He smiled, handing her his card. "Any at all."

It was obvious he was drawn to Charley. She had that effect on people.

"I'm sorry about Dr. Roisten," Charley said.

"Yes," he answered softly and headed out the door. "We all are."

After a brief consult with him in the hallway, Jackson and Chance entered.

"Did you find out any more details?" Charley asked.

"They say that after finding out about the scheme, Roisten opted to take whatever he had left and let it ride on his favorite number," Jackson offered. "It didn't come in."

"So he took himself out," Chance said, pointing his finger to his temple. "Pow."

"Abani said we can go," Jackson said, changing the subject. "But he wants us to find you a professional to talk to."

"I have someone," Charley answered. "Dr. Evans."

37  *THE HARBOR*

"DID YOU SEE THE *SPECTATOR* THIS MORNING?" GEMMA SAID in a conspiratorial tone as lobster Benedict with gobs of beluga was placed in front of her.

"What's the *Spectator*?" the plasticized socialite to the left of her said.

"The hottest place for news since the *Enquirer*," another guest said through overly plumped-up lips.

Eight nipped-and-tucked middle-aged women, who would have preferred being called cougars, were seated around the highly polished agarwood table on the upper deck of Serge Kasagian's *K*.

"Olivia Gaines's photo was on the front page," one platinum blonde chortled. "Looking pretty fucking good for someone who'd had their head bashed in," she added.

"Who is her doctor?" a cinnamon-colored ex-model asked.

"Blake Masters, obviously," Gemma offered. "Why else would he have been at the funeral?"

Gemma dug into her food with the finesse of a truck driver.

She took a bite. "Kelsey?" she bellowed.

Kelsey made a beeline for Gemma. She knew when the lady called, you answered. Otherwise you were out the door, and right now Kelsey needed this job.

"Too much lemon!" she wailed. "Take all of them back to the chef. What was he thinking?"

"Mine's delic—" the platinum blonde started. She nearly choked on her words as Miss Plasticized kicked her under the table. They all knew Gemma was no one to contradict. Not if you wanted to be in the most publicized social circle in Monaco.

"I'll have it taken care of, Mrs. Kasagian," Kelsey said apologetically.

She punched a button on her beeper, and four hunky waiters in tight white polo shirts and shorts appeared from their positions at the edge of the deck.

"At least Olivia's not here to deal with this fucking disaster Richie's in," Cinnamon Girl said. "What an ass. At least he'll be behind bars so he can't make any more lame promises to the dozens of bimbos he's had on the side."

Kelsey dropped one of the plates on the table, splashing béarnaise sauce and egg yolk all over Platinum Blonde.

"Kelsey, what is wrong with you?" Gemma roared.

"I'm so sorry," Kelsey said, near tears as Platinum Blonde pushed away from the table.

"Go, just go! Get Misty a robe, and go buy her whatever size 0 she wants." It was a Gemma order, so it would be followed.

Kelsey was at her breaking point as she followed Platinum Blonde to the elevator.

"The only promises Richie'll make now are to stock Santa Maria Novella soaps in the prison showers." Cinnamon Girl laughed.

"Oops, he dropped it," Miss Plasticized said, putting her tightened hands to her lips, which were filled with fresh collagen.

The claws were out, and all the women were giggling.

Kelsey was not amused. In fact, she felt her heart sink to the pit of her stomach.

"Enough about them," Gemma scowled playfully. "While we wait, who wants to see my new jewelry?"

∞

"Can you believe it?" Marlena said, her smiling eyes beaming as she watched Claire pulling John and her da into the deep azure of the Mediterranean.

"When did all this happen?" Belle said, truly curious. She and Marlena sat in pale blue and white beach chairs with floppy hats. The marina was full of yachts, including the *K*, with its bitchy ladies' lunch in full swing.

"He's been having intense physical therapy for months, which coincided with the feeling returning to his body," Marlena explained. "Which I knew nothing about."

"Nothing?"

"He wanted to be the best man for me he could," Marlena answered. "At least, that was his excuse."

"That's important to men, isn't it?" Belle stated.

"Men of your dad's generation, and I believe even younger," Marlena said. "These are such confusing times for both sexes, but I still believe men need to know they're needed. And not just for sex."

"Not even that, since babies can be grown in test tubes now," Belle said ruefully. "Or at least without the parents doing it."

"Sometimes science is a bit scary," Marlena admitted.

"Being pregnant is a bit scary," Belle said. "I am so happy though, Mom."

Marlena pushed back the blonde hair that drifted into her daughter's eyes.

"Claire having a brother or sister is a wonderful thing," Marlena said. "I still miss Samantha every day."

Marlena's twin sister, Samantha, for whom her daughter Sami had been named, had been murdered over twenty years ago.

"She had such a good heart. Like yours," Marlena said.

They heard a squeal coming from the water. Claire was in a major water fight with John and Shawn, and she was winning.

"Claire's a bit more like her dad," Belle said. "At least I hope."

"Uh-oh," Marlena said, her eyes widening. Claire was running straight for Belle and Marlena.

"Come on! Come on, come on!"

Before they could protest, Claire dashed behind them and tried pushing them out of their chairs.

"Baby, no!" Belle laughed, but Claire was insistent.

"It's fun!" Claire insisted, pushing even harder.

Her exuberance was intoxicating, but the girls weren't interested in getting wet. On top of that, the beach was crowded with European sunbathers soaking up the hot August rays and not in the mood for rambunctious American tourists.

"Hey, party poopers, what are you waiting for?" John called as he and Shawn made a beeline to their wives.

"John—" Marlena warned.

"Shawn!" Belle warned.

But their protests went unheeded as the men swept them up in their arms and carted them into the bay.

Belle immediately threw up all over Shawn.

Marlena yelped happily as she was tossed into the water.

She didn't hear her BlackBerry. A call was coming in, and the caller ID simply read: "Private."

If the name hadn't been blocked, it would have read: "Charley."

∞

By the time Abby and Chelsea arrived, Belle was back in her chair, slathered in sunblock. Marlena stayed in the water, cavorting with Shawn, John and their granddaughter.

"Sorry we're late," Chelsea said.

"You're not swimming?" Abby asked.

"Puking is more my style these days," Belle said. "I told you both, right?"

"We figured." Chelsea smiled. "Look at you, happily married with a kid and another on the way."

"Look at us, still us," Abby said.

"You're doing just fine, Abs," Belle offered a bit wistfully. "Great job, great life, the two of you both in London."

"Regrets?" Chelsea said, responding to Belle's expression.

"None," Belle insisted.

Chelsea and Abby knew their friend well. Simultaneously, they cocked their heads.

"Okay, I'd been hoping to meet Olivia Gaines here." She grimaced. "I designed a whole line for next spring that I'd wanted her to see. To even bring it up to you guys, under the circumstances, is tacky."

"Is this too tacky?" Abby said cautiously.

"What?"

"Chels and I are late because I was on the phone with my folks. Could we ask your dad for a phoenix rising feature on his journey for the *Spectator*?"

Mention of the phoenix hit a nerve. Stefano DiMera's brand on her father's back was still a reminder of the pain and agony he'd put John through.

"It's a fabulous story," Abby added.

Belle glanced to her parents, thoroughly enjoying life again.

"Fabulous is right," Belle answered.

"But?"

"Should the whole world know about dad's recovery yet?" Belle asked pointedly.

Abby and Chelsea exchanged confused glances.

"The whole world, meaning Stefano DiMera," Belle clarified. "No one should ever, ever trust that man. And the last thing my dad needs right now is to be looking over his shoulder for the man who personifies evil."

38  *THE TOXICOLOGIST*

THE HOTEL DU CAP-EDEN-ROC, BUILT ORIGINALLY IN THE LATE 1800s as a private mansion, had become the most famous hotel in the south of France. Once a winter escape for the wealthy, some of its guests included literary greats, including Ernest Hemingway and F. Scott Fitzgerald.

The month of May had been especially buzzy at the hotel, as many of the stars who attended the Cannes Film Festival stayed there. Everyone from Brad Pitt to Michael Douglas to Johnny Depp parked there when they attended the event, which, truth be told, was nothing more than a very glamorous sales convention.

Willy was waiting in the high-ceilinged lobby in one of the overstuffed white sofas when Jackson and Chance entered.

"Nice to see you again," Willy said, rising to shake Jackson's hand.

"You too," Jackson said, taking a good look at Willy for the first time. Chance was right. He actually looked very together.

"Thanks for this," Chance said, motioning to the room.

"I thought you two walking into my office might be a little suspicious," Willy said. "Drinks?"

"Do we need them?" Jackson asked.

"You might."

They moved through the massive hotel to the restaurant, which overlooked the crashing sea below. The salt air invigorating. The atmosphere, yes, spectacular.

"Bloody Mary for me," Jackson ordered.

"Make that two," Chance agreed.

"The usual," Willy said to the mature waiter, who was a professional at the job.

"While you know how great it is to see you, I can't wait any longer for the news," Chance said with a sincere smile. "Lay it on us."

Willy understood; he was nothing if not professional. "The toxicology reports indicated alcohol, which we knew. She had relatively high levels of mercury, from all the fish she ate, I assume, but nothing extraordinary," Willy said.

"But?" Chance asked, sensing Willy's hesitation.

"There was a significant amount of hydrogen cyanide in your mother's system."

"Cyanide?" Jackson gasped.

"From?" Chance blurted.

"She had to have been given it," Willy told the stunned brothers.

"In other words—"

"Your sister was right," Willy said. "Olivia Gaines didn't die from that accident."

Chance was thunderstruck. "Somebody killed her."

39   *THE JOHN BLACKS*

"WE HAVE VERY SPECIAL KIDS," JOHN SAID AS HE KISSED MARLENA on her all-too-vulnerable neck.

"They knew we'd only had one night alone so far." Marlena sighed as she melted at the touch of his tongue on her skin.

"You don't mind?" John asked.

"I love it that you asked them to stay." Marlena gazed into his blue, blue eyes. "I really do."

"We're going to have plenty of privacy for years to come, and they'll be back at sea soon."

They heard a brisk cough. A uniformed waiter who stood before them.

They were in Le Louis XV, the glorious Hôtel de Paris venue with Alain Ducasse as the chef. As Blake had told Marlena what seemed like aeons ago, dining in this belle epoque restaurant was a gastronomic experience one had to share.

"Sorry, didn't see you there. But can you blame me?" John asked.

"Not at all, sir," he said with a nod to Marlena. "May I take your order, or do you need a little more time?"

"We'll leave it to the chef," John answered him.

The waiter nodded and made his way to the kitchen through the elegant setting in whites and golds. Massive white fresh flowers graced the tables covered in white linen, and Lalique crystal chandeliers cast a soft, warm light.

"Beautiful." John smiled warmly.

"It's considered one of the most exquisite dining rooms in the world," Marlena answered.

"Not it. You."

Marlena could feel herself actually blush. She hadn't done that in so many years, but as corny as it was, she felt as if she were on a first date with her real-life James Bond.

John was indeed drop-dead handsome in the tux she'd shed him of the night before. Marlena was in a shimmering opalescent Armani Privé white dress John had had Belle pick up for her that afternoon. She might have simple taste, but for this first dinner date with her husband, Marlena would bend to his every desire.

"When do we tell the world?" she asked.

"When the time is right," he answered simply. "Not yet, though. I just want to get to know you intimately again first."

That made her blush even deeper.

"If I didn't know better, I'd think I was having hot flashes," she teased as she fanned herself.

"To a life with you and a love with you always," John said, raising his champagne glass.

Their fine crystal flutes pinged as they toasted.

The waiter brought the first of four courses. It was fresh cod salad with warm potatoes and black truffles.

"Not quite the Brady Pub, but it'll do." He smiled.

The Brady Pub, one of the main gathering places in Salem, was not exactly gourmet, but it stirred a lot of lovely memories.

"Do you think you'll ever want to go back there?" Marlena asked.

"To Salem?" he said. "I miss it, sure. But once again, it's all about timing. For now, Europe ain't so bad."

The food was incredible as was the talk. They reminisced about the good times and none of the bad that had haunted them in the past.

When they were about to be served the classic bittersweet citrus dessert, the waiter brought them a phone.

"I'm sorry, Dr. Evans, but there's a call for you," he said.

"Here?" Marlena said surprised. John shrugged as she answered. It was Shawn.

"Marlena, I am so, so sorry to bother you, but Charley Gaines is trying to reach you," he said. "She's sounding pretty desperate."

John could see by her expression he knew so well that this was important.

"Charley Gaines," Marlena told him. She was deeply torn.

"Doc, we've got a life full of romance ahead of us," John said as he signaled the waiter and indicated they wanted the check.

"Let her know I'll be there as soon as I can," Marlena said into the phone.

She hung up as the waiter returned.

"I love you, John," she said.

"You'd better, 'cause you're stuck with me," he answered, signing the check to their suite with a flourish.

40  *GREED*

"GREED, FOR LACK OF A BETTER WORD, IS GOOD," GORDON Gekko proudly proclaimed to the assembled investment brokers in the Oliver Stone film *Wall Street*. Not surprisingly, it was Richie's favorite movie, and he'd seen it at least once a year since its release in 1987.

"You should never have gotten caught," Richie slurred as he wagged his finger at the screen.

The screening room at the villa was the place Richie had stayed most in the last few days. Although the August weather was gorgeous, and the house had over 12,000 rambling square feet, the longer he was confined, the more he wanted to be in a cocoon. The screening room afforded him that. Plush crimson walls and deep purple sound-absorbing drapes enveloped the room, which had leopard-print lounging chairs and a fully stocked bar.

"Michael Douglas, you lucky son of a bitch," he chortled to no one as he poured himself another shot of vintage Macallan from its nearly empty Lalique bottle. He swirled it in the snifter, then took a swig.

"You've still got that face and that un-fucking-believable wife." Richie laughed. "A divorced sex addict who went through rehab and ended up with Catherine Zeta-Jones. You know you're my hero?"

The film played on as Richie mused about how his life mirrored Gekko's. Top of the game, reviled but respected, and then landed in the clink for a dozen years.

"Maybe when I get out I'll write a book," he said. "You listening to me?"

Of course neither Gordon Gekko nor the man playing the role replied.

Richie swirled the deep caramel liquid again. "No one's ever gonna listen to me again, are they?" he muttered.

His life was in shambles, his wife dead, and his Macallan nearly gone. He'd also fired Kelsey, the housekeeper so willing and so curvaceous under her short white uniform, and he certainly couldn't pay for one of the dozens of girls he'd had stored around the Côte d'Azur.

He picked up the remote and turned up the volume.

"I don't like losers, sport. Nothing ruins my day more than losses," Gekko spouted.

Richie raised his glass to the screen.

∞

The scathing words about Richie's womanizing rang in her ears.

"How could I have been so stupid about him, Emilio?" Kelsey cried softly to her brother.

They were in her cabin on the lowest desk of the überyacht, as she lay on her bed in the staff quarters of the *K*. They were utilitarian with no windows, but the beds were comfortable, and at least she had a job. This wasn't a time to be out of work.

"Men are pigs," Emilio answered. "Especially the Gaineses and Kasagians of this world," he continued while wiping her tears.

"I know…" she answered, sniffling. If she hadn't known before, the bitchfest at Gemma's lunch would have sealed it.

"If Serge Kasagian makes you any promises…" He scowled.

"I learned my lesson, *irmão*," she insisted. "Mama would be so upset with me."

"She never has to know," Emilio said, giving her a half smile.

"I was so, so bad…" Kelsey said.

A chirp sounded on Emilio's mobile. It was Serge.

"Wonder where he wants me to drag her to this time?" he said and answered the call. "Mr. Kasagian, sir?"

"Get my wife out of here for a few hours, Emilio, and I couldn't care the hell where," the philandering Serge Kasagian snapped.

Emilio hung up.

"So he can have his booty call," Emilio said, getting up to leave. "It had better not be you," he warned again.

"Never," Kelsey answered. She would not allow herself to be taken in by another misogynist liar, no matter how charming or rich he was. Richie Gaines had promised to marry her if he was ever free, and now he was.

Instead he had fired her.

And now she hated him.

41  CLUES

JACKSON AND CHANCE WERE IN THE LIVING ROOM LOOKING AT the portrait of Olivia by the contemporary Spanish master Enrique Senis Oliver that hung over the fireplace.

She was in gauzy white amid a sea of phalaenopsis orchids, wearing rows and rows of pearls that dipped deep into her ample cleavage.

"Cyanide," Jackson said.

"How and why?" Chance was incredulous.

"I'm more interested in knowing who," Jackson said, straightening the shoulder on his six-foot frame.

"And how we find out how and who," Chance added.

"Right now we're not exactly the poster boys for honesty and decency," Jackson said. "Will anyone care?" He sighed.

"While we're 'in great news' mode, you should see this."

Jackson picked up his iPad from the side table and opened Spectator.com.

"Jesus, Mary, and Joseph." Chance winced as he saw the first full list of investors who'd been royally duped by their father all these years.

"So many in the medical profession," Jackson said, shaking his head in shame. "Nurses, technicians, even hospital workers. I remember Dad telling us how he liked to help the little investors too."

"Helped them out of their retirement," Chance said, sadly.

"Wiped so many people out totally."

"It always sounded too good to be true, but whenever anyone asked for a distribution, he gave it to them," Chance said, trying to defend them.

"Because he could in the beginning," Jackson said as much to himself as his brother. "That's how Ponzi schemes work. The new investors' money is used to pay off the older ones."

"But we were his CEO and attorney. How can anyone believe we weren't involved? How could we have been so stupid?" Chance countered.

"He's one smart motherfucker, bruv. Our crime is that we trusted our own father."

Charley entered in time to hear the exchange. The words cut deeply, and she opted to ignore them.

"Dr. Evans called, and she'll be here any minute," she said softly.

"Would you like us to go?" Chance asked.

"Just while I bawl my eyes out." Charley answered.

The security-gate buzzer buzzed. On the monitor, they could see a town car with two passengers in the back.

❧

"Hi, it's Dr. Evans," Marlena said into the speaker.

The gates swung open, and the town car pulled into the drive.

Chance opened the front door as the driver opened the rear door for Marlena.

"I have no idea how long I'll be," Marlena said as she leaned in to John, who was sitting on the other side of the backseat.

"I've waited this long; a few more hours won't kill me." He smiled warmly and waved his iPhone. "I've got my toys."

Chance came out to greet her. "Thanks so much for coming so late," he said. Unable to not notice how well-dressed she was, he added, "Armani Privé?"

"My husband and I were having dinner," she said, "but we'll pick up where we left off later."

"He doesn't need to sit out here and wait," Chance offered. "Why doesn't he join my brother and me in the den for a drink?"

"That'd be lovely; thank you," Marlena said.

For a houseful of crooks, she thought, *they certainly know their manners.*

∞

Charley felt the weight of the world lift off her shoulders the minute she saw Marlena. She had never had an actual psychiatrist before, and the relief she felt was overwhelming.

"I took you from something," Charley lamented, noticing what Marlena was wearing.

"Anticipation makes the heart grow fonder," Marlena assured her. "But this isn't about me; it's about you."

∞

John was fascinated by the Gaines Villa. While he now had a vast amount of money, he had lived a large portion of his life in the Salem PD and loved the simple life as a cop.

"You mind?" he said, loosening his tie and popping open the top buttons of his shirt.

Through his tumultuous and exciting adulthood, he'd had many personas but always felt best as just one of the guys.

"Please," Jackson said. Both he and Chance were in typical Monaco fine light linen, but even in his Brioni tux John made them feel at ease.

"What's your poison?" Chance asked him, indicating the bar.

John laughed. "You don't know how funny that is actually."

He knew if he told them of the poisons that had crippled him for the last few years, they wouldn't have believed him. "Have any Budweiser?"

In fact, they did. No matter how much the French hated Americans, they had to admit their beer was one of the truly great thirst quenchers.

"Your wife reminds me of someone," Chance said as he retrieved the icy can from the refrigerator. "Not sure who."

"Me too," Jackson realized. "Those eyes that light up, I think."

"Like Charley's," Chance said. "She's a mess, Mr. Black."

"John," he said. "If anyone can help your sister, it's Doc."

John took the beer in the bottle and drank the elixir. Say what you will about the finest champagne, when it's beer you crave, there's nothing better.

"John?"

Marlena was in the open doorway.

"We all need to talk."

Marlena saw their confusion.

"If anyone can help tonight, I think it's you." She then turned to Jackson and Chance. "My husband was the most successful undercover agent the ISA ever had. If anyone can solve this puzzle, he can."

"I don't think we should meet in here," Jackson said. "Dad's in the screening room, which is right above us."

∞

Charley was sitting on one of the suite's four overstuffed sofas, her legs tucked under her, when Marlena entered in front of Jackson and Chance. John took up the rear, and when he saw Charley, he was startled.

"Didn't realize you were quite so gorgeous." He smiled with that crooked smile that made Charley feel at ease.

"I'm pleased to meet you—"

"John," he interrupted before she could finish. "I'm really sorry about your mother."

I'm sorry about Olivia too, she thought. *Devastated. But she wasn't my mother.*

"Thank you," she answered.

"What can you tell me about the night of the accident?" he asked gently.

Charley recounted the details as she remembered them.

She recalled the frantic day at OMG and Olivia's early departure to have her hair done by Beverly Hills' finest. That Olivia had been overly excited about the bash on the *K* because of all the celebrities who loved her, and that she had been drinking her favorite Dom Pérignon rosé with caviar and tea sandwiches when Charley joined her downstairs.

Charley's voice was shaky as she told John that she didn't blame them, truly, but Jackson and Chance were supposed to have been with them and driven to the party. When they hadn't shown, Olivia had taken the driver's seat instead, not wearing her seat belt. Chance had broken the news to her that there had been cyanide in her system, which had to be why she was dizzy and nauseated as they had driven the Route de la Grande Corniche.

"And then you hit the railing," John concluded.

"I tried to control the car, but I couldn't," Charley said, choking back tears.

"This wasn't your fault," Marlena assured her.

"If I'd seen that man on the bike earlier, I could have reacted faster," Charley said, feeling guilty.

"What man on a bike?" Jackson asked.

"Just some guy. He appeared out of nowhere," she answered.

John let it all ruminate. "Cyanide reacts really quickly in the body. Can you show me where you were before you left the house?"

"We can show you," Chance offered.

He and Jackson led John toward the infamous bar off the foyer as Marlena poured Charley a fresh glass of water with lemon from the ready tray nearby.

"Would wine be okay?" Charley asked ruefully.

"It usually makes things worse," Marlena told her. "As a doctor, I'd tell you to avoid it, but it's your call."

Charley studied Marlena's face, and the warmth in it was

appealing and convincing. She took a long, satisfying sip from the crystal tumbler.

∞

"You were really with the ISA?" Jackson asked.

"For a number of years, yes," John answered. "Now and then, I get called back into duty."

"A real James Bond," Chance said.

"I've been called a lot of things," John answered. "But yes, that's been one of them. Where is the wine cellar?"

"Downstairs through that door," Chance said as he pointed to a carved door next to the game room. "But the Dom is always kept here for Mum. Or was."

John opened the cabinet, and there were eleven bottles of the premium champagne ready to be iced.

"And any food comes from where?"

"The help brings it from the kitchen," Jackson said. "And nothing's ever kept more than twenty-four hours. If it's not fresh, it's out."

"Delivered by whom?" John asked.

Chance and Jackson realized quickly that John asked all the right questions.

"All gourmet from Royal Food and produce from Place des Armes. They cater to the palace, so it's all the best quality you can find," Chance explained.

"And what's L-cytokine?" John asked as he took out a vitamin-supplement bottle that was behind several jars of olives, candied cherries, and perfect pearl onions.

"That? A supplement Mum thought would help ward off hangovers."

"Empty," John said. He opened it and smelled the empty bottle. "'Scuse me."

John headed back into the living room, where Marlena was going through photos with Charley.

"Charley, did your mother take any capsules before you left for that party?" he asked.

"Yes. She took them every time she went out."

"How long before you left the house did she take them?"

"A few minutes, maybe," Charley answered.

"What about you?" John asked.

"I was going to take them to humor her, but there were none left."

"Are you sure?" John asked.

Charley nodded. "That's what Kelsey told me. She was the maid. Dad fired her the next day. I was sorry too; she was pretty special."

John's ISA mind was spinning. "Where is she now. Do you know?"

"She was with Gemma Kasagian at the funeral," Chance said. He was a fine observer.

"Mind if I take this bottle, guys?" John asked.

It was obvious to them where he was going with the question.

"How would cyanide get into that bottle?" Charley asked.

"That's a $64,000 question," John answered.

"Take whatever you want from the house," Jackson said.

"Unless it's something we have to inventory for the authorities," Chance added sardonically.

"I'll have to send it to the ISA lab in London," John said apologetically. "I think it's best if we keep this on the down low until we have some answers."

"Wait, could the medical examiner's office test it? That would be faster," Chance asked.

"Too public a forum," John said.

"Not for us." Chance smiled. "At least not for me."

42 BLACK TIME

On the ride back to the Hôtel du Cap, the town car took the same route traveled by Olivia and Charley on the night Olivia died.

Marlena rested her head on John's shoulder as they rode in silence with the beauty of the Mediterranean spread out in front of them.

Hundreds of tourists and residents were partying the night away, while Charley was in the villa trying her best to forget the horrors she'd been through and get much-needed sleep.

"She's a very sweet girl," Marlena whispered.

"She's got to drop the guilt. But you know that better than anyone," John said.

Marlena had once been accused of heinous crimes. While it had ultimately been proven that she didn't commit them, she remembered the pain, doubt, and gut-wrenching insecurity she had felt until that happened. Even when she had been proven innocent, residual guilt lingered on.

"Stop here," John instructed the driver as he noticed the dying yellow flowers and melted candles by the side of the road.

The driver pulled the car over, and John got out to take a look.

He could see up the highway, and it was a clear shot. Anyone heading in their direction could be clearly seen.

Looking behind him, he saw the same. Yes, it was a hairpin turn, but the approaches were both easily visible.

Marlena got out of the car and joined him.

"Thoughts?" she said.

"Strange that a bicyclist would appear out of nowhere," he answered.

Marlena smiled. He was indeed the old John. He was the John whose powers of deduction and observation had helped him out of the most unthinkable positions. No wonder he was an ISA favorite.

"You miss the ISA?" she asked.

"The ISA, Salem, Titan Industries, Basic Black, the Toscana Foundation...I actually miss them all. Except DiMera Enterprises, for obvious reasons."

She knew it was because of Stefano's involvement. The man had wreaked havoc on so many decent people that John regretted ever finding out that he and Stefano were half brothers. It was like finding out you were a Gaines. Thank God John didn't carry the DiMera name.

"What I missed most of all is you," John said, wrapping her in his arms. The moon was full, the night air heady.

"You ever done it in the back of a town car overlooking Monte Carlo Harbor?" he asked, yes, cocking that eyebrow.

Her response was to hit him playfully.

"Not when we have the most exceptional suite in all of the principality." She smiled.

He kissed her fully, deeply. She rested her head on his shoulder.

"We need to help Charley," she said.

"I know," he said, kissing the tip of her nose. "But there's nothing we can do tonight, so how 'bout we take up where we left off this morning?"

"With the kids in the suite?" she reminded him.

"You mean the humungous suite with bedrooms on either side of the living room?" he reminded her.

John helped her back into the car and went around to his side to get in. Before he did, he stopped to survey the area one more time. The wheels kept turning in his mind.

∞

Belle and Shawn were on the terrace of the suite when John and Marlena returned. The table was littered with plates. After spending a few hours with Abby and Chelsea, they had ordered the best room-service hamburgers and frites in the Riviera.

Shawn was up and inside in a flash when he heard them enter.

"How is she?" he asked.

"Charley's gone through a lot, Shawn, and it's going to take a long time for her to heal," Marlena said.

"Well, thank you for helping her, Marlena," Shawn answered.

"Mom and Dad, you look amazing." Belle beamed as she entered through the French doors. Even though they'd been through an emotional and mind-bending few hours, the two of them did still look incredible.

"Not exhausted and ready for bed?" John asked pointedly.

Shawn caught on immediately. "Oh, bad, you look really, really bad. Really exhausted. Really tired."

"Thanks." Marlena laughed.

"We're heading off to bed anyway, Mom," Belle assured them. "And tonight's been absolutely great, thank you."

"Night," Marlena said.

"Night, Mom. Dad," Belle said as she went into John's arms. "Life couldn't be much better, could it?"

It was a question that didn't need an answer.

"I've got some work to do tomorrow, but you'll still be around, right?" John asked.

"Our next stop was your place, so the time schedule's up to you. Unless you don't want us to visit now since we've seen you."

"Go to bed," Marlena scolded.

"Yes, Mommy." Belle smiled.

"Let's go, CB," Shawn said.

For the first time, John and Marlena noticed Claire was on one of the sofas, asleep, snuggling with one of the squishy silk pillows. Shawn scooped her up and carried her toward the second bedroom.

"Ice cream?" Claire muttered in her sleep.

"Good night," Shawn called back as he disappeared with the nearly four-year-old bundle, Belle following behind them.

"Good night," John and Marlena said in unison.

Alone at last, they waited until Shawn and Belle's door was securely closed, then bolted into the bedroom.

❧

"What are you thinking about?" Marlena asked John as she snuggled against his chest.

The bedroom was lit by candles and moonlight, and John was

staring at the ceiling. Their clothes were scattered around the room, and they'd had a very hot night once again. Hey, it had been years, so they were both more than ready.

"What?" he said, coming out of a fog.

"I'll bet I know," she said. "Cyanide."

He couldn't help but smile.

"Offended?"

"You know better," Marlena said. "I was just thinking about Charley."

John and Marlena were both professionals who knew each other well. In fact, they found each other's dedication incredibly sexy.

John kissed Marlena and pulled her close.

"This is good," he said.

"No, it's perfect," she responded.

They lay totally secure in each other's arms with the connection that only comes with familiarity. The passion of commitment.

∞

Claire was sound asleep between Shawn and Belle in the massive, luxurious bed in the second bedroom. Their hands were clasped as they gazed into each other's eyes.

They smiled and blew each other a kiss, then closed their eyes and drifted off to sleep.

The passion of family.

43   *THE JACKSON FIVE*

"GUINNESS ON TAP, MARTIN," JACKSON SAID TO HIS BUDDY the bartender at Le Big Ben, the most popular pub for locals in Nice.

The English pub was a short drive from the Gaines Villa, as was pretty much everything on the Côte d'Azur, and Jackson needed air, but not the warm breezes that wafted through the coast; he needed the familiar stale air of a pub sandwiched between shops on the narrow Rue Alberti. The south of France might have been the Gaineses' base camp every summer, but home for him was still London.

Charley had gone to bed for the night, and Richie, well, he was drinking and watching *Wall Street 2* in his screening room. Chance had gone off to meet Willy, leaving Jackson alone to ruminate on everything they'd been hit with.

An icy-cold draft and some peace and quiet were what he needed. True, Le Big Ben catered to the sophisticated pub crawlers, but they were pub crawlers just the same.

Jackson downed the first one in two swigs from the pint and

ordered another. Martin slid the glass over to him, and Jackson snatched it up.

"Nice grab," a voice said behind him.

He turned to come face-to-face with Abby. From behind, she'd just noticed his broad shoulders, slim waist, and dark floppy hair.

"I know you." He squinted through the smoke swirling around them.

Abby was not in the mood for a confrontation but steeled herself.

"Abby Deveraux," she said, then addressed the bartender. "Two pints for my friend and me." She nodded to a nearby table, where Chelsea sat observing. "Excuse me," she said as she moved in front of Jackson and placed her euros on the bar.

"How do you live with yourself?" Jackson asked.

"My intent wasn't to hurt your family," she said simply, not looking at him.

The pints were put in front of her, and she took them back to her table.

Jackson shoved his empty pint toward Martin. "Another."

Martin poured the third stout for his friend, whom he wasn't used to seeing drink this way. Jackson studied Abby sliding into the seat opposite Chelsea.

Martin slid the drink across the bar. "Jackie."

"Nice creamy head, mate," Jackson said as he reached around and hefted it, studying the pale golden foam. "Put it on my tab."

"Your credit's no good, mate," Martin said carefully.

Jackson cocked his head.

"Boss's orders. Sorry."

Word had gotten around quickly that the Gaineses' assets were all frozen.

"Bollocks," Jackson said, rummaging in his pocket. He had a wad of euros and tossed them at Martin. "How about cash?"

Martin pushed it back. "On me, Jackie," he said. "For tonight, anyway."

Jackson took another swig. It was a pity pint, but at this point, he wasn't in the mind to argue.

∞

Chelsea and Abby were finishing their ale when Jackson stumbled to the table.

"Do you even have a conscience?" he asked with steely anger.

People at the next table turned sharply.

"Where is your compassion?" he sputtered. He curled his right hand into a fist. He'd been a varsity boxer in prep school, and they had called that fist the Jackson Five. "If you were a man, I'd knock you to kingdom come."

Abby took a moment and then bolted from her seat and got right in his face.

"If you were a man, you'd admit you looked the other way while your father destroyed the lives of thousands of people."

"I had no idea what he was doing," Jackson spit.

"Then you're either a liar or a fool," Abby retorted.

"What do you think your paper does, report the news?"

"We let the world see what already exists," she said.

"Clever girl," he sneered.

Abby grabbed Jackson's fist and forced it down.

"Don't you dare condemn me for doing a job to protect my family. My parents nearly lost everything, and I figured out a way to help them. Was I lucky to get those photos? Lucky and smart. Unlike your father, we prey on the guilty, not the innocent!"

A round of applause came up from the pub's patrons.

Jackson was steaming.

"Let's go, Chels," Abby said, grabbing her bag from the back of the chair.

Chelsea was up in a flash, and she and Abby made their way out the door.

Once outside, Abby collapsed against the side of the building. She was breathing heavily.

"Are you okay?" Chelsea asked. "You were just fabulous in there!"

Abby held out her hands, which were shaking badly. She started to laugh from nerves and relief.

The door to the pub slammed open, and Jackson stormed out.

Abby and Chelsea froze as he whirled and moved right into Abby's face again.

Grabbing both of her shoulders, he yanked her to him and kissed her with intensity and passion. Jackson then turned on his heel and strode down Rue Alberti to his red Ferrari.

Abby was dumbstruck.

"So hot," was all Chelsea could mutter.

44   *COMMAND CENTRAL*

THE CHURCHILL SUITE HAD BECOME COMMAND CENTRAL FOR John, Marlena, and the family since he had stunned her with his romantic recovery. It was costing him well over $10,000 a night, but this reunion was worth it. Besides, what was money for?

John sat at the sleek contemporary dining-room table drawing a schematic of the Route de la Grande Corniche while Marlena had breakfast on the terrace with Shawn, Belle, and Claire.

John's mind was clicking again, and he was in his element.

The bell to the suite rang. It was Jackson and Chance, the former looking a bit worse for wear.

"Hey, guys," John said. "Coffee?"

"Do I look like I need it?" Jackson asked.

"Maybe hair of the dog?" John asked.

Jackson grimaced, and Chance answered for him, "Strongest coffee you've got, and make his a double."

John poured each of them coffee from a silver-and-crystal French press and shoved the porcelain creamer and sugar to them.

"Appreciate your coming here," he said. "Those walls in your place have ears."

"Named Richie," Chance said.

"Do you think he was involved?" Jackson said, not wanting to believe it. True, their father was a crook, but they didn't think he was a killer.

"No," Chance insisted too strongly before John could answer.

Jackson and John gave him a quizzical look.

"The other day I asked him about Mum's hangover tablets, and he said there were none left," Chance admitted.

"We can get the bottle dusted for fingerprints, if I'm right," John said.

"You are," Chance said, chagrined. "I picked this up from Willy on the way over. There are traces of cyanide."

"Bingo," John said.

The word was punctuated by the ringing doorbell.

"My prints are definitely on it," Chance said. He pulled the white plastic bottle out of his pocket and set it on the table.

John thought for a long moment. "We need to know who had access to this that day," he said as he picked up the bottle with a napkin. "I need to talk to your sister."

From the other room, they could hear giggling and laughter.

"I'll call her," Jackson offered.

He moved toward the terrace for mobile reception and ran smack into Abby.

"Oh!" She jumped.

"Hi," was all he could manage. He was a mixture of embarrassment and attraction. "'Scuse me," was all he added as he went outside.

Abby's hand went to her lips as she watched him go.

Belle appeared in the doorway, apologetic. "Dad, I didn't real-ize you were having a meeting. Abby and Chelsea came over to say good-bye."

"It is what it is," John said graciously. "Do you know Chance Gaines? Chance, my daughter, Belle."

"So nice to meet you," Chance said and offered his hand.

"And her sister-in-law Chelsea Brady," John added as Chelsea appeared.

Chance recognized her name. "Are you the one who tried to help our mum?"

Chelsea nodded. "Shawn and I were at the accident site."

"He saved Charley's life, not only then, but with the blood match." Chance was truly grateful.

Chelsea nodded again.

"Did I hear that it was your camera that took the photos of the crash site that ran in the *Spectator*?," he continued.

"Uh, yeah."

"Your brother and I already had this out," Abby chimed in to Chelsea's defense.

"Photos?" John said behind them. "Chelsea, were there oth-ers that none of us saw? Maybe the surrounding area? Anyone in the vicinity?"

"Quite a few."

"I need to see them," John said simply. "All of them. Did you delete them?"

"Nope. They're right here in my camera," Chelsea offered as she pulled the camera out of her bag.

∞

Abby's MacBook Air was now on the dining table, and John was scrolling through the myriad photos of a dead Olivia Gaines and the crumpled bright yellow Aston Martin that lay in a heap in the street behind Chelsea and Shawn.

Shawn had joined them, while Belle took an excited Claire for fresh pink polish in the hotel spa. With all the talk of death and destruction this was no place for Claire.

John studied the trajectory of the car and made notes as the doorbell rang once again. This time they heard Marlena answer it.

It was Charley.

"How are you feeling today?" Marlena could be heard as she asked gently, "Are you sure you're up for this?"

"I can be stoic when I have to be, Dr. Evans," she said. "Don't know where that came from, but I can."

When Charley appeared in the dining area, the first person she spotted was Shawn. She lit up like a Christmas tree for the first time since the accident.

"Great to see you," she said warmly.

"You too," Shawn answered as he gave her a light peck on the cheek.

"Take a seat," John said warmly.

Charley's smile was beautiful, and she had a glow about her like Marlena. He could see why they responded so well to each other.

"You've been through this a number of times, I know, but I needed to know who else was in the house the day of the accident," John said.

"I'm not sure of everyone. I wasn't in for part of the day. But when I was it was just—Dad—" Her voice cracked as she said it. "Kelsey, of course, and the landscaper was there, I know."

"Do you know his name?" John asked.

"Sam," Charley answered. "Mum hired him away from Trump when she was in Southampton."

John added his name to the list. "He's not who you saw on the bicycle?"

Charley blanched. She might be stoic, but she had to shake off the memory. "No, Sam's African American."

Abby raised her hand. "Man on a bicycle? I think he's in one of the photos." She moved to the computer and leaned over to scroll through them.

Jackson couldn't take his eyes off her.

"There."

"Blow it up as large as you can," John directed.

With a few keystrokes, Abby enlarged the photo as much as she could. It was heavily pixilated, but you could make out the shape of his head and that he had short-cropped but curly dark hair and a golden skin tone.

John tapped his pencil on the table.

"Why would that mean anything?" Chance asked.

"Are there any other photos?" John asked.

"Not of Chelsea's, but of course I've got a slew of photos I took with my phone," Abby said as she avoided Jackson's gaze.

"All synced?" John asked.

Abby got where he was going. "Faces in iPhoto."

For those uninitiated at the table, John explained that it was a software program that used face recognition to identify and organize a user's photos by the people in them.

"Hang on," Abby said as she named the face "Bicycle Man"

and clicked on Faces. After a few seconds, eight photos showed up, including three different people.

"Not perfect," John said. "But a start."

"Wait," Abby said. "Him." She pointed at a shot from Olivia's funeral. In the background behind Richie's car was the Kasagians' stretch Phantom.

John turned the computer screen toward Charley.

She gasped as she flashed back to that fateful moment on the road. Her mother dizzy, the wind through their hair, the bicyclist appearing out of nowhere, and her vain attempt to stop the car from slamming into the guardrail.

"That's him," she said firmly. "The man on the bicycle is Gemma Kasagian's driver."

It was no secret that Gemma resented Olivia's beauty and talent. But what was her driver doing in the hills when he should have been at that party? And how did he tie into any of this in the first place?

"John, look there," Charley said, noticing two pictures below. "Is that him at Dalita's party?"

John turned the computer around again, and Abby studied it with him.

"Absolutely," John said.

"How could he be in both places at once?" Chelsea asked. She too was curiouser and curiouser.

"Check the time code on the photos," Abby suggested, but John had already started.

"Eight thirty and eight fifty-two," John reported. "Enough time to get from the crash to the yacht?"

"On a bike? Easily," Chance offered.

"And he was late to the party," Abby declared. "He's the guy Dalita's father was reading the riot act to as I was leaving."

It all began to fall into place.

"What we'd have to do is link him to the house," John presented coolly.

"The security cameras in the house are motion-activated," Jackson said.

"I guess we know what we need to see," John said, rising from the table. "Where is the security company? They should have tapes archived."

John Black was back in spades

❧

"We need all the data from last Friday backward for a week," John told Manny, the burly Russian owner of Monte Carlo Sécurité, the premier home-security company in the principality.

"Who's gonna pay?" Manny asked Chance and Jackson, fully aware that the Gaineses' assets were frozen solid.

"I am," John said, handing over his black American Express card.

Manny bit the card playfully and growled happily.

"Let's start with Friday, as early in the morning as possible," John said. "And the camera covering the foyer and the front bar."

After a few moments, Manny pulled up the Gaines Villa tapes, and they all watched. Nothing. Nada.

Manny scanned through several hours' worth of footage. Once again, zip.

"The lives of the rich can be so boring," Manny complained.

A third round of tapes and there was no movement.

"Wait," John said firmly. "Go back."

"Why?" Jackson questioned.

"I hear someone arguing."

The tape was played again, and John asked the boys what was to the left of the foyer.

"The maids' quarters," Chance said.

"Any camera covering that?" John asked.

"Nope. That's an invasion of privacy, man," Manny said. "How twisted are you?"

"It shows the hallway, though," Jackson reminded Manny. Why he needed to remind someone they'd paid handsomely over the years, he wasn't sure, but this was no time to be picky.

Manny inserted the tapes from camera four, and they could hear the arguing more loudly. It was in Portuguese, however, and none of them understood the argument.

"We need an interpreter," Chance said, frustrated as hell.

"Or we check the supplement bottle for those fingerprints I mentioned. Maybe they'll match his." John said, pointing at the screen.

Coming from Kelsey's room was a male figure, the only parts visible, his side and arm. But in his hand was a white bottle that looked a lot like the one that held Olivia's favorite red capsules.

∽

"Shane, I need a connection here in Monaco," John said into FaceTime on his phone.

Shane was in his office in London and pleased to hear from his friend.

"The Monaco Police Force can't be beat," Shane assured him. "It's new, but they have a link to our fingerprint base here at headquarters."

"Thanks, my friend," John said.

"Before you go, how are things?" Shane asked.

"It's as though we've never been apart," John told him. "When we're back at the ranch, you and the kids need to visit."

"Be well," Shane said, then cautioned, "and don't push too hard. Though I know saying that to you is like pissing in the wind."

John hung up and turned to Chance and Jackson. "I'd better go this alone. If you're at police headquarters, there'll be all kinds of questions."

"How long should this take?" Jackson asked.

"The databases are unbelievably quick these days," John told him. "By the time we get back to the hotel, we may have answers. Then again, maybe not."

"I need to get back to the house sometime today," Jackson said. "Starting a full inventory for the Security and Exchange blokes."

"Abby Deveraux is leaving today," John said with a glint in his eye.

The attraction between Jackson and her had been palpable.

"I guess I can start it tonight," Jackson said casually. "It'd be rude not to say goodbye."

Chance gave him a "what the hell?" look.

Jackson said, "She's the one with all the pictures."

Then admitted to himself wryly, *The thing I nearly clocked her for might very well solve this murder.*

45  *OIL AND WATER*

"Dad's arraignment is next Tuesday," Chance told his brother as they were heading up to the Churchill Suite in the private elevator.

"Will he go?" Jackson asked.

"He has no choice," Chance admitted. "And he initially said he was pleading guilty, but now that he's in a drunken haze, I have no idea."

"What if he refuses?" Jackson asked.

"It'll only prolong the inevitable."

"Jail time."

"Look, he only screwed the investors out of a billion or so. He may only get thirty years, and be out in twelve with good behavior."

"Good behavior?" Jackson scoffed. "Our father? Right…"

"If he doesn't pay somehow, he'll be a pariah forever. And so will we," Chance said.

"Not that we aren't now," Jackson rued, recalling his humiliation at Le Big Ben.

They crossed the hall and rang the doorbell to the suite.

Marlena answered. "Hi," she said. "Where's John?"

"He'll be here soon," Jackson said as they entered. "Thought I'd get back to say good-bye and thank Abby and Chelsea."

Marlena looked confused. "Abby got a call, and they left here about twenty minutes ago. She said they were meeting you."

"We haven't spoken," Jackson told her.

"Guess what that means?" Marlena said. "That girl's up to no good."

Little did Marlena know, it was actually quite the opposite.

∽

The gangplank to the Kasagians' überyacht was longer than Abby remembered.

"It's got to be amazing inside," Chelsea said to Abby, who was wearing glasses and had her hair pulled into a ponytail.

"Are you here for the job interviews?" an officious gay crew member crooned. "Step it up, girls."

They hustled up the ramp and inside, where there was another crew member with a clipboard.

"Make sure you include all your references." The petite blonde smiled. Abby recognized her as one of the bartenders at Dalita's party, but luckily, the ditz looked right through her.

"Thank you." Abby smiled as they took job applications.

"French, German, Italian, English, Chinese…" Chelsea said as she looked at the form in multiple translations. "Covering all the bases, I see."

"Gotta be able to impress all the guests," chirped the bosomy blonde. "At least one waitress for every language."

"I worked at the Brady Pub," Chelsea said under her breath. "Wonder if that qualifies me as Irish?"

"Probably." The girl smiled and moved on to other no-doubt totally unqualified job hunters.

"There's Kelsey," Abby said as she poked Chelsea in the ribs.

"Very pretty," Chelsea said with a bit of sadness as the stunning young Portuguese woman walked toward them.

"You made it," Kelsey said.

"Yes, thanks for the call. You said they're hiring ten girls, so I brought a friend," Abby said. "I met her at Olivia Gaines's funeral," she continued, lying.

"Really? I met Abby there too," Kelsey said as she studied Chelsea's face. Chelsea had spiked her hair and changed her makeup drastically at the suite. She looked more punk than proper and was barely recognizable.

"Could we talk privately?" Kelsey asked Abby. "You don't mind, do you?" she added to Chelsea.

"No, not at all," Chelsea said. "I need to fill this out anyway," she continued, indicating toward the form.

Abby and Kelsey moved a short distance away, behind one of the many majestic Mediterranean fan palms that graced the first deck of the ship. Kelsey's nerves were showing as she quietly asked, "How much will you pay me?"

"That depends on what I get at the party. It's for Carla Bruni and President Sarkozy, right?" Abby asked.

Kelsey nodded, making sure no one was listening.

"Five-hundred-euro minimum," Abby said. "Up to five thousand if I get something scandalous."

Kelsey steeled herself and nodded again. "I'll make sure they hire you. As for your friend…"

They looked over to Chelsea, who was pretending to be taking in the spectacle of the multimillion-dollar surroundings

"She really needs the job," Abby said. "She's been having an affair with that felon Richard Gaines for a year, and now he's dumped her. They were going to get married."

Kelsey burst into tears and wailed, "Emilio was right."

"What?" Abby said, wide-eyed, as the line of other applicants swiveled their heads to stare.

"He's a bastard!" was all Kelsey could say, and she fled the room, crying.

Abby shrugged and joined Chelsea.

"Bingo," she chimed, echoing John's word from earlier.

The bosomy teenager approached. "Done with the forms?" she asked Chelsea and Abby as if she hadn't seen Kelsey's meltdown.

Abby put on her most self-deprecatory frown. "After seeing your choices, I don't think we could cut it." Abby mourned as they handed back the blank applications.

"But thanks." Chelsea smiled.

As they'd gotten the info they needed, they sashayed through the crowd and onto the dock.

Chelsea's phone rang. It was Belle, freshly mani and pedied. "Where are you guys?"

"ISA'ing, why?" Chelsea smiled.

"My dad's on his way back, and there's news," Belle said with urgency. "And what do you mean you were ISA-ing?"

∞

"You did what?" Shawn said, wide-eyed, to Chelsea and Abby as he faced the assembly in the dining room of Command Central.

"Both Dad and my mom were cops, Shawn," she reminded her brother.

"So was he and Hope," Shawn said, stunned. "That doesn't mean I'd go undercover."

"Well, we did, and did a pretty damned good job, if I say so myself," Abby added, pretending to polish a badge on her perky breast.

"You look like sluts!" Claire declared, then scampered off, flashing the new Hello Kitty decals on her bright pink fingernails.

"Claire Brady, we're going to have a little talk," Shawn scolded as he went after her.

"We may look like sluts, but we know who is one," Abby said to Chelsea. "Kelsey Silviera."

"Did you say Silviera?" John said, catching the end of Abby's statement as he entered.

"Yep," Abby said. "Why?"

"Shane called on my way back, and the prints matched an Emilio Silviera," John said as he pulled his iPad from the side table. "He's emailed all the stats."

John turned on his iPad and checked his email. There indeed an email with the subject "Silviera."

The image of Emilio Silviera popped on the screen with a series of mug shots. There were at least eight different photos with long hair, short, bearded, mustachioed, and on and on… each with a different alias. But one thing was sure: he was Kelsey Silviera's brother.

"His record's a long one across the board," John said, scanning the report.

"Unbelievable," Chance said, stunned.

"Petty larceny, male prostitution, sales of coke and heroin, and attempted murder," John continued.

"This time he got it right," Jackson said flatly.

Abby touched Jackson's shoulder, and he clasped her hand.

"But cyanide, John?" Marlena asked. "How would he get that?"

"He worked on the Kasagians' yacht, right?" John asked.

"He's actually Gemma's driver," Abby said. "But all the permanent help live on the yacht."

"Cyanide is commonly used for fumigating ships," John said. "And I'll bet they have a boatload."

46  *SPECTACULAR*

"WHERE DID YOU COME FROM?" JACK BEAMED AS HE VIDEO-chatted with Abby. Abby sat on the dock amid a sea of policemen, as Emilio and Kelsey were led down the gangplank in handcuffs. Kelsey was in tears, but her brother was stone-faced.

"I didn't do anything," Kelsey pleaded to Abby as she was taken to a waiting police car. "I didn't know."

Chelsea was at Abby's side and watched as the door shut on the girl who'd trusted too many people.

"I don't know why, but I believe her," Chelsea said as the car drove off, sirens blaring.

"I don't know why, but I believe her too," Abby admitted. "But she gave Olivia Gaines those pills laced with cyanide."

"What, Abs?" Jack said, bringing Abby back to his image on the mobile.

"We need to talk to John, Dad," Abby said. "Tell Mom I'll get back to you later."

"Will do, but you're just spectacul—"

Jack was flummoxed as Abby hung up the call.

Tourists and locals went back to lounging on their yachts, drinking rosé, and soaking up the sun. The sounds of music and laughter filled the harbor, but Chelsea and Abby didn't feel like partying.

"Thank God this happened before the president got here," one of the Kasagian crew members muttered as he headed back onto the yacht.

"Yep, hate to spoil a good party." Chelsea sighed.

∞

Jackson, Chance, and Charley stood on the terrace of the Churchill Suite, watching the arrest of their mother's killer in the distance. From their vantage point, they could see the police on the deck of the *K*, slapping the cuffs on Kelsey and Emilio, and Gemma stomping around as if they'd spilled red wine on her Persian carpets. They watched the police cars as they caravanned to the station, only several blocks away.

"I always hated supplements," Charley said sadly as they saw the cars pull into the station. "But if I'd taken those, Mum might still be here."

"And you'd be gone, Little Sis," Jackson said.

"I know you miss having a mummy," Chance said as he kissed her on top of her shining brown mane. "But we'll fill in."

Charley stared at her brothers. "Did you both know I'm adopted?"

Both Jackson and Chance looked at her as if she were crazy. But before they could question it, John appeared from the living room.

"In case you're interested, there's a CNN crew at the police station, and Emilio's asked to make a statement."

Not sure they wanted to hear him, the siblings still were drawn to the television like magnets.

Shawn cradled Belle, and John wrapped Marlena in his arms as Claire sat fiddling with her newly painted toenails, oblivious to the drama unfolding on international television.

Emilio, unemotional but strong, faced the cameras and pleaded for his sister's release.

"My sister had nothing to do with the murder of Olivia Gaines, except for being my motivation for doing it." He continued as nearby Kelsey choked on her tears, "I will plead guilty to all charges and take lie-detector tests, if necessary, to prove her innocence. Her crime is loving an evil man who didn't love her but lied and said he'd marry her if he was free. I had to prove what a monster he was to save her. And I did. God bless you all."

John clicked off the television, and they all stared in silence.

❧

In the darkened screening room at the villa, Richie sat with a bottle of tequila in his hand, watching Emilio and Kelsey being escorted into the station. He took a swig directly from the bottle, then used the remote to turn off the widescreen television.

Click, and the movie screen rolled into place.

Click, and the movie started.

Wall Street.

Again.

❧

By the time Abby and Chelsea had returned to the suite, the

Gaines siblings had gone. Although Olivia Gaines's murder had been solved, the mood was somber instead of celebratory.

"You've heard, we're sure," John said to them both.

"We didn't think Kelsey was guilty," Chelsea said. "Something in our guts just told us."

"It's the breeding," John said. "Reporter and cop blood flowing through your veins and your's," he added, pointing to each of them.

"I never wanted to be a cop," Chelsea said. "So much of it in the family, and I've seen the heartache it can cause."

"You've also seen the good," Shawn offered from the sofa, where Belle still sat wrapped in his arms.

"I haven't had real focus since I moved to England," Chelsea admitted. "All the craziness with Max has had me at loose ends."

"Maybe now you'll get it together," Abby said. "You were pretty damned good in there."

"We'll see," Chelsea said.

A loud *crack* that sounded like a sonic boom filled the air.

"Fireworkings!" Claire said, bolting upright from her fascination with her toes.

Through the window they could see bursts of light as fireworks illuminated the sky. They were accompanied by glorious Spanish music that was punctuated by the crackling spectacle in the harbor.

"The International Fireworks competition," Marlena exclaimed. "Tonight's entry is from Spain."

She had read about the annual festival that remained one of Monaco's most popular summer events and had drawn thousands to the principality every August for the last forty years. The winner of the dazzling show over Port Hercule garnered not only bragging rights, but also one hundred thousand euros.

"Our terrace is one of the best viewing sites," she told them, encouraging them to join her as she moved outside.

Shawn swept Claire up in his arms, and he and Belle joined Marlena and John, with Abby and Chelsea following.

They oohed and aahed as the lights in the city dimmed, and a profusion of color filled the starry sky.

Next to two of the most romantic couples they knew, Chelsea and Abby linked arms. "You like him, don't you?" Chelsea asked.

"I do not," Abby protested.

"You don't even know who I meant," Chelsea said accusatorily.

"We both do," Abby admitted. "And yes, I do, dammit."

A blaze of color crossed the sky.

∞

Jackson drove their Range Rover slowly up into the rocky hillside as the fireworks exploded over the city. It was one of the most romantic nights of the year along the Côte d'Azur, and he was thinking of Abby.

Charley was in the passenger's seat, and she was lost in the beauty of the pageantry. Her mother's killer had been found, and all was right with the world, aside from a few small things—if one considered a drunken international felon for a father and a total loss of identity small.

The gates automatically opened as they pulled into the front courtyard and parked next to the Bentley, Maserati, and Ferrari that would all be confiscated soon. They all silently got out of the car.

Richie was now in the living room, waiting for them. Drunk, sad, and filled with remorse.

When they entered, he rose to greet them. The man who they had always seen as their hero, their father, their support was gone. In his place was a shell of his former self. In less than a week, everything had collapsed around him.

"I know sorry isn't enough," he choked.

"I'm sorry, Dad, but it isn't," Jackson said. "Hey, we're not stupid. We always knew you had your faults, but didn't realize they ran as deep as the Mediterranean Sea."

"Charley, baby?" Richie smiled sadly. He tried to reach out to her, but she stood frozen.

"Mummy really loved you." She sighed. "We all did. You gave us everything we ever wanted, when all we really needed was someone to be proud of us and to love us more than himself. Good night…Richie."

His hand went to his chest as her dismissal stabbed him like a knife.

Charley went into Jackson's arms for a tight hug. Then she took Chance's hand and kissed him on the cheek.

"Let me go up with you," Chance said and walked out with her without another word.

"I'll be inventorying everything in the villa, then the offices and the London flat," Jackson said. He was cold and businesslike. "Can't imagine who'll be coming out of the woodwork next," he added. "Unfortunately for them, there's nothing left to blackmail you for."

Jackson turned to go, then stopped. "One more thing…I pray

to God I can forget everything you ever taught me." He turned and walked away.

Richie was alone again.

A bright flash of light illuminated the sky as they walked out of the elegantly casual room that reflected Olivia so thoroughly. The finale of the fireworks competition was a grand finish to a fateful day.

Richie caught sight of Olivia's portrait, and it was as if she were watching him and smiling.

He began sobbing uncontrollably.

47  *WHO?*

THE DOOR TO THE HOTEL SUITE OPENED, AND TWO WAITERS entered, pushing room-service carts with ice buckets and silver-domed porcelain plates.

"Be careful, we have a child sleeping," Marlena said, motioning to Claire, who had fallen asleep on one of the massive sofas.

"Once that girl's asleep, there's no waking her," Belle told her mother. "A bomb could go off, and she wouldn't know it."

"Sounds like a little girl we knew." Marlena smiled as John pointed at Belle.

"What's all this?" Shawn said as he emerged from the bathroom. His hair was still wet, and he was shirtless but wearing light cotton drawstring pants. He looked every bit the hunk that Belle had married.

"Remind me to keep my shirt on." John grimaced.

"Yeah, right," Shawn scoffed.

"Where would you like these, Madame?" the young waiter asked Marlena.

"One goes in each bedroom, thanks," John instructed.

The waiters did as they were told, moving the fine linen-covered carts to opposite sides of the suite.

"Enjoy, guys," John then said to his daughter and son-in-law.

"Thanks, Dad," Belle said as she wrapped her arms around him. She then kissed him lightly on the lips.

Belle then kissed her mother, took Shawn's hand, and they disappeared into the bedroom as the waiter held the door for them and then closed it behind them.

The second waiter came out of the master bedroom and nodded. "Extra crème fraîche, as you asked, sir."

"Thank you," John answered as he handed them each a large tip.

"Thank you," they said in unison as they saw the generous offering. "Anything else you need, don't hesitate to call."

"All we want now is privacy," John said.

The two quickly crossed the plush carpet and closed the door behind them.

"Alone at last." He smiled. "That's not weird, is it?" he added. "Our setting up a night of romance for our little girl?"

"She's married with a child, and she's pregnant," Marlena reminded him needlessly. "And she's happy, John," she said with emphasis. "Isn't that what we want for all our children?"

He kissed her on the tip of her nose. "Every last one. You know, I feel sorry for the Gaines kids."

"Me too. Finding out your father had feet of clay."

"Maybe it's a good thing she's adopted." John said.

Marlena gave John a surprised look. "Was that in her file?" she asked.

"I overheard her ask her brothers about it on the terrace. Apparently, she didn't know."

"So many secrets, so many lies," Marlena said, shaking her head sadly. "I'd like to help her through it. Any way I can."

"Yet one more reason you're perfect."

"That's me," she said with a self-deprecating tone.

"You are, you know," he said. "Just perfect."

"I love you, John Black," she murmured.

"Not nearly as much as I love you." He smiled. "There's no way you could."

John held her tightly, the warmth of their bodies comforting, inviting. After a few moments, he lifted her off her feet and into his arms.

"You're still in recovery," she cautioned.

"I told you I had to be whole before letting you in on this, Doc," he said. "Don't you worry."

Marlena gazed into his eyes seductively, then buried her head on his shoulder as he carried her to the bedroom.

"What did you say the name of your physical therapist is?" she asked. "I've got to remember to thank her."

∞

Charley sat in the bay window of her bedroom, looking across the front courtyard and into the harbor. She had planned to go to bed but couldn't sleep.

Small wonder.

A tap on the door and Chance entered with a bed tray with hot cocoa with marshmallows and graham crackers.

"Hi." She smiled wanly.

"Hey." He smiled. "Know it's summer, but when we were kids, this always cheered you up."

He gently put the tray on the Belgian lace bedcover and patted the bed for her to join him.

"Is cheering up what I need, or answers?"

"Hey." She heard a voice from the doorway. It was Jackson. "Didn't think you could do this without me, did you?"

He had his own cup of cocoa and a small bottle of Kahlua.

"Good thinking." Chance nodded.

Jackson joined them on the bed and poured an ample amount of the coffee liqueur into each of their cups.

"To us," Chance said, raising his mug in a toast.

"To us," Jackson complied.

"Is there an us?" Charley asked pointedly. "Look at the two of you, and look at me."

"You're gorgeous," Chance started.

"And obviously not blood related," she said.

Chance lowered his mug and addressed her sweetly. "Sis, we know this has been an incredibly bad time for us all, and especially you, but we have absolutely no idea what you're talking about."

"Nada," Jackson concurred.

"We don't look anything alike," she said with a hint of desperation. "We don't have any of the same tastes or talents, and my blood type did not match either Mum's or...Richie's. It doesn't take a rocket scientist to put two and two together."

"You were born at New York–Presbyterian Hospital, Sis," Chance reminded her.

"So we thought," she replied.

"I was ten when they brought you home," Jackson reminded her.

"You were both away in prep school during Mummy's entire pregnancy," she reminded them.

"There are photos of her," Chance added.

"She hardly showed. Why would she if she wasn't really pregnant?" Charley insisted. "Dad kept her away from both of you and all their friends. Oh, right, and why don't I just ask him?" The set of her beautiful jaw was firm. "He's a big fat liar, or haven't you noticed?"

"There have to be answers," Jackson said.

"Unfortunately, the only one alive who probably knows is Gram, but somehow I doubt she'd remember."

It was true. Olivia's mother, a beautiful soul who she adored, had been suffering the torture of Alzheimer's since Charley was two.

"Does it matter, little one?" Chance asked. "Does it really, truly matter?"

"I don't want to be Richard 'Ill Gotten' Gaines's daughter," she admitted. "It matters to me."

⬥

The strawberries and cream had been devoured, as had Marlena. She and John lay in one another's arms.

The Monte Carlo moonlight shone in; the scented candles were nearly burned down. Marlena's smile faded as her thoughts drifted to the events of the day. John knew his wife well. "Why can I guess what you're thinking, Doc?" he smiled. "And for the record, I'm not offended.

"Can you help her, John?" Marlena asked softly.

He smiled at her tenderly. "I'll do my best."

"That's all I can ask," Marlena replied as she drifted off to sleep in his arms.

48  *WHAT?*

JACKSON WAS IN RICHIE'S HOME OFFICE AT THE COMPUTER, completing the inventory, logging in item after item. He picked up the Baccarat crystal Encounter Man and Woman figures that Richie used as bookends, and checked the computer.

$1,740 each.

They were expensive but hardly going to pay back the hundreds of investors who were seeking restitution.

Chance entered, dressed in simple white slacks and a Ralph Lauren Black Label shirt rolled up at the sleeves.

"Sorry I can't help you with this, bruv," Chance said.

"You've got the legal eagles to deal with," Jackson answered. "I'd rather do this."

Chance sat on the edge of the Biedermeier desk. "What do we do about Charley?"

As if on cue, Chance's phone rang.

"Private caller," he said, checking the caller ID. "Do I answer?"

"Your call."

He decided, *What the heck?* "Chance Gaines here."

"Chance, it's John Black. There's something we need to discuss about your sister."

Chance listened, fascinated as John told him what he and Marlena knew about Charley's belief that she was adopted and her need to have answers. When he hung up, he sat silently for a moment.

"Well?" Jackson asked, especially curious from Chance's expression.

"John Black thinks he may be able to track Charley's DNA," Chance offered.

"Okay," Jackson said skeptically. "And?"

"He doesn't want to get up her hopes, so he wants us to get a DNA sample, and he'll have it tested," Chance said.

"Against whose?" Jackson asked.

"Apparently, this ISA has recently compiled a main database from 40 percent of the hospitals and police stations in the world."

"So if her DNA matches a sicky or a sicko, she'll have some answers?" Jackson sighed. "Sounds fab," he said, tossing a pencil across the desk.

"If he doesn't find any matches, no harm no foul," Chance countered. "Look, it's something."

❧

Charley was out on the terrace having fresh summer fruit and eggs, when Chance and Jackson came out to join her.

"Gorgeous day," Chance said, sitting on the wrought-iron chair across from her.

"So now we're discussing the weather?" Charley remarked.

SHERI ANDERSON

Jackson sat between them and joked, "Okay, what about them fireworks? Think Spain'll win this year?"

Charley had to appreciate her brothers, whether they were by blood or not.

"You don't have to worry about me, I'll be fine," she said, popping a ripe piece of cantaloupe in her mouth.

"We know you will," Chance said. "Just know we love you."

"I do." She smiled.

"Would you like some more juice?" Jackson said, picking up her juice glass and not waiting for an answer. "Sophia's squeezed more fresh."

Before she could protest, Jackson disappeared into the house.

"What are you doing today?" Chance asked.

"I should go to the boutique," she said. "Since...Dad...was co-owner, it's bye-bye to OMG."

Chance held her hand tightly. Fashion wasn't Charley's love, but the thought of losing Olivia's legacy was painful.

Jackson returned with two full glasses of orange juice and set one in front of Charley.

"I'm full, Jackson, really," she said. "But you have it, Chance." She pulled away from the table. "I'd better get dressed."

Chance watched her cross into the house, then turned back to the glass. "Well, that worked," he said sarcastically.

Jackson pulled out a small juice glass wrapped in a linen napkin.

"I switched hers with a new one." He smiled.

"Well, well, my good man." Chance smiled. "Guess it's time to go see John Black."

49  *IDENTITY*

JOHN WAS CHECKING THE TIME ON HIS PHONE WHEN THE SILVER Maserati pulled up curbside. He was at the Nice airport, and his flight was leaving in less than an hour.

"Perfect timing, guys," he said to Jackson as he leaned in the car's window. "What've you got?"

Jackson produced the juice glass with Charley's lip-gloss print clearly visible. "From breakfast this morning."

"Great," John replied, impressed. "What does she know?"

"Nothing," Chance said across his brother. "We thought it best."

"Good call," John answered as he put the evidence in his jacket pocket. "With any luck, we could have answers tonight."

Jackson and Chance were stunned.

"So soon?"

"Yep. The technology's been in place for decades," he added. "The databases are just catching up now." John heard the boarding call for his flight to London.

"Keep us posted," Jackson said.

The brothers watched as John sprinted into the airport.

"I don't care what he finds out," Chance said. "She's always going to be my sister."

Chance revved the 4,691-cc Maserati engine whose roar was known to ignite the pheromones of men and women alike, and headed back to the villa.

Back to Richie. And grief.

"Hey, if we're lucky, bruv," Jackson said over the noise, "maybe we could find out we're not his either."

John was in club class on the British Airways flight to London and took the time on the flight to email Shane and also the house in Lausanne. Desiree was in shock at the news of John's recovery but asked—no, begged,—to keep her on to ensure he didn't relapse.

The flight was smooth and short, less than two hours, and Shane was waiting outside customs when John arrived.

The customs official sent John through immediately, and he embraced his old pal.

"Helps to have friends in high places." John smiled.

"This could be a long shot, you know?" Shane reminded his former ISA partner.

"That much hasn't changed," John admitted. "Technology gives us a lot, but only if it has the right input."

"You want to join me for a lunch while we wait?" Shane said as John handed him the bagged evidence.

"If you can email me the results, I'd like to get back to my girl," John said. "No insult intended."

"None taken," Shane said with that mellifluous British accent that made women swoon. He then paused and looked at his friend. "Why are you doing this, John?"

"Doc wants to help this girl, Shane," he said. "Charley feels that she doesn't know who she is right now."

"Ah, for Marlena," Shane said, not totally buying it.

"And for me too, I guess. If anyone knows what it's like to not have an identity, Shane, it's me."

Shane got it in spades. John had been through so many incarnations it made his head spin.

"When you know your biology, it doesn't change who you are, but it sure changes your understanding of yourself."

"I'll get back to you as soon as we have news or no news," Shane said. Then he embraced the man he felt as close to as a brother.

John headed for the departure gates. Back to his future.

50  *OMG*

Since the accident, no one had been in what had once been the hottest boutique in Casino Square. Before she opened the door, Charley picked up the freshly placed flowers and candles that fans had brought.

The shop was exactly as she'd left it before rushing home to change for Dalita's party. Stocked with the most expensive items from Olivia's line, it was a celebutante's dream.

She picked up a pair of white sunglasses encrusted with the logo in pavé diamonds and put them on. She looked in the mirror and posed with them for a moment, chuckling at the superficial girl she saw in her reflection.

On the counter by the register were proofs of the preliminary shots she'd taken for the upcoming collection.

"Guess we won't need these anymore," she muttered.

The bell at the front rang as the door opened.

"I'm sorry. We're not open," she said before she realized it was Shawn, Belle, and Claire.

"Those are silly!" Claire said, pointing to the oversize glasses

Charley was still wearing. "Can I have them?"

"Claire, that's not nice, and no, you can't have them," Belle scolded. "Sorry," she said to Charley.

"No, they are silly, and yes, you can have them if your mommy and daddy say it's okay." Charley smiled. She liked Claire. In fact, she liked all of them.

"We were just headed down to the boat and saw you here," Shawn said. "Wanted to say hi."

"Hi. And I'm, well, worse than I'd like to be, but better than I could be," Charley said, answering the question they hadn't wanted to ask.

"We're all headed out in the next day or so, depending on Belle's folks," Shawn said. "We're headed up to their house in Switzerland."

"We'll see you before, I hope," Belle offered. "If you're not doing anything tonight…"

"Not making any plans at the moment, but I'll see," she said. "Thanks. Belle, do you mind if I kiss your husband?"

Belle laughed.

Claire's eyes widened. "I mind!"

"It's just to say thank you one more time for his saving my life, twice," Charley said. "I've got his blood in me now, so maybe I'm like your auntie, you think?"

"I like that," Claire said succinctly. "Did you know I'm almost four?"

Charley grabbed a small white leather OMG hat from one of the racks. "Then this is for you."

Claire plunked the hat on her head and the glasses over her ears. One happy little girl.

Charley moved to Shawn and kissed him lightly on the cheek, lingering a bit longer than she'd expected. "I mean it, Shawn. I owe you my life. We'll always have a bond."

He gently kissed her back.

Belle faked coughing. "Ahem." She knew her relationship with Shawn was stronger than ever. But Charley was so naturally beautiful, so much more down-to-earth than someone with her upbringing had a right to be.

"See you later?" Shawn asked.

"Hope so," Charley smiled.

"Bye!" Claire said, grabbing both Belle and her da's hands and pulling them out of the shop.

Charley watched as the door closed behind them.

Just my luck that he's married. She smiled to herself. *He's exactly the type of man I've been saving myself for.*

∞

"That was quick," Marlena said as she saw John moving to join her on the terrace.

"Less than three hours door-to-door," John said. "Even though I was on the 'screaming baby' express, I couldn't have cared less. Getting back to you was all that was important."

He settled in one of the chairs next to hers.

"Shane said we might have results tonight," he told her.

"It's all so confusing," Marlena admitted.

"I had time on the plane, so I used my ISA connection and contacted New York–Presbyterian—the guys had said that's where Charley was born—and they do have birth records there. But—"

"What?" Marlena asked.

"An in vitro procedure on Olivia there. Olivia was carrying someone else's baby."

John's phone rang. It was Shane.

"Talk about quick," he echoed to Marlena as he answered the call. "He didn't email. Not always good news." Then into the phone, "Shane, hello, buddy…"

"We've got a match," Shane said evenly.

"Mother or father?" John asked.

"Both."

Excited, Marlena took the phone. "Shane, you found a match on both of her parents?"

"Good news or bad?" John asked.

"Are you two alone?" Shane questioned.

"We are. Why?" Marlena was getting anxious.

Shane took a deep breath. "Could you put me on speaker." It was a request, not a question. Marlena complied.

"We're here, partner," John said.

"Her DNA matches John Black and Marlena Evans Black."

"What?" Marlena sputtered.

"It's impossible. No, seriously, Shane…" John added.

"I double- and tripled-checked the results before making this call," Shane insisted. "We all know that DNA does not lie. Neither do I. It matches the two of yours."

Marlena's hands began to tremble, badly. The phone slipped from Marlena's grasp and tumbled to the gardens below, neither of them even noticing. They just stared into each other's eyes.

"Charley's our daughter," John said with conviction.

In that instant between them, they knew that somehow, some way, this incredible revelation was true.

❧

John and Marlena were still frozen in place on the terrace, when they heard a key in the door, and Belle entered, followed by Shawn and Claire. Shawn was now wearing the oversize white glasses, and Claire proudly wore the floppy soft leather hat.

"Look at Da," Claire squealed as she danced a jig in the room.

"Bathroom, CB?" Shawn asked, recognizing the signs.

"I'll take her, honey," Belle said as she guided the little one to the loo.

"We just saw Charley," Shawn said as he removed the signature frames. "Gifts for Claire."

Marlena and John were both quiet.

"Did we interrupt something?" Shawn asked.

"We have interesting, confusing—"

"Yet exciting—"

"News," John completed. "I think we should wait for Belle to tell you."

"No need to wait. I'm here," Belle said, drying her hands. "Did Shawn tell you we saw Charley?"

"He did," Marlena said carefully.

"And?" Belle frowned. Marlena's tone was strange.

"If we didn't know better ,we'd think we were back in Salem," John started. "Belle, you have a younger sister."

Belle sank to the sofa. John and Marlena explained what they'd learned and what they still needed to know. How? Why? When and where?

Before it had a chance to sink in, there was a knock on the door.

"Whoever it is, tell them to go away, Shawn," John instructed his son-in-law.

He couldn't. When he opened the door, it was Charley with one of the bellmen.

"Oh, hi. Didn't think you'd see me again so soon, did you?" She smiled ruefully. "But I found this phone in the grass when I was leaving the shop, and I recognized the case. I think it's John's."

John and Marlena exchanged glances. This was neither the time nor the place, but there they were facing their daughter.

"Is everything all right?" Charley asked cautiously. The tension in the room was thick.

"That depends on you," Marlena said as she moved to face the biological daughter she had never known.

∞

"You are my biological parents?" Charley squeaked in a voice she'd never used before. One of shock, surprise, and total disbelief. "The two of you? The most amazing two people on the planet are *my* parents?"

She sank onto the arm of the sofa, in total shock.

"And you never knew?" Charley added. "Of course you didn't, or you would have told me, and—" She stopped herself. "You're telling me this is true?"

Marlena nodded.

"We're as shocked, but happy, I guess, as you," John added.

The details they had were still sketchy, but Marlena held Charley's hand as John carefully explained all he knew.

Charley had indeed been conceived by artificial insemination in New York, but that's all Shane and John had been able to decipher. John and Marlena had no answers about how they had become involved, but there was no doubt it was real.

Charley looked between the two of them. "You're my parents," she said again in disbelief.

"Biological," Marlena said, confirming.

"Which means a lot," Charley said as she laced her fingers with Marlena's. "In France, there's a theory, you know, that the touch of a mother's hand is like no other," she added. "I never felt this with Mummy; it's true."

"She still was your mummy, you know, because she raised you," Marlena said supportively.

"Nature and nurture both count," Charley said wisely. "I know that." Then she smiled and started to cry. "Even if I never see you again, I am so happy that it's the two of you."

The room was filled with emotion that couldn't be put into words.

"I have a new little sister." Belle leaned in. "And you stay away from my husband," she teased. "Our older sisters are the pros at that."

"Other sisters?" Charley said as she drank it all in.

"Oh, it's an extended family, all right." John laughed. "And we're all crazy about each other, warts and all."

"Do Chance and Jackson know?" Charley asked.

"Not yet," John told her. "But we did have a little of their help getting your DNA."

"They're the best," she said as she shook her head in amazement.

"They love you," Marlena said. "We all do."

"There's just one person I need to see," John said. "If I have your permission."

"Richie," Charley said as the smile faded from her face.

"If anyone has the answers, he will."

51  *WHY?*

"Dad, there's someone here to see you," Jackson shouted into the darkness of the screening room.

"Not interested in company, Son," Richie said quietly.

"Maybe not, but this isn't a social call, and you're going to see him," Jackson said as he lifted Richie from his four-thousand-dollar chair.

Jackson guided him out of the room and down the long hallway to the curved staircase that led to the main floor.

"Chance is my mouthpiece; he should talk to the authorities." Richie chortled. "What does he think I pay him for? Oh, that's right. Now I'm not paying him anything."

"This isn't about the investigation, Dad," Jackson said, guiding his broken father down the stairs.

Charley was there, waiting.

"Charley? I thought you said it was a him, Jackson?" Richie said as he shook his head.

"It is. John Black has something to ask you," Charley said evenly.

"John Black?" Richie said as John moved into the room with Chance. "Have we met?"

"Not personally, no," John said evenly. "But you may have heard of me and my wife, Marlena Evans."

Richie was confused.

"Dr. Evans? She's been helping Charley," John reminded him.

"The shrink," Richie realized. "That pretty blonde."

Richie's mind was whirling in a sea of alcohol and *Wall Street* overload.

"She's more than that, 'Dad,'" Charley said. "She's my biological mother."

Richie just stared. Slowly, it started to sink in. "Marlena Evans and John Black. Evans and Black...Oh my God," he said as his knees buckled, and he grabbed on to the railing.

"To quote my friend, 'DNA does not lie,' and we have the proof," John said. "So now we need to know how, what, when, where, and, what's more, why?"

"I love you, Charley," Richie said. "Your mum and I loved all of you more than you know."

"Are we your sons, Dad?" Chance asked.

"Or is that another lie too?" Jackson asked as he moved to join his brother.

"You are my sons!" Richie insisted. "We loved all of you!"

"But why this?" Charley implored.

"Your mother always wanted a daughter, and she had three miscarriages after these two," he said, tossing his head at the boys. "She wanted a daughter."

"Your daughter deserves an explanation, Richie," John continued. "We all do."

Richie snapped. "It was Stefano DiMera's idea," he spouted.

John reeled back. "Stefano?"

"You know him?" Jackson asked.

"Know him and revile him," John said, his eyes blazing. Of all the explanations he had thought of, this was one John wasn't expecting.

"Olivia desperately wanted another child, a daughter, and Stefano owed me a favor," Richie railed as the story spilled out. "We'd met in Paris, and he invested his entire fortune in my company. He was a powerful man, a devious man, and still is. We drank together, laughed together, and he became my confidant and my friend—"

"Stefano has no friends, just—" John interrupted.

Richie overrode him. "Let me finish! When I realized Stefano would lose everything if he stayed with me, I realized I could use him."

"Go on," John said as he saw the Richie's glazed eyes.

Chance, Jackson, and Charley were all spellbound.

"Did he ever tell you about those twins he created?" Richie asked.

"Rex and Cassie," John answered. Stefano had indeed at one time used a surrogate to carry two children created from sperm he'd harvested from one of his enemies.

"You and your wife were captured by DiMera at one time, remember?" Richie offered.

"And he harvested specimens from us," John said, realizing the diabolical truth.

"He thinks you are both perfect. You do know that, don't you? He wanted to give me the perfect child as a gift, and he did. Look at her, John. Isn't she perfect?"

The truth was out. And as preposterous as it seemed, John knew. "She is perfect, Richie."

"I always wanted only the best for her," Richie said, trying to defend him. "For her and the boys and Olivia. Dear God. Olivia's gone now too."

He started to cry. He was drunk, emotional, and spinning out of control.

"I never wanted to hurt her, John. I didn't even deserve her, and when she wanted a little girl I couldn't give her, what was I supposed to do?"

"Cheat on her, lie, and steal?" Charley interrupted. "Can we go, please?" she pleaded.

"No," Richie demanded.

"Dad, this is enough for tonight," Chance said, stepping in. Richie's dignity had been stripped away.

"That's probably best," John agreed. "We got what we needed here."

But Richie's world was crumbling further around him.

"No, please…we need to talk, Charley. I love you." Richie bit back tears.

Charley was torn. The man she'd loved for so many years had disappeared before her eyes.

"Like you loved Mummy? No, thank you," Charley said, trying to regain her composure. She could barely breathe. "I'd like to stay at the hotel with you, if I can," she said to John. "I can't be here anymore."

John smiled warmly to the girl who was now integral in his life. "We have a lot to go over. With Marlena."

Chance and Jackson nodded in agreement.

"Let me get a few things," Charley choked back as she headed to her room.

Richie was frozen as he watched his only daughter head up the winding staircase. "Charley, please," Richie pleaded. "Just stay until I leave for London."

She stopped in her tracks. "I'm sorry…Daddy," she stated. "Truly. But…it's not about you anymore."

To keep from breaking, she quickened her steps and dashed to her bedroom.

Before anyone could stop him, Richie bolted up the stairs behind her. As he stumbled to her room, Charley slammed the door in anguish. From below, John, Chance, and Jackson watched Richie recoil.

He was in pure agony. Unable to face them, he slunk down the upstairs hallway.

The house was eerily quiet, except for the sounds of Charley's packing coming from her bedroom.

John turned to Charley's brothers. "You don't know DiMera, but I'm sure what your father said is true. That man is capable of anything."

"As bizarre as it sounds, I believe you," Chance added.

"Gotta say. I'm glad it's you two," Jackson offered. "What a coincidence."

"Coincidence or fate," John said. "Not sure anymore the difference between the two."

Again, the room was quiet.

"Why don't we give her some time," John offered.

"Good idea," Jackson answered. "We can have a drink while we wait."

But before they could do that, Charley's door opened, and she appeared with a small carry-on.

"Let me get that, Sis," Chance said as he headed up the stairs.

"Thanks," she answered softly.

Charley headed down to the man she'd just learned is her biological father. She nodded in Chance's direction. "They spoil me, you know,"

"A spoiled brat, I see that." John smiled wryly. "But you ain't seen nothin' yet."

"Something tells me this is going to be an interesting new chapter for us all," Chance remarked.

"Any chance you like to ride?" Jackson asked, making small talk as they headed for the door.

"Bikes and horses," John answered. Both boys were impressed as they began to learn more about these new people now forever in their lives.

Charley led the way, John resting his hand on Jackson's back, the comfort level apparent as they continued to get to know one another.

After the four of them had exited to the front courtyard, the house was quieter than ever. Until Richie appeared from the direction of the screening room, another bottle of scotch in his hand.

"Charley?" he mumbled through tears.

But there was no answer.

"Chance? Jackson?" he continued.

No response. Only the sound of John's car starting in the driveway.

"No." Richie gasped. "Not yet…"

Desperate to say good-bye to his daughter, Richie bolted down the steep incline. At least, he attempted to.

In his drunken state, he stumbled down the entire eighteen stairs. All the while, he tried to catch his footing but clumsily plummeted nonetheless. Reaching the last step, he pitched forward and was catapulted toward the antique coffee table. His head hit the corner of the marble top with a loud *bang*.

He lay on the floor, bleeding profusely.

The left side of Richie's face was caved in. He was dead on impact.

Just like Olivia.

52 ANOTHER FUNERAL

THE FUNERAL FOR RICHARD GAINES WAS THREE DAYS LATER AND was only attended by a few. There were no press, no hangers-on, no Gemma and Serge Kasagian. They were all going about their extraordinarily glamorous but empty lives.

Dressed in simple black, Marlena and John were there for Charley, as was her newfound big sister Belle. Claire was with Shawn on the boat as she packed up before the trip to John and Marlena's. This was no place for a nearly four-year-old.

Willy, who'd connected with Chance once again over a dead parent, was by Chance's side as they listened to the brief nondenominational service that was held graveside. Jackson was alone, and when Richie was lowered into the plot next to Olivia's, he sidled up to Belle.

"If you hear from Chelsea and Abby, let them know I said hi," he said. "Is that tacky, considering?" he added, indicating the cemetery.

"Life goes on," Belle reminded him. "And give her a call."

"Who?" Jackson asked knowingly.

"For what it's worth, Abby's a great girl. Don't hold her profession against her."

"I think I can give her another exclusive. What do you think?"

"That's totally up to you." Belle smiled.

John approached.

"We're heading to lunch, baby girl. You joining us, Jackson?" he asked.

"Thanks, but I've got a lot to do at the house before heading back to London. And you might need to change Belle's nickname." Jackson smiled.

"Nah," John said. "She'll always be my baby girl." And he hugged Belle tightly.

∞

Lunch at Le Jardin Côté was simple and beautiful. Charley sat between John and Marlena and listened to their love story, which had started so many years ago on the docks of Salem.

"There's so much to know." She smiled.

"You have no idea," Shawn chimed in as Claire tossed a pommes frites at Charley.

"Claire!" Belle scolded.

"It's fine." Charley laughed. "I've never had a little niece before."

The pain of losing the mother and father who had raised her, both beautifully and badly, was salved by the love she felt around the table. This was a new family, an adjunct family, and for now, it was no one's business but their own. John and Marlena, along with Charley and her brothers, had decided that the Stefano connection died with Richie. Until it ever came out, if it ever did, for now, it was their secret.

"Dr. Masters!" Charley called as she saw Blake take a nearby table.

"Hi, all," he said as he realized it was Marlena, John, and family.

"Would you like to join us?" John asked.

"Meeting a client, but thanks," Blake said. "We've got some unfinished business, though," he said to Marlena.

"It's fine now," Marlena answered. The tattoo she had thought was killing John was obviously her grasping at straws. He was the old John again, only stronger and better.

"Good to see you," Blake said. As he nodded to each person, he stopped as he noticed something.

"What?" Marlena asked.

"Do you realize you and Charley have the exact same nose?"

They began to laugh.

"And smiley eyes," John added.

Blake took his table as Miss Plasticized from Gemma's luncheon joined him.

"Good luck with that one." John grinned as the rest of the table laughed. It was comfortable, settled, and secure.

"When can you join us in Lausanne?" Marlena asked Charley.

"Soon, I hope," Charley said. "But I have to help Chance and Jackson wrap up things here and in London."

"They're still your brothers, you know," Marlena said.

"I know, Dr.—"

"No, not Doctor. How about Marlena for now?"

"Okay. And I know, Marlena. I know they will always be my brothers."

A cloud crossed Charley's face.

"But?" John asked.

"They're going to suffer the most fallout from what Richie did, how he destroyed all those people," Charley said. "We're going to carry that guilt forever."

John saw the pain she felt. His mind began to turn.

53  *LAUSANNE*

DESIREE WAS AT THE WHEEL OF THE BLACK V-8 RANGE ROVER that picked up John, Marlena, and the kids from Geneva International Airport.

John and Marlena each only had hand luggage, while Shawn and Belle had backpacks—plus a huge duffel bag with toys, clothes, and snacks for the nearly four-year-old.

"I'm Claire," she piped up as Desiree helped her into the V-8. "Who're you?"

"A former nurse, who at the moment is very thankful to know your grandparents."

"Grandparents." John grinned. "You know, I'm beginning to like that title," he said as he patted Belle's tummy.

"Dad!" she said, shoving his hand away.

"I like that title too," John added as he helped Marlena into the passenger seat. "I'll drive."

Desiree climbed into the backseat while Shawn and Belle settled Claire into her car seat.

"You look *splendide*, Monsieur Black," Desiree said from behind him.

"Did you know he was getting better?" Marlena said, tilting her head and glaring at the girl who'd nursed him for nearly a year.

"They all did, Doc," John answered for her. "Haven't you heard of confidentially agreements?"

"Shut up and drive." Marlena sneered as she kissed him on the cheek, then snapped her seat belt.

"Yes, ma'am." He saluted and gunned the supercharged engine.

❦

"Wow," Shawn said as the Rover pulled through the winding drive toward Maison du Noir.

"What're those?" Claire asked as she pointed to the fields.

"Grapes," Marlena told her. "We sell them to the local wineries and have a very nice wine cellar because of it."

"Wine." Belle sighed. "No more for me for a while."

They pulled into the drive and piled out of the car.

"The guesthouse is by the pool, but we'd love you to stay in the house with us," Marlena offered.

"There's a state-of-the-art gym and a game room inside," John said to Shawn.

"I like games." Claire giggled as she started her jiggly dance.

"Let's find the loo." Belle grimaced, her hand going to her lips.

"Puke time!" Claire laughed as she ran to the front door.

Marlena and John entered behind them, and Marlena stood looking at the home they'd shared for two years.

"I'd forgotten how beautiful it is, John," she said. "Do I thank you often enough?"

"Save it for later," he said with a twinkle in his eye.

"Your room's that way, Shawn," Marlena said.

Shawn hauled his, Belle's, and Claire's gear toward their quarters.

"Thank you for picking us up, Desiree," John said.

"Thank you for keeping me on." She sighed.

"I know you were part of that Ponzi rip-off."

"My friends, my father," she said and started to choke up. "How that man could ruin so many lives is unconscionable. Especially to people whose lifework is to help others." She tried to steel herself. "I'm sorry."

"See you in the morning, Desiree," Marlena said soothingly. "We're all fine."

"Good night," Desiree said and exited.

"Well," Marlena said.

"Well," John answered. "Time to go up?"

"I am exhausted," she said. "We can clean up and then get dinner for the kids."

"One question," he said as they started up the winding staircase. "Where do we sleep?"

Marlena punched him playfully. "Wherever we want."

John smiled to himself. Little did she know what was in store for her.

At the top of the stairs, Marlena stopped in her tracks and gasped as she'd never gasped before.

The hall that had separated John's and Marlena's bedrooms was gone. In front of her, covering the entire second floor, was a huge master suite. It looked right out of the pages of *Architectural Digest*, with one floor-to-ceiling window the length of the room that overlooked the valley across to Lake Geneva.

"Welcome home." He smiled.

54  *RESTITUTION*

SHAWN AND BELLE SPENT A FEW GLORIOUS WEEKS AT MAISON du Noir, savoring their time with John and Marlena before they continued their worldwide journey on the *Fancy Face IV*.

The purpose of the trip had been to recement their relationship, and it had done it in spades. They had learned about life with each other in the most intimate setting and given their daughter memories her formulating mind would remember.

Marlena had taken Belle in to see the top ob-gyn in Geneva before they left, and she was right on track with her pregnancy. He'd given Belle referrals in all the cities they planned to dock in, and assured Belle she should be fine for Shawn's coveted deep sea fishing trip in Trinidad in January.

Charley was planning on taking an extended trip to Lausanne as soon as she could. Marlena and John were waiting for the right time to introduce her to the rest of the family.

In the meantime, Charley, Jackson, and Chance were still working on cleaning up Richie's mess. They were closer than ever to being done with the whole scandal. The investigation had proved they were indeed innocent, and John promised to help them with referrals for new jobs if they needed them.

And then, an odd thing happened. One afternoon, Desiree flew into the house, absolutely elated.

"Monsieur Black, Docteuer Evans!" she squealed as if she'd learned how from Claire. "You won't believe this!"

Marlena took an envelope from her hand. Inside was a cashier's check for thirty-two thousand euros. "Exactly what I lost in that scam!" Desiree proclaimed. "And I called my father. He received a check too!"

Marlena was thrilled for her. "From who?"

"No idea," Desiree said, snatching the check and fanning herself to keep from fainting. "An angel, it has to be an angel!"

Marlena drank it in and then decided to call Charley with the news. But Charley had heard already.

Not about Desiree, but Dr. Roisten's family, the nurse at Princess Grace Hospital, and hundreds of the victims on her father's list whose lives had been ruined. Now, someone, somewhere was coming to their aid.

It was a miracle.

∞

Marlena had a bottle of their finest white wine chilling when she heard the Range Rover in the driveway. John had been out all day, and she hadn't been able to reach him on his new phone.

She opened the door, beaming.

"Hey, Doc, what gives?" he asked.

"An anonymous donor has sent checks to hundreds of the

victims of Richie's scheme," she told him. "I spoke to Charley, and she's absolutely thrilled."

"So she's happy?" he asked, pleased.

"Did you hear me? She's thrilled! She and the boys feel like they can face the world again," Marlena said, near tears.

"That's what money's really for, isn't it, Doc? Making people happy?" He took the wine from her hand.

"Thank you," she said simply.

He stared into her smiling eyes. She knew.

"You don't mind? It was a lot of money. A lot!"

"What's money for, if not to make people happy?"

She kissed him and put her arms around him.

He winced. She pulled back.

"What?" he asked.

"Take your shirt off," she insisted.

"Doc," he said with a grin.

"I mean it, John. Where were you today?" she asked as he shrugged out of his shirt.

"Seeing a friend of yours," he answered. "Blake Masters."

Marlena turned him around, and the phoenix tattoo that had scarred his back and his mind was gone.

"He said it was some mutant cell that'd never go away, and the only way was to cover it," John said. "So he did. What do you think?"

Over the phoenix tattoo, Blake had designed a gorgeous eagle with soaring wings.

"I love it. And I adore you."

With a glass in one hand, John scooped her up in his arms.

"Let's see if he can fly." John smiled as he carried her up to their bedroom.

ACKNOWLEDGMENTS

I owe a debt of gratitude to those who helped in a variety of ways to make this book possible. To Greg Meng for his passionate support of my work and Ken Corday for allowing me to bring the romance and power of *Days of our Lives* to print and to expand on its canvas. To my editor at Sourcebooks, Peter Lynch, whose overview and excitement about the characters and story made submitting to him a pleasure, and to Andrea McKinnon for her effervescent commitment to promoting the book in the best way possible. I would be remiss without a bow to Pat Falken Smith, who was my mentor and who knew the power of good storytelling.

A big thanks to those who helped me along the way with details and color to make the pages come to life, with a nod to Google for making research not only easy but fascinating; special kudos to Jodi Airhart and Michele Riley, who filled in moments that helped make the characters sing; to the other *Days of our Lives* writers who created a number of the beloved characters I was able to explore; and to my sister, Judy Speas, I cannot say enough. She took over as my unofficial editor from our mother, who passed away last year, and did an exemplary job. To my business partner, Paul Cohen, for his input and understanding during the writing period, and to Lawrence Zarian for his continued encouragement. To my husband, Paca, without whose love and belief in me the books would not have been possible or as romantic; I adore you. To the fans, old and new, who have made *Days of our Lives* a part of their own, and to the new audience of readers, I hope you have as much fun reading as I did writing.

The story continues in these
new releases coming soon from
Days of Our Lives Publications
and Sheri Anderson

A *Stirring* in Salem

Spring 2011
978-1-4022-4477-3
$14.99 U.S./$17.99 CAN/£9.99 UK

A *Scandal* in Salem

Summer 2011
978-1-4022-4480-3
$14.99 U.S./£7.99 UK

Also available from Sourcebooks

The Days of our Lives

The True Story of One Family's Dream and the Untold History of *Days of our Lives*

On a November day almost forty-five years ago, the first episode of *Days of our Lives* appeared on the NBC Network, NBC's first color soap opera broadcast. Eleven thousand episodes later, millions excitedly tune in every weekday to watch one of the 260 original one-hour episodes

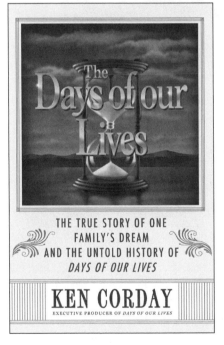

THE TRUE STORY OF ONE FAMILY'S DREAM AND THE UNTOLD HISTORY OF *DAYS OF OUR LIVES*

KEN CORDAY

EXECUTIVE PRODUCER OF *DAYS OF OUR LIVES*

produced each year. What few know though is that the show started as the dream of one family, the Corday family, who still owns and runs the show to this day. These are the days of their lives.

Days of our Lives is the first insider account of the history behind one of our most beloved soap operas. It is about the family who believed in it, conceived it, and sometimes seemed to live it along with millions of viewers, as they struggled to emerge from nowhere to create and produce one of the most successful and enduring television shows in history.

978-1-4022-4222-9 • $24.99 U.S./$29.99 CAN/£12.99 UK

Days of our Lives
45 Years

A Celebration in Photos

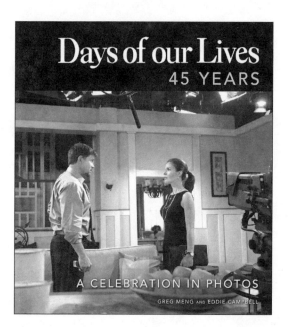

Days of our Lives 45 Years: A Celebration in Photos is an unprecedented photographic journey behind the scenes of the longest-running scripted program in NBC's history, *Days of our Lives*. Including both vintage and recent behind-the-scenes photos, this book showcases the beautiful cast, dedicated crew, and familiar sets of a television icon that continues to this day to bring the beloved world of Salem to its loyal viewers.

978-1-4022-4349-3 • $29.99 U.S./$35.99 CAN/£19.99 UK